AMERICAN
CALIPHATE

AMERICAN CALIPHATE

By William Doonan

Oak Tree Press Taylorville, IL

Oak Tree Press

Oak Tree Press books may be purchased for educational, business or sales promotional purposes. Contact Publisher for quantity discounts.

First Edition, March 2012

Cover by Reese-Winslow Designs

Book Design: Linda W. Rigsbee

978-1-61009-045-2
LCCN 2012930762

DEDICATION

For Carmen

Acknowledgement

I am indebted to many people who worked tirelessly to bring this book to life. Thanks first and foremost to Sunny Frazier at Oak Tree Press, my sensei and editor, for her relentless insights, instructions, and illuminations. Thanks also to my editor and writing partner, Dan Stuelpnagel, who spent countless hours hammering this story into shape. Many additional thanks are due to my family for their support, and for giving me time away from diaper duty to write. Yet more thanks are in order for my mentor, Jeff Quilter, who brought me down to Peru in the first place to work on the most insanely-fantastic excavation project I've ever been part of. And gracias always to my cherished colleagues on the north coast, who are engaged in the important work of archaeology, and who have lots to do with my story, except for the parts that relate to: a) spies, b) drugs, and c) Moors. I hope to join you again soon for yet another field season.

CHAPTER 1

RIO AMADOR, CALIFORNIA

Early November was a confusing time of year, if neighborhood decorations were any indicator. The last of Halloween's skeletons and ghosts vied for window space with the first pilgrims and smiling turkeys. Ben Juarez stared at the sign in front of the little museum – Rancho Maidu.

Due to an unforeseen shortage of midsize cars, the rental place had upgraded him to a Mustang convertible. And because it would have been an insult to the car to leave the top up, he drove the ninety miles from San Francisco with the top down. As such, he nearly froze to death, and that kept him focused on something other than abject fear. He had a question to ask this morning, and he well understood that its answer might determine the course of his life.

If she said no, she'd stay and have nothing to do with him, have some turkey soon and give thanks. But if she said yes, if she agreed to come back to Peru, to a land without a single turkey, Ben might want to be very careful with her, because there were a lot of skeletons lying around the north coast, and more than a few ghosts.

Rancho Maidu. Inside sat an older man who had to be ninety if he was a day, pants up to his ribs and a bolo tie. He was sitting behind a counter laid out with postcards and Native American craft kits. Beads and bits of feather were everywhere.

"You can look around for yourself," the man said, pointing toward the exhibit hall with the glass cases, the dioramas. "It's self-guided. A donation is all we ask. There are tours as well, but you've missed that. The last one is almost over."

"Can I catch the tail end of it?"

"Suit yourself." His hand shook as he strung a bright green bead onto a leather cord. "They'll be down by the middens. Just go out the back and hang a right by the smoke house. You should run into them."

"Middens," Ben said.

"A midden is basically an old pile of shells that the Indians made."

Ben smiled. "I know."

He heard her voice before he even got to the smoke house. She was hidden by a group of kids, three women hanging back, looking like they wanted a cigarette but not in front of the kids. School trip. Ben moved closer.

"This is a bedrock mortar," she said, running her hands over a punchbowl-sized depression in the rock. "Remember, the Maidu Indians were the original inhabitants of this part of California. They lived here for thousands of years, in harmony with nature. Now, who remembers what the Maidu's favorite food was?"

"Antelope," said a girl in the front.

"Pizza," a boy in the back chortled.

"Well you're right, antelope might have been their favorite food, but their most important food was acorns. Around October the harvest would start. The men would climb the trees while young boys gathered the acorns that had fallen to the ground. The girls would help their mothers weave the large baskets they used to store the acorns. When it came time to prepare a meal, the acorns were ground right here. The women used rocks to pound the acorn into flour."

Then she stood and Ben felt a rush of adrenaline. "Little Bird," he whispered. Her hair was tied back and she looked thinner. It had been two years. Still lovely. Ben forgot all about the Mustang listening to her.

"The problem," she continued, brushing a bug from a girl's hair, "is that acorns are poisonous. So after they ground the flour, they had to put it in special baskets and pour boiling water over it to leech out the poison."

"How did they boil the water?" a skinny boy asked as he held up his backpack so the bigger boys wouldn't unzip it and fill it with dirt.

Ben cleared his throat loudly. "They used their finest woven baskets, with leaves on the inside to make them watertight. They filled them with water and then heated rocks in the fire. When the rocks were hot enough they put them in the water and stirred them around."

She stared at him. Surprise, not like the harder stares from the teachers which were more appraising, more technical.

"Hello, Jila," he said.

She said nothing for a moment, just stared at him. "Well, folks, we have a special guest today," she said, having missed more than a beat or two. "I'd like you to meet Dr. Ben Juarez, an archaeologist and professor from Michigan."

"Mississippi," he corrected.

"Mississippi. Dr. Juarez, meet Rio Amador Unified's Fourth Grade class."

"It's a pleasure."

"Do you believe in vampires?" one of the children asked.

"No," he said, "But my uncle is a werewolf."

Nobody laughed.

"OK," Jila told them, "now if you go back inside, Duncan will show you how the Maidu made their stone tools."

She didn't take a step, even when the children had left. She brushed off the dirt from her hands on her vest. "I used to wear a hat when I did the tours but I stopped. I'm not sure why."

"How have you been, Jila?"

"What are you doing here, Ben?" She noted the new denim and the pressed shirt. Not field clothes, these.

"I came to see you."

"Why?"

"Missed you. Love you, remember?"

"Shit, Ben," she said, turning, walking down the path toward the stream. "Do you want to see the burial mounds?"

"I do."

"You're still teaching then, in Mississippi?"

"No," he said, picking up a stick, reaching into his pocket for his knife.

"No whittling," she said without turning to look at him. "It's a rule."

Ben tossed the stick away and walked after her. "No, I left after last semester. It wasn't a good fit. Tupelo Baptist couldn't quite wrap its faith around an atheist Latino professor. They decided that I had about as much chance at tenure as salvation."

"You were left behind."

"I was."

Rounding a bend behind a sycamore, the path turned them out in a meadow marked by two small hills and behind them, across the road, a housing development.

"Have you excavated them?"

"No," she said, still not looking at him. "People live there."

Ben grinned. "I meant the hills. They're the burial mounds."

"Why did you come here, Ben?"

"Proposition for you."

"Marriage or just sex?"

"A job." Ben fiddled with the car keys and the coins in his pocket.

"I have a job. Are you jingling things in your pocket? I can hear you jingling."

He stopped. "Sandy asked me to come see you."

She spun around.

"To see if you would think about working with him again. With us."

"You're joking," she said. "I don't even want to know. Where?"

Ben hadn't had a cigarette in almost two years, but he wanted one now. "Santiago de Paz. To finish what we started."

"Peru?" she shouted. "You want me to go back to Peru? I got shot, Ben. Remember?"

"So did I."

"In your arm," she reminded him. "Do you have a scar from that one stitch or did it already fade? I was in the hospital for four months. I almost lost a lung."

"I didn't come here to compare shark bites with you," he said. "Things have changed in Peru. It's a lot safer. Even the remnant guerrilla movements have disbanded."

Jila frowned, her fingers absently tracing the chip in her rib that the second bullet had taken out. "And Sandy is back in Peru, is he?"

"Yes. He was in Mexico last year. He excavated a Maya coastal trans-shipment site near Merida. Did you know that the Mayas had canoes thirty meters long and employed accountants to log in the cargo and prevent theft?"

She held out her arms. "Who doesn't?"

"You knew that, really?"

"Yes, there was a thing on TV. They also had court astrologers to tell fortunes before the canoes left. Probably incantations too. The new codex they found in that collection in Prague was for shipping. A captain would consult it before sailing to learn his odds at shuffleboard."

"Don't joke. They found a new codex in Prague?"

"I think, or a dinosaur bone."

Ben nodded. "So Sandy was working on a couple of articles but he wanted to go back to Peru. And it's safe now, or as safe as it's going to be. I went down last month, took a look around. Otherwise I would never have come here to ask you."

"Well you asked me and I said no."

"Have dinner with me."

"I can't," she said. "I have a date."

"Your nose wrinkles when you lie."

"I could get a date in five minutes," she said, snapping her fingers. "Watch me. Do you have a cell phone?"

Ben shook his head.

"Okay. But early and Mexican. I have to be home by nine; I have cable TV and there's really a lot on."

• • •

"I heard you got married," he said, layering chicken and peppers in his fajita. The smell of cilantro always took him back to a barefoot childhood.

"I did. It didn't take. Enough chitchat." Jila ordered a large draft beer and another after that. They came with limes in them, and that was reason enough to go to a Mexican restaurant. "What about you? I never heard from you after Chicama."

"Don't even joke," he said. "I sat by your bed for three weeks. Then I wrote you for a year. I called until you disconnected your phone."

"I needed some time."

"Two years?"

Jila sat back and tucked her hands under her legs. "I don't know, Ben. I had to rethink things. Almost dying does that to you. I saw a therapy guy for a bit. Took some pills for a bit longer. Then I dated the therapy guy and fell in love with the pills, so I moved to California. Original, no?"

"You like it here?"

"I do. I get to work as an archaeologist. There aren't that many jobs for us out there, though I might look into something recently available at Tupelo Baptist."

Ben shook his head. "They wouldn't have you. An unmarried woman in her thirties; you'd stray before midterms."

"It's quiet here," she said. "And nobody shoots at you."

"Come back to the north coast with me. Sandy said he can't do it without you."

"Then Sandy can't do it."

"He says you're the brains of the outfit."

"He's full of shit. Sandy is five times as smart as I am. If he wants me there it's because he's my friend and yours, and he wants things back like they were."

"Please, Jila. This could be one of the greatest archaeological discoveries of the century. We'll get inside that pyramid, and we'll excavate the plaza. You know the script better than anyone alive; we need you to work it out."

"It's not really a script," she said, stirring her tortilla soup. "They're maker's marks, remember."

"Yes," said Ben. "That's what the textbooks say. But you found something different, some measure of context, of textual information. That's what we were working on. We had taken the notes and the drawing and the photographs to...to Chicama."

"I don't do that sort of work anymore." Jila waved at the waitress, pointed to her glass. "I'm a site interpreter at Rancho Maidu. Last year I ran a field school and taught thirty kids how to excavate."

"I'm talking real archaeology, Jila, the kind you were trained to do."

She frowned. "This is real archaeology. You don't need a pyramid to make it real."

"Don't you miss it though?"

"No."

"How much do they pay you?"

Jila dug into the nachos. "Thirty-nine, five. Full dental."

"No co-payment?"

"Five dollars per visit, but I haven't been yet."

"Not shabby."

"No. You're looking sharp these days," she said. "Prosperous, I might say. I've been hanging out at the mall a lot, so I can spot quality when I see it. That jacket of yours is calfskin, four bills. I'm not even going to ask but you were maybe pulling forty-eight at the University, fifty with summer school. Did you come into some money?"

"Something like that," he said. "Sandy has a grant. We're going to do the whole excavation in thirty days, so we can finish before the storm comes. There's going to be a storm this year, a big *El Niño*. It's a big team, forty workers and a security detail. You're our best hope at working out the maker's marks. Otherwise, we have to move ninety million adobe bricks to find the box."

"The box," Jila repeated. "Do you still believe there is a five-hundred year-old Muslim box hidden in that pyramid?"

"Either in the pyramid or on the plaza, but yes, I'm certain it's there, and when we find it, we'll change the whole world."

"It might be just fiction."

"It's real, and you know it. We have the documentation."

She nodded. "Where did Sandy get the grant from? Did his fairy godmother come into some more money?"

"Yes."

"These are great nachos," she said. "Did you know that Maidu women wove skirts from willow bark as well as grass? In the rain they wore caps that were woven like baskets."

"Twenty thousand dollars for thirty days. Twice that more if we find the box. And you'll be famous! You could work at any university in the country, even Tupelo Baptist."

"That's a lot of money, Ben. But I'm safer here."

"No denying that."

"Maidu songs were very short," she said, staring at the guacamole. "Only twenty or thirty seconds long."

"Come to Peru with me. We'll talk to Sandy. If you're not happy, you can be back at work Monday morning."

"Only twenty or thirty seconds," said Jila. "That's long enough to change your life forever. I had two different kinds of bullets in me, Ben, from two different guns."

"I know."

"I get to keep what's in the box?"

"It's probably just dust."

"Can I keep the dust?"

"Of course not. But you get to look at it, and that's worth something to you, and to me."

"I can't just pick up and leave. I have rent to pay. Also, I bought a jet ski, and the payment is almost $200 a month. It's too much."

"I don't see you riding a jet ski."

She shook her head. "It's awful, really. It's incredibly loud. I was trying to change my image. Why thirty days?"

"Like I said, there's a storm coming, a big *El Niño* this year. If we don't do it now the storm will wipe out half of the work we did before, and the wind and rain will tear the friezes from the walls. We need to get them shored up at least. Two grand up front if you come for the weekend. If you decide to stay for the month, it's a bonus, otherwise you come home having made two grand as a consultant."

Jila's soup had cooled. She stirred it and the tortillas broke apart. "Okay."

"Okay?"

"Okay. I'll come for the weekend. To Santiago. Not to Chicama, right? I'm not ever going back there."

"Agreed."

"You know, Ben, I don't think it was guerrillas who shot us."

"I don't either," he said.

CHAPTER 2

1542
CORDOBA, SPAIN

As fate would have it, the secretary charged by Tomas Ibanez to carry a message to his son and crossed paths under the midday sun with a messenger entrusted by the younger Ibanez with a letter to his father. Though the streets were empty, the men did not take notice of each other. Both carried requests for a meeting that evening, after dinner, when music and laughter would be heard throughout the city, and plans could be made without undue concern.

Diego Ibanez fastened his cloak and set his hand on the iron latch, seconds away from a perfect escape when his wife's candle cast his shadow on the stone wall.

"A late night meeting with a wine merchant's daughter?" she asked, standing in the archway. "Herring on coarse bread with the young wife of the lawyer from Granada?"

Diego turned and walked slowly toward her. "Not far from the truth," he said, his lips almost touching her ear. "Cider on the roof with the young wife of a shipping agent."

Mina laughed. "I am not so young anymore."

"But you must wait up for me while I answer my employer's call."

"This late?" She put her arms around him. "Your father has no mercy. He works you like a peasant."

Diego kissed her quickly. "He works me lest we be peasants. Wait up for me."

"Careful," she said. "The streets are not as safe as they used to be."

"The streets were never safe, Mina," he said as he lifted the latch and opened the thick oak door. "We have just for so long convinced ourselves that they were."

Tomas Ibanez traded in wool, olive oil, hard woods, and Dutch matchlock pistols which had to be packed carefully in wool under the hard woods so as to pass the customs men in Cadiz who would otherwise forbid their export to Genoa and Venice and Larnaca. Over the decades he had made a fortune, building on the success of his father and grandfather.

Tomas paced the floor of his warehouse. Though his packing agent was quite good at his work, Tomas had developed the custom of nervously checking the inventory list against the lettering on the shipping containers.

"I have made a decision," he announced as his son entered. He poured two glasses of juice made from the oranges that had just come in from the north. "We are leaving. I have made up my mind."

Diego removed his cloak and locked the door behind him. The warehouse occupied the first floor of his father's large house. Upstairs were the offices and apartments, but there was only one door, next to the loading dock, and Diego wanted to be sure they would not be interrupted. "You were frightened, that is all. It is over now."

"Never over. Never over." Seven months ago, Tomas Ibanez had politely declined the Cadiz Trade Minister's request for an increase in his already-steep monthly bribe. Authorities were notified and a charge made that Tomas Ibanez was a practicing Muslim, still making the prayers five times a day. Heresy is punishable by death.

"Not five hundred families in Spain have our wealth or power," Diego said.

"Power," Ibanez repeated. He held out his hands and looked down at the fingernails, now almost grown back. He remembered the look on the Inquisitor's face as he brought the forceps. That hurt like nothing he had ever known, and Ibanez swore his allegiance to the Crown, to the Lord Jesus, when he should have screamed that there is no God but Allah. But naked, whipped, exposed, he could not. "It is my nature to be skeptical," the Inquisitor said, teasing a poker in the coals. Ibanez's business acumen stronger than his faith, his Christian piety was demonstrated by the transfer of a small property in Marbella, and a brace of German carriage horses, assuring his eyes and genitals would not be harmed.

"Power," Diego repeated. "We have work to do, work that progresses. And we have powerful friends. Friends who defeated our own King Charles last year in Algiers. The Caliphate is strong."

Tomas Ibanez sat gently on the edge of a small barrel of cheese and wept. "I have not been to the meetings. Not since...not since my arrest."

Diego dragged a stool and sat in front of his father. "I know. You are frightened. We are all frightened, but the time will come. We are gathering arms. Damascus will lend its full might. King Charles, if he lives, will spend his days hunting foxes in Castile when Granada rises again."

Tomas took his son's hand in his. "I am a man of commerce, of equations and balances. And the equation now, this day, does not favor us. The balance...."

"No." Diego stood. "It is your fear alone that makes you say that."

"Charles will have the Dutch as keen allies within the year, and the Hapsburgs will rule Europe for a century or more." Tomas wiped his eyes with a silk scarf. He was talking business now and that kept his fears at bay. "We cannot win this. We will dream and plot and our children's children will do the same, but Damascus will never give the word."

"I go to the meetings, father. They are optimistic. Emissaries from Cairo are encouraging."

"And they always will be. But you will never see their ships anchor in Spanish bays, or their soldiers marching on Seville. Damascus will calculate the equations, they will figure the balances; realize the cost. And even if the cost is met, Diego," Tomas paused, sensing the anger in his son, "the battle cannot be."

● ● ●

Diego stood by the great window overlooking the Guadalquivir, where six stout Ibanez river barges sat laden, ready to leave at dawn, each watched by a pair of men with long guns and a coal fire that made the night air sweet. He said nothing as his father read from the heavy ledgers brought up from the vault under the floor. Arrangements had been made to sell the family holdings in Cordoba and Cadiz, all save the houses that Diego and his brother occupied, and the estate in Oporto with the vineyards. Diego remembered the summers of his youth when they fled to Oporto to escape the heat. Grapes like melted honey and pretty Castilian girls with paper bows in their hair. "How long?" he asked.

"Seven months. Maybe eight. The Cadiz properties will go to Ovando Jimenez, who bought also the cargo ferries and has a bid on the little caravel that the courts in Genoa awarded us."

"The San Sebastian."

"Yes. I've never had the heart to put into service a ship named for a saint."

"You could rename it."

"It is said on the wharfs that this brings bad luck. The sailors demand an additional payment before embarking."

"And the facilities here in Cordoba? This house?" Diego spread his arms to indicate the warehouse and the apartments above.

"The Grijalva brothers, and an outfit from Malaga." Tomas Ibanez closed the ledger and returned it to its place beneath the floorboards. "You will have enough money for five lifetimes, and for women who wave from balconies."

"Do not confuse me with your first-born son, the one who loses your money at the tables, doughy from tankards of wine. I do not keep women in rooms with balconies.

"Miguel will mature in time."

"He is forty years old. Where will you go?"

Tomas said nothing.

"Did they take away your faith, father?"

Tomas made a quick path across the sawdust-covered floor, faster than his son would have thought possible, and slapped him hard across the face. "Do not ever ask me that again. I lost my courage only. Not my faith. It is because I've grown tired of secret prayer meetings that I leave. Spain is no place for a Muslim."

Diego walked quickly to the door and drew the bolts.

"To Alexandria," Tomas called after him. "But should anyone ask, you will say Genoa."

Diego froze, the door now open to the night. "Alexandria?"

"You could come as well. Bring your family. Your children could grow up proud of their faith."

"They would grow up proud of their faith even if they lived on the moon," Diego spat. "Are there not enough Muslims in Alexandria? Would we not be just another refugee family of peeking out of windows onto the Nile?"

"We will prosper."

Diego slammed the door behind him, his cloak draped over his shoulder despite the evening chill.

● ● ●

Javier, the older of the Grijalva brothers, wiped his hands on the tablecloth which was now thick with herring oil. "I will surely miss you, my friend," he said. "Your competition has kept me sharp. Now I will own everything and grow fat and dumb."

"You're already dumb," Tomas Ibanez answered, poking at the man's enormous belly.

"I am to believe you're going to Genoa, then? That is your story?"

"Of course. That's what I told you. The land is already purchased and construction has begun on the main house, Venetian marble for the columns. You must visit me."

"If ever I am in Tripoli, I shall," Grijalva said, reaching for another herring.

Ibanez froze.

Grijalva refilled his cup with heavy Port. "Speculation, Tomas. You have been a good friend to me. I am a Christian man and a loyal Spaniard. But it is because I am a brilliant and honorable man that I have grown wealthy and happy. And I have known you since the king wore short leather breeches."

"Do not speak to me like that," Ibanez said sharply. "I have proven myself even to the Inquisitors."

"Friend," Grijalva said softly, "I meant no disrespect. I thought only that you might need one day to call on an old friend, and to know that this old friend would meet you on short notice at one of the coffee houses in Cyprus and make no inquiries or reports."

Tomas nodded. "Then I shall take comfort in that knowledge as I lounge on my marble piazza in Genoa."

"The marble was for the columns."

"And for the piazza as well."

A servant came to clear the plates and bring a platter of duck and salted lamb surrounded by broiled vegetables in hot oil.

"I had inquired about the two Flemish boats you bought two summers ago, the ones you almost lost in the Normandy storm. Thirty-tons, three masts."

"Thirty-five tons, yes. They are due to return to Cadiz by the end of the month."

"And you will not sell them to me?"

Tomas cut into a chunk of lamb. The smell of garlic was making his mouth water. "Yes, of course," he said. "I thought we had already invoiced them."

"We had I but your son indicated that they were no longer for sale."

"Did he, now? I shall have to inquire. I am certain that the boats were not included in the Ovando Jimenez purchase."

"They were not. I spoke with their agent yesterday. They are not buying any of your caravels, just the river craft."

"I know they are buying at least one caravel." Tomas remembered the San Sebastian.

"No. That was withdrawn as well, by your son." Grijalva reached for a duck leg and speared a small white vegetable with his knife. "What in heaven is this?"

"It is called a potato," said Tomas. "They are new. I will discuss this with Diego this very night."

Grijalva bit into the potato. "I've heard of these. Never had one before. It is quite bland."

• • •

The servants asleep after the luncheon, Mina herself answered the chime and found her father-in-law at the door.

"Hello, Aminah," he said, kissing her cheek.

"It has been some weeks since you've come to the house. You must see Delia. She has grown quite big."

Ibanez frowned. "Unless you have had a child and hid her away I cannot imagine who Delia is."

Mina laughed. "That is one of the few things I would not hide. Delia is the puppy, the little French puppy that came on the post boat."

"Yes, I remember."

Diego rose from his chair when his father entered the room. "Leave us please," he said to Mina, who was already halfway down the hall. "You'll have some wine?"

"How is it we drink wine when it is forbidden?" Tomas asked, pouring himself a small cup.

Diego poured a cup as well. "We hold on tightly to what we can, to what is important. You taught me that."

"Tell me about my ships."

Diego began pacing the room.

"You have no right to alter the terms of a contract once the contract has been set. Your brother was signing papers on a crate of sail cloth when he learned the ships had been removed from the offer."

"I doubt that very much, father. If Miguel had a pen in his hand it was because his wallet was empty and his cards showed promise. I don't believe he can read papers, much less sign them."

"Your brother is more complex than you think. He prays every day and he keeps his nose in the wind. He is simply bored. Will you not answer my questions?"

"Yes. I have been giving this some thought," Diego said. "I do not wish to accompany you. I have tried to imagine myself in Alexandria. I could walk the long sea wall with Mina at my side, looking out at the sea."

"And Delia."

"Delia," Diego paused. "Yes, the dog. We could pray in a Mosque. We could look up at dusk and see the minarets. We could employ servants and gardeners without the need to investigate their every prior moment and movement. And call out loud to Allah. Have you ever prayed out loud?"

"Yes, as a child. Before Grenada fell to the Queen.

"I have never prayed out loud," said Diego. "Even when business took me to Morocco or to Alexandria, I could not. Knowing I would have to go back, I could not. My voice betrayed me."

"So you will stay here and manage shipping. There is fine cloth from Burgundy that brings delight in Mali."

Diego shook his head. "No, I will not stay. I will go."

"To where?"

"To the Americas."

Tomas Ibanez refilled his cup and stared into it. "To the Americas, Diego? What on earth would you do in a such godless place? Have you not heard the stories?"

"I have heard the stories."

"They will cut your head off faster than talk with you, for their own fancy. Or tear out your heart with a knife made of glass."

"Yes. It would be so much more civilized if they drew out your fingernails, broke your knees, and burned you alive."

Tomas drank deeply from his cup, refilling it again. "I fear I shall be drunk when business reopens."

"You said they were godless, father. What if we were to change that? We could bring the words of God to the godless."

"I'm afraid the King is already in that business. They have bishops already in the Americas. Inquisitors, Diego. They will burn you there just as quickly."

"I would rather burn there than smolder here like an old coal, growing dimmer with each passing year."

Delia, the puffy white dog bounded into the room, Mina close behind, chasing after. "The Inquisitors don't burn you," she said, "the soldiers do. The Inquisitors only pass sentence."

Tomas was outraged. "How dare you listen to our private conversation! Such insolence!"

"No father." Diego beckoned for Mina to sit down. "A wife is an equal partner in all things."

"So you have shared this nonsense with her?" Tomas shook his head sadly.

"Your son has faith," said Mina. "He learned that from you."

"Do you know who these Spaniards are? Tomas asked. "These men who board ships to seek fortune in the Americas? They are the ninth and tenth and eleventh sons of every dimwitted turnip farmer from here to Aragon, and half the purse snatchers in Iberia who never mastered their trade. And those are just the priests."

"Father, you said it was a measure of equations, of balances. You said that the only minarets in Spain will be found in cellars and hidden rooms. That Spain is lost to us."

"It is. Spain is lost to use forever."

"Across the oceans, that need not be. We will build a new Caliphate."

"Our families have been close for generations," Mina said. "We have grown wealthy and strong by handpicking our causes, leaving others behind like the olives that are not yet ripe. If we have no chance in Spain, must we also concede all the world?"

"Think, father," Diego said. "We can bring the light of God to the men with glass knives who cut heads and hearts. Pizarro is dead now eight months. We've heard nothing but talk of Peru for eight years now. It is time. It is written, father, written in the Qur'an, those who believe fight in the cause of God. The oppressed of the world call out to Allah. Shall I read it to you, father? I can go downstairs to the locked room, shove aside the old rugs and look under the trunk to the secret place and get the book. Shall I get the book?"

Tomas shook his head. "Save us from this land whose people are oppressors and bring to us from You someone who will protect us and bring us to You."

"That is it," said Diego, now pacing the room. "That is it."

"And you would be that person?"

"I would give my life to be that person."

"And you would go as well, I suppose," he said to Mina.

"No," she said, stroking the dog. "I will go to Alexandria with you. We have people to organize, and a network to create. Organizational structure and fundraising are required. I am pregnant with your grandson; a man, I can tell as much. I will call him Jibrail."

Tomas's hand shook as he poured still more wine into his cup. "This is going to take some thought. Some planning. A lot of planning."

"It will," said Diego. "I am fortunate to have a father who is a master of thought and planning."

• • •

Two months later, on the roof of the offices in Cadiz, Tomas Ibanez broke off a piece of coarse bread and dipped it in peppered olive oil. The sweet beef sausage left him full but he ate when nervous. "It is almost dusk," he said, tapping the lambskin purse that held the permits. "Your men are on board and your ships are heavy, yet you look fearful."

"I said goodbye to my wife," Diego said softly. "I am more fearful of being without her than I am of this endeavor."

"She will want for nothing. Help me finish this plum wine. It's quite bad but it will be a long time before you and I sit together again."

"Yes," Diego said. "But we have less than an hour before the tide. You will come to the dock?"

"I'll watch from here, from the roof. From here one can see the masts. I will make my prayers when I lose sight of them."

Diego shut his eyes. "How much did it all cost?"

"Do not ask."

"It was quite a lot?"

"Yes. Now you must hear it one more time to be sure. The Council of the Indies prohibits Moors from traveling across the ocean."

"There are no Moors in Spain," Diego interjected. "Isn't that what the law says?"

"Yes, but the rules apply even so. You have a trade license for Mali. If you are stopped by Crown revenue ships, it will be north of the Canaries. The permits are from the House of Trade in Seville, not local from Cadiz, so you won't be searched. But if anyone does try to board you, you must engage. Fire on their ships and kill them. Your cargo is illegal, as are your armaments. And remember, once you pass the Canaries, you are legally a pirate. Are you certain now you only want three ships?"

"Colon had only three," said Diego, stabbing another piece of sausage.

"Cristoforo Colombo, yes, but that was fifty years ago."

"Even so."

"Your charts are the most current. Once out at sea, you must move south. Portuguese cutters now prowl the coast of South American; they will take you without even looking at your papers, and they outgun you. Run from any ship you see in open ocean or you will have to fight them."

"South around the tip of the continent," Diego said before his father could. By now he had the plan in his heart. "Following the Portuguese charts, not the Spanish. We dare not enter the Caribbean and make for Panama like Spanish Catholics. We'll circle the tip of South America and sail north to Peru."

Tomas pat him on the shoulder. "As you approach Peru, you will encounter Spanish ships. At this point, you do not run and you do not engage. As you have Spanish flags, it is unlikely you'll be challenged. If you are, you have forged papers from the Council of the Indies that will hold up if you are boarded, but they will not fool a trade minister. So if it comes to that, start paying whoever you need to. Stay away from the coast until you're far north of Lima. It is at that point that any advice I can devise or purchase expires."

"When I put to shore, the first day, I will pray five times out loud. On the second day we will begin building a mosque."

"They have no wood there, I'm told," said Tomas. "The Indians build their houses from bricks of mud."

"Then we will build a mosque from bricks of mud. The crew is excellent; I have spoken with every man.

"As have I." Tomas had drawn on networks that had survived centuries of oppression, and made inquiries, made offers of employment to men of the faith, to seamen and captains, to armorers and soldiers, doctors and mullahs. One hundred and thirty men, a light crew for three ships laden with more wheat and meat and olive oil and wine than any Spanish master of conquest had ever seen. The cannons were from Genoa, the guns were Dutch, and the swords and armor were cold Spanish steel.

"Take care of Mina." Diego felt himself close to tears.

"It is time now."

Diego nodded. "I have renamed the ships you know. Not on the prows or on the papers but in my mind."

"And what have you called them?" Tomas walked with him toward the stairway.

"The twin caravels are Jinn and Mina."

"Those are fine names. And the San Sebastian?"

"I call her Isha, the night prayer."

Tomas Ibanez embraced his son. "An angel came to me in my dreams last night. He told me that a son of mine would sire a dynasty of kings."

Diego held his father tightly. "Give my love to my son when he is born."

"I will. And one thing more. On board there is a cask of flour marked with white striping. Hidden in the flour is a small wooden box wrapped in oil cloth. Open it when you have arrived and are safe."

"What is inside the box?"

"Something that will bring faith, even to a Spaniard if need be. May Allah guide your voyage."

"I will see you in Alexandria in four years," Diego said. "Perhaps just three. And we will eat lamb, say prayers, and speak of our new American Caliphate."

CHAPTER 3

2010
LIMA, PERU

Jimmy Segura figured he had a shot with the new girl. He was thirty pounds overweight but he paid good money to the good tailors in Lima for clothes that drew attention to his broad shoulders.

He figured he had a shot with the new girl but he wasn't going to rush it. The full-forward, 'this is how it is' that played well with the local talent was unlikely to win her over. He had met her three times now, twice at embassy functions, and once at a UNICEF picnic, but this was the first time he was going to have more than just a few moments at her. Ranking officer, he was, but she was from a different division, so there was nothing in the regulations prohibiting a romantic engagement as long as it was reported.

Jimmy Segura tugged at his shirt, trying to keep it loose around his belt. On a big man, an extra thirty pounds was easily overlooked. He was late because that was part of the thing. He had planned to be late but the Lima traffic was almost unimaginably fluid, making him early, so he sat in the car reading the newspaper, and then out of boredom, the Toyota owner's manual.

After twenty minutes or so, he got out of the car and made his way inside. He was halfway up the escalator when he spotted her. He walked across the promenade of the museum, a ghastly poured concrete structure from the seventh level of architectural hell; equal parts art-deco, East German functionalism, and third-world incompetence.

Aleza Sabatini had been waiting.

Jimmy waved but her expression didn't change. No return wave, that was never a good sign. "Apologies," he said, "I was out the door an hour ago but had to take a call from Langley. There is still this issue of missionary planes and their involvement in the cocaine transshipment, which is nonsense. Try to convince anyone in Washington of that!"

Aleza smiled. Sometimes they blow a little too hard, she thought. She'd been standing by the window for the last twenty minutes smoking, watching him as he read some briefing in his car. She was two weeks into Peru; she was thirty-two.

Jimmy shook her hand. "They set you up in a nice place?"

"Yes," she said. "Overlooking the ocean, and it has a Murphy bed."

"The kind that folds up."

"That's right."

"So you found your way without a fuss?"

"Yes, thank you. I took a cab."

"My directions were good? Sometimes I worry."

"It's the National Museum."

"That's true," he said. "I expect the drivers know how to get here. Come look at something with me." He led her down a long hall to a glass case illuminated by a bank of lights, half of which were burnt out.

"They sure knew how to make jewelry in the old days," she said, staring at the golden artifacts, medallions shaped like birds and little statues of men with their hands held high.

"Inca gold," Jimmy said. "From 1476 - 1534, the Inca were kings of the largest empire in the world."

"It would seem," she said, pointing at the sign on the wall that said just that.

"Beautiful, aren't they?"

"They are."

"Most of them are fake," he told her. "Two years ago, the President brought in appraisers from Geneva to see what they might be worth on the auction circuit, but it turns out that they were mostly fakes. The museum staff had been replacing them, one every couple of months, to pay for their daughters' fifteenth birthday parties. The President was going to have the Minister of Antiquities shot unless he paid restitution. Then the guy asked if could pay in gold. They say the President shot him himself."

"But he didn't really, right?"

Jimmy shrugged. "Probably not. But they are all mostly fakes."

"Why did you ask to meet me in the museum?" she asked.

"Take a walk with me," he said, leading her into one of the galleries.

He got halfway down the hall when he realized she wasn't following. Maybe he didn't have a chance with this girl at all. Too bad about that, the local talent would suffice. "You're going to have to come with me if you're going to listen to what I have to say."

She followed him into a dimly-lit room dominated by a diorama of Indians kneeling in their cane house cooking fish.

"Local inhabitants were living in settled villages here 4000 years ago," he said, "on the coast, fishing and growing squash and cotton."

"Cotton," she repeated.

"For nets. To catch fish." Leading her quickly past the diorama, "monumental architecture by 1800 BC."

"Fascinating," she said, lagging a little.

He stopped at the entrance to a hall called Chavin. "The mother culture of Peru. Chavin were farmers. This is where it all starts," he said, "royalty, and a pattern of symbolism that would carry for two thousand years."

Aleza pulled a little Minolta digital camera from her bag and aimed it at him.

"Don't even joke."

"But the light is just right," she said, returning the camera to her bag and following him into the next hall.

"Moche," he said. "This is the earliest state-level society in South America, getting under way at about 250 AD. It was a time of lords who built massive pyramids, irrigated the deserts and controlled the talent and strength of millions. The people were farmers who grew the corn, fattened the guinea pigs, and paid hefty labor taxes to the Moche lords, building their pyramids. And as soon as they were done, they built them again over and over again for the next six hundred years, right on top of the old pyramids, just making them bigger."

Aleza found a cigarette in her purse, and rolled it between her fingers, knowing she couldn't light it here.

Jimmy stopped in front of a display case that featured a series of boxes, eleven across by nine deep, each bearing a different inscription, some just lines, some dots, some both. "Maker's marks," he said. "The Moche lords required their serfs to pay taxes in the form of adobe bricks. Each community supplied a certain number of bricks per year. They marked the bricks to indicate which communities paid service."

"Sir, I'm an archaeologist. I know all this. Is this important to us?"

"It is," he said, "but I'm not sure why. Sandy Beckham is a Moche archaeologist."

"And he's important to us?"

"He is," Jimmy continued. "The Moche were lords of it all, until the Inca took them out. Like an army from hell, they swept down onto the coast and took out the rulership in one fell swoop."

Aleza smiled. "I have a Masters degree in Andean archaeology," she said. "You know that, right?"

Jimmy Segura didn't care much now. "Aleza, you almost had a Ph.D. until you blew off your dissertation. Twenty-six months ago, Ben Juarez and Jila Wells, two archaeologists working for Sandy Beckham, rented a beach bungalow in Puerto Chicama. They had pages of this stuff taped all over the walls; pages of maker's marks. We only know this from the crime scene photographs. The pages and the notes were gone before our boys got there. Why do you think you got assigned here?"

"It wasn't the Inca who marched in," she said. "It was the weather, and you're saying my name wrong. It's Aleza, like lay down to sleep. 'Lay,' not 'Lee.' Aleza. And it was the weather that took the Moche out; long periods of drought. And they deserved it too. The Moche were bastards, cutting off heads every time the storms blew, thinking *El Niño* was an angry god."

"*El Niño* is an angry god, Aleza," Jimmy said, letting his stomach puff; it didn't matter now. "It takes out the whole economy every twenty years or so. If I were an angry god, I'd do the same. Let them get complacent, then hit them hard; take away their fish and wash away their crops and guinea pigs for kicks."

She walked ahead, stopping before a segment of adobe wall adorned with the image of the Moche Decapitator god, a snarling figure holding a severed head on one hand, a metal sword with a rounded blade in the other."

"It's called a tumi," he said, pointing to the weapon. "It was made of copper, sharp enough to cut off a head or at least to cut a throat. They found one in the tombs at Sipan."

"They found three," she said, her fingers tracing the edges of the tumi until a heavyset woman in a blue blazer came over and looked at her curtly.

"It all fell to the Inca by about 1450."

"Not yet," she said. "Not until about 1480 did the Inca control the north coast, giving them about fifty years before the Spanish came."

• • •

"Why didn't you finish your dissertation?" he asked, sitting across from her at the cafe.

She shrugged. "I wanted to make a difference. Archaeology started to seem a little esoteric after awhile, a little pointless. I wanted to change the world."

"So you decided to join the CIA?"

She stared at him. "I think normally we don't say things like that out loud, in public."

"Fine. What do you know about Sandy Beckham?"

The waiter brought the wine immediately, filling both their glasses to the rim.

"I don't generally drink during the day," she said.

Jimmy, not a wine connoisseur, inhaled the fruity bouquet and took a deep drink. "I get four weeks vacation each year, and free airfare plus a stipend when I visit home. I can never be arrested, and I have a little account that I can use to brief agents. Regulations say I can use that account to purchase alcoholic beverages if I feel they are in order."

"I'm not certain they are in order."

"I wasn't asking," he said, taking another drink. "Tell me what you know about Sandy Beckham."

Aleza stared at the wine glass, already hating Peru. "I'm sure you know as much, but Sandy Beckham was a professor of archaeology at Columbia University. He did some seminal Moche archaeology work until about 1993 when the guerrillas all but took over Peru and threatened to kill foreigners, including archaeologists. They even shot at a few. So Beckham went to Panama or some place."

"Ecuador."

"Then he came back, right?"

"Yes, he came back in 2005 and started excavating a Moche pyramid."

"So what?"

"So he's building a new team, going back at that pyramid at Santiago de Paz. It's up north, on the coast."

"Again," she said, sipping her wine. "So what?"

Jimmy Segura sat back in his chair, ran his fingers through his hair. He was feeling the old insecurity that an overweight man feels when faced with a pretty girl who was having none of his wisdom. He inhaled deeply and adjusted his shirt.

"Why are we interested in Sandy Beckham?" she asked.

"Two reasons. First, because we're bored," he said. "Peru is at a crucial stage in terms of its evolution as a democratic state. The bad guys are in jail, the good guys are not so good, but they at least have a shot. Everything is just groovy, though there's not a lot of economic investment."

"And the problem?"

"Sandy Beckham was married for three years to Helen Tower."

All her training and Aleza couldn't even control her look of surprise. "Senator Helen Tower?"

"Yes. Helen Tower is a member of the Senate Foreign Relations Subcommittee on Latin American Affairs."

"I didn't see that anywhere in the files," she said, angry at herself, angry the way only a former doctoral student can get when the documents are not where they should be. "But even so, why is it significant that he's continuing his excavations?"

"It's significant because his wife is a public figure, so Sandy is a civilian of interest for us. Consular affairs keep an eye on him, just like they keep an eye on the guy from the Grateful Dead who has a house down here. Okay? So we've been paying attention to him. And here's the second reason; Sandy just came into some money."

"Yeah," she said. "So what?"

"Stop saying that. Eleven million dollars paid to an account at BancoCallao. Not to a foundation, not to a project, the money was paid to his landlady."

"From who? And why to his landlady?"

"From Twinberries Hamilton, a holding company in Bermuda. But the money originally came from Jibrail Holding, bankers in Cairo, Egypt."

"They really named a company Twinberries?"

"Bermuda," he said. "It's a nation of fruits. Even the police wear short pants."

"Interested in the ancient Moche, are they?" she asked, getting interested, getting her hands around the wine glass. "Aren't banking records private?"

"Normally. Bermuda wasn't saying much, but the local boys working for the Finance Minister here in Lima gave us this info, and in turn, we gave the Presidency an old B-12 bomber that had been sitting mothballed in Arizona for a decade. It looks nice with new paint."

"That's a lot of scratch for an archaeologist," she said.

"Yes." Jimmy poured himself another glass. "As a point of fact, it's an archaeological record."

"That's very funny."

"I'm serious. I checked it out. No excavation project has ever had close to that kind of money. They did Tut's tomb on about sixty grand."

"That was ninety years ago. Why channel the money through the landlady?"

"That's a good question. Sandy Beckham rents an apartment in Barranco, just a few miles south of here. It's the same apartment he's had for decades. It overlooks a little bistro where they play guitar; Che Guevara posters everywhere."

"That's a lot of rent paid in advance."

"Yes. His landlady is a Peruvian woman named Edith Heydr. She raises canaries and does local charity work, feeding orphan girls and such. She's clean, she doesn't have any paper on her at all. And I mean nothing, no birth certificate, no passport. Then a year ago, she shows up in a surveillance photo taken in Luxor, Egypt. Now she has eleven million dollars."

"Is she romantically involved with Beckham?"

Jimmy shook his head. "I doubt it, she's about eighty years old. But they're tight. She bailed out his project twenty-six months ago when it went bad. She sent in a helicopter and major security guys to get his people out of danger."

"That's exceptional service from a landlady."

"It is," he said. "Guerrillas shot up two senior members of Beckham's team. One of his principals, Jila Wells, was almost killed. They tried to take some documents from her."

"Tried? What do you mean tried?"

"I mean they failed. There were four assailants. The field director, a guy named Ben Juarez, jumped in front of Jila when the shooting started. He got hit. But they were after her. They hit her four times."

"She lived, right? Did they ever figure out who did it?"

"She lived," he said. "And no, they never figured out who did it. The police got there about five minutes after the shooting. By then, three of the gunmen were already dead and the fourth was wailing like a banshee, gut shot. He would probably have talked, but Jila shot him clean in the head right there as the cops were talking to him."

Aleza's eyes opened wide. "Jila, the archaeologist working with Sandy Beckham? She shot him?"

"Yes. Jila Wells. She was hurt badly. She had already killed three of them. She got this last guy while she was bleeding on the floor. The police would have done her right there if she wasn't already half dead."

"Fuck me," she said under her breath.

"Right."

Aleza shook her head. "Why did she have a gun?"

"Many of them do."

"Many of who?"

"Archaeologists. Bandits have been working them since the 1960s, first for cash and cameras, more lately for computers and cash and cameras. So the archaeologists got wise, got guns."

"Okay. Okay, so the girl survives, and now is back working with Sandy Beckham."

"That's right. But here's the thing. The documents that the assailants were trying to steal went missing."

"How did they go missing? I thought she killed all four gunmen."

"That's the rub. In the crime scene photographs the documents are taped up all over the walls. The police sealed the beach house and by the time Sandy Beckham got there the next morning they were gone. The police searched, and Edith Heydr hired detectives to search. Nobody knows, so now Sandy and his team have to start over without them."

"What do you think was on them?"

"I told you, maker's marks. You can see them on the crime scene photos, but not clearly enough to make out the patterns or the archaeologists' notes. And we've had the best guys go over the negatives with electron microscopes."

"What were they looking for?

"That's the eleven million dollar question," Jimmy said.

"So what's the plan? Do I have an assignment here?"

"Get chummy with Sandy Beckham. You're an archaeologist, and he's building a team. Be part of it."

CHAPTER 4

PERU

Jila said little during the flight to Lima. She ate Chicken Kiev, drank two little rum bottles plus the dinner wine and refused Ben's offer to watch the in-flight movie with him. Instead she watched a documentary on jellyfish. Jila learned that not all jellyfish had all their internal organs. Some lacked reproductive systems and some lacked brains. Yet all the jellyfish, genetically identical by virtue of asexual reproduction, worked as a single organism. Individuals who lacked one organ system or another hovered at the outer edges of the jellyfish community and were the first to be eaten by predators, preserving the innermost important individuals.

Jila imagined herself a less than perfect jellyfish. Had fortune and taxonomy not made her a flawed but sentient mammal, she might be swimming in a swarm of jelly. And she understood something very clearly on Flight 906. She understood she'd be one of the peripheral jellies, lacking something internal that would matter little to the cuttlefish that ate her.

"Say something," Ben said, pulling out the new Vanity Fair.

"It won't matter. They're going to eat me anyway."

"You want to read the magazine with me?" he asked.

"I don't." She sat back in her seat and grabbed the in-flight magazine, reviewing the airline's top choices for best seafood restaurants in Lima. She made a plan to say nothing more for the duration of the flight.

"Are you going to talk to me now?" Ben asked, once they cleared Customs.

She shook her head again as they boarded the little jet to Trujillo, the only city of any size on the north coast. The jet was nearly empty, and she drank two more little bottles of rum just after takeoff. "I could kill you with a pen," she said.

Ben yawned. He had heard it before.

The car was waiting at the airport. Ben didn't know the driver but didn't care this late in the evening. There was only one road, and his nose filled with dust as they spun out of the parking lot. The view was slightly more appealing at night because you couldn't see as much. Political slogans screamed from every conceivable surface, kids on bikes moved recklessly into the street, and every four seconds, another three-wheeled motor-taxi screamed by. Forty minutes of this before the car turned onto a smaller road and into the cane fields.

The cane cutters were still at work, even in the dead of night. Once the chaff was burned and the cane cut, it had to be processed within about twenty-four hours or else it would ferment. The foremen would whip you for that; Ben had seen it happen. The fires at the Santiago de Paz distillery burned day and night, as the cane was refined into sweet sugar for the domestic market, and the byproduct, molasses, distilled locally into a fine export rum.

Jila woke up when the car lurched onto the cracked pavement leading to the town center. Santiago de Paz. "My god," she said, "Can you gain weight just by smelling molasses?"

"It's pretty bad," Ben agreed, taking in the sights. "My nose feels sticky."

Jila took in the sights too. Santiago de Paz was a land reform community of nearly identical concrete block houses, home to seven hundred inhabitants who made a living cutting cane. Its commercial hub was pretty bleak: one church, one school, and a general store that sold toilet paper, baby chickens and a lot of rum. There were also a couple of little bars for the workers. Half a kilometer past the town center stood the massive walled compound that housed the distillery. 'Chimu Azucar y Ron' read the sign. Chimu Sugar and Rum.

"This place sucks," Jila said, half drunk, half not wanting to be here. The car turned a corner, came to a curve by the entrance to the distillery compound, then headed past the edge of town, down toward the ocean, toward the Moche kingdom, to Sig's Place.

Sigmund Klein owned the second largest bank in Peru before the world economy went into a downturn. He loved archaeology almost as much as money, so he built this hacienda as his retirement home, hoping to bring researchers to the Moche heartland. He died six months into retirement but he got his wish nonetheless. The researchers were here. The bank hated having to pay the upkeep, but legal documents being what they are, Sigmund Klein having served as Treasury Minister to three presidents, nobody was going to mess with him even dead. Besides, nobody wanted to buy a hacienda at the tail end of nowhere, fancy though it was.

"Sig's Place," said Jila. "How I've missed it."

The car bounced onto a firmer road and drove over the air strip, passing the small cluster of labs and facilities that comprised the research station. Out the window to the left, if the moon was right, Jila knew she could see the top of the pyramid, but she didn't care to look tonight. She sat quietly as the car passed through the gates and pulled up in front of the hacienda.

Toro, not his real name, but the guy they called Toro, the caretaker, majordomo, husband of the cook, opened the car door and drew her into his arms. "I told you," he said in Spanish, "I told you I had a place here you would be safe. Here, nobody touches you while I still live."

"I want to see Margarita," she said, pulling away quickly because she was about to cry, and she didn't want him to see that.

"Not now. Sandy wants you inside."

"Sandy can wait," she said. And when Ben went inside, she followed Toro along the path behind the big house where men's voices rang hard.

Margarita was sitting on the edge of the bed, shelling some legume, watching a soap opera on the TV. She almost jumped. "Sweet little angel," she said, her Spanish cracking with emotion. "You don't know how many prayers I've said for you. I thought you were dead until the papers came and we heard you were in Texas or somewhere in a hospital."

Jila couldn't stop the tears. She had friends, lots of them, maybe three if there was an accounting to be made, but who had ever loved her more than this woman? You find your family where you find them. "And your daughters?" she asked.

"Both in school. The little one in Trujillo, the fat one we sent to Lima."

Jila laughed.

"The boss has been waiting for you," Margarita said.

"You kept something for me," Jila said.

"Yes, doll. You want me to get it now, or maybe after?"

"You looked in my bag, Margarita. You did, right?"

She smiled. "After you got killed, yes, I looked. I took them out. Then when I heard you didn't die, I put them back."

Jila stared at the TV, watching as two masked men fought with swords while a young woman stared from behind a curtain.

"I kept them cleaned and oiled," Margarita said, ambling into the back room. "Toro said you can leave them alone if they're not being used but I took them out now and again, when he was out cutting figs for the guinea pigs." She came back and handed her the bag.

Jila hugged her, then gave her the envelope that held twenty hundred dollar bills, the advance money Ben had given her. "I think you're my best friend," she said, unzipping the little Nine West backpack, looking at her guns in the low light, for the first time in two years.

• • •

Jila peeked out through the kitchen door. There were lots of people in the big room. Sandy was sitting on the overstuffed leather couch on which she had fallen asleep dozens of times. Ben was next to him, and Toro was across the room, now in a white blazer, behind the little bar mixing drinks. Bottles of Scotch were displayed like trophies, next to bottles of the local fizzy water with dolphins on the labels. Toro was grinning, happy to be doing something new, anything but feeding the guinea pigs.

Jila edged her way in, and walked up to the nearest guy. "You're Bill Field," she said, "from the Field Museum. I always thought that was funny."

He turned to her, a big man, with a big beard. "Field from the Field Museum," he repeated. "It's given me endless amusement."

Jila held out her hand. "I'm Mildred Pine. Entertainment. Rodeo mostly, my parents were circus people. I couldn't read or write until I was seventeen but I could tame a lion. You're the sonar guy."

He switched the drink to his other hand and shook hers. "Sonar is for submarines. I do remote sensing, ground penetrating radar. And you're Jila Wells. I read the briefing document."

"There's a briefing document?"

"The whole cast of characters," he said, waving across the room. "That's Gordon Maybach over there; has to be close to ninety. He wrote the Moche Lords volume in 1972. Look at him working that little girl."

Gordon Maybach had taken one of the rusty pistols from the wall and was rubbing it with an old hand, showing it to young woman.

"That gun has to be as old as he is," Bill Field said.

"It's a Colt. 1890s," she said. "Who's the girl?"

"Can't remember her name. Last minute addition to the program."

"She's cute. What's her story?"

"Ceramics. She's doing a Ph.D. at Trinity College, Dublin. She was already in country so Sandy hooked her up."

"I don't like people I don't know," Jila said. "I didn't like you either until we bonded."

"I'm flattered."

Jila made her way to the bar, kissed Toro on the cheek and asked for a big mug of anything, conscious of the hush. When Sandy stopped talking, people listened.

Then he was there, all of him, Sandy Beckham, right in front of her. Five-nine, maybe a hundred and seventy pounds, sixty years old, but a big man in any room. He didn't say a thing, just reached out and took her hand, looked her in the eyes and still said nothing.

"If you make me cry, I'll leave right now," she said.

"Jila." He wrapped himself around her. "We'll talk later," he said. "I've got guests."

• • •

Sandy Beckham stood in the middle of the room and held his glass high. He might have said something to get their attention if he had been the kind of man who needed to. "Ladies and gentlemen," he began, "damas y caballeros, welcome to Sig's Place, Santiago de Paz, Peru, where we are about to make prehistory."

Clapping.

"I know you all have questions," he continued.

"I've got questions," said Bill Field, standing behind the big oak table, lighting a cigarette.

"We all do." Sandy was calm, no matter who said what. "We'll do a site tour tomorrow. I'm going to talk a little about our project tonight. But first, how about some introductions."

"I might suggest," Gordon Maybach interrupted him, the old pistol still in his hand, the new girl's arm in his other, "that you introduce us, Sandy, since you've brought us all together."

Sandy didn't miss a beat. "Right then. We'll start with you," he said, raising his glass. "Gordon Maybach, Professor emeritus at Oxford University now, though Harvard for much of his illustrious career. Physical anthropologist. It would take hours to tell of his accomplishments, but Dr. Maybach is best known for his work on the excavations at Cajamarca, where the Inca emperor, Atahualpa, was captured by Pizarro. Also, of course, for his definitive Moche Lords volume."

Gordon Maybach nodded.

"Dr. Ben Juarez," Sandy continued, "archaeologist at Sonora State University, then Mississippi State, I believe?"

"Something like that," Ben said.

Sandy rolled an unlit cigar back and forth between his fingers. "This is going to take too long if I tell of all your accolades so forgive me if I'm brief. Mark Cox," he said, pointing to a chubby little man by the door who held tightly to an almost identical woman. "Geography and Geographic Information Systems, and beside him, his lovely wife, Dr. Brenda Cox, cultural anthropologist, who recently completed a study on the fisherman of coastal Peru."

Sandy clipped the cigar, lit it with an enormous Mount Everest type high-temp lighter and puffed. "Dr. Bill Field will be doing our side-scan radar," Sandy continued, "and Juan Carlos Cortez, site archaeologist for Santiago de Paz is our resident field director. We call him J.C." Juan Carlos smiled, already a little drunk. "Dr. Jila Wells, archaeologist and specialist in archaic writing systems, and please meet Ms. Aleza Sabatini from Trinity College, who will be analyzing our ceramics."

The girl had a beautiful smile. Jila didn't like her for that, nor for her breasts which seemed to glow; they'd be handy in a blackout.

• • •

Dinner was masterful. Cream of asparagus soup from an old recipe, salad dressing tangy with lime, ceviche, the raw fish fermented in lime that Jila didn't care for but everyone else raved about, and much of a goat that had been dispatched earlier before the guests arrived. Potatoes, and Chilean wine rounded out the meal.

"We have a big day tomorrow," Sandy said, holding his court. "So let's get some of the basics out of the way. Many of you have visited the pyramid before, but we'll have a long look tomorrow."

"Huaca," Jila said, then bit into a potato.

"Huaca, yes," Sandy continued, "pyramid to us, but in this part of the world, they're called huacas. Just a short walk from here, the Moche built the massive adobe brick structure that the locals call the Huaca de los Espantos, the pyramid of the ghosts."

"Ghosts?" Brenda Cox said. "Is it haunted?"

"Very likely. Construction began around 250 AD," Sandy continued, "and the pyramid was continuously modified for the next six hundred years until some El Niño, or some political event brought a cease to its construction." He tossed a wine cork into the fireplace where two skinny logs blazed.

"Roughly seven hundred years later," he went on, "long after the Moche were gone, the Inca Empire was in power but they paid little attention to the north coast. Then the Spanish came. Francisco Pizarro ransomed Atahualpa, the Inca emperor, for fifty-four million dollars in gold."

"We've heard the story," said Maybach.

"Some haven't," Sandy snapped. "Atahualpa had just defeated his brother in a war of accession to the Inca throne. He was marching to Cuzco, eight thousand men strong, another forty-thousand or so within two hours march. Pizarro met him in Cajamarca with one hundred and eighty men. Atahualpa figured he could sneeze a bigger army than that."

Toro was grinning, still at the bar, pretending he didn't know English.

"Pizarro offered peace. He sent over a priest with a Bible, but royal bodyguards stepped in front of the priest and the Bible fell to the ground."

Gordon Maybach looked tired. "They were going to kill him anyway," he said.

Sandy nodded. "The Spaniards started firing. Even with all those soldiers, the Inca were powerless against Spanish guns, armor, and Toledo steel swords. Atahualpa never knew what hit him; he was a prisoner within the hour. Over the next three months as the ransom came in by llama caravan, Atahualpa learned to speak Spanish and to play chess with Pizarro. Once the ransom was paid, Pizarro tied him to a stake and lit the fire. Atahualpa would have been about thirty years old."

Toro was still at the bar, still pretending he didn't know English, but not grinning anymore.

"A refreshing history lesson," Bill Field said. "But this is not an Inca site, it's a Moche site. And why are we rushing to finish it in thirty days?"

Sandy smiled, found another cork and threw that into the fire too. "We are expecting an *El Niño* this year, bigger than most and within the month. Our work might be curtailed. There are other matters to discuss, but first, pie and ice cream."

• • •

Later, all of them in the living room, Toro ferried Scotch in the little green glasses that had once been the bottoms of wine bottles. The men all had their Cuban cigars, acting like kids with the forbidden.

"Bill raised an excellent question," Sandy began, "why are we in a hurry to finish in thirty days? And my answer was truthful, we are facing a major storm. But my answer was only half of the truth."

"How I love a prologue," Gordon Maybach said.

"1548," Sandy began, striking a match for effect and to light his cigar, "fourteen years after Pizarro took Peru for himself, the Theatine Order of the Roman Catholic Church sent a delegation to Peru, where they built a church on the plaza right here in front of our pyramid."

Jila frowned. What nonsense was this?

Maybach shook his head. He was old in body but sharp as a bronze tack. "All of Peru was Franciscan."

"Ultimately, yes," Sandy said. "The Franciscans had great influence in Spain, but the Theatines were here first, and they built a church."

"Why do we care?" Bill Field asked.

Sandy held up a hand. "About five years after the church was built, in 1553, a priest named Giovanni Carafa sailed to Peru. You'll not find this information in the Vatican library because he made the voyage in secret, and made it round-trip in only eleven months. We have authenticated documentation of this voyage."

Toro moved quietly, making himself almost invisible, like in the jungles up north when he was younger. He refilled glasses from a decanter as if it were a privilege.

"Carafa entrusted a book to his priests here in Santiago. His benefactor, Pope Julius had charged him with this task, but Julius died before Carafa returned and another Pope had been seated."

"So many Popes," Gordon Maybach said. "It's difficult to keep up."

"So true," Sandy said. "This next Pope lasted only 22 days. And upon his untimely death, Giovanni Carafa became Pope, Pope Paul IV."

"And what of the book?" Maybach asked.

"Yes." Sandy stared at the fire. "One thing had to haunt old Pope Paul IV."

The room was silent.

"The book he gave to the priests at the church at Santiago de Paz was no less important than the Domesday Book of 1086."

Jila shook her head, wondering if Sandy was making it up as he went along.

"I don't remember what Domesday was," Bill Field said. "I'm not a medieval scholar."

"Perhaps Professor Maybach can illuminate," Sandy suggested.

"I'm not a medieval scholar either," Gordon Maybach said, "but since I was there at Domesday's inscription, I can perhaps help. Toro?" He held up his hand, and Toro was there like a shadow, lighting the man's cigar, not a Cuban, a genuine American Philly.

"Domesday was a census of England commissioned by William the Conqueror to ascertain Crown revenue. I can't imagine what this has to do with our endeavor."

"Nothing whatsoever," Sandy said. "Just that Carafa's book was an accounting of the Vatican's land holding in all of Europe, much of which was illegal. Should this book come to light, the Vatican would find itself embroiled in lawsuits that might take down the entire church."

"But the book never surfaced?" Bill Field asked.

Sandy shook his head. "Not yet. The Theatine order is still around. They have a monastery near Denver, Colorado, and they're rich as thieves because they invested early in Microsoft. And they want the next Pope to be a Theatine, when the time comes."

"I have a question," said Aleza, the first time they had heard her voice, "and for those of you who can't see me through the cigar smoke, I'm over here on the couch, hoping that there's enough oxygen left in the room to refill my lungs."

"What is it?" Sandy asked, ignoring her comment.

"If it was a book, wouldn't it have disintegrated long ago?"

Silence, then everyone was looking at her, knowing which way the wind blows on the Peruvian coast down by Santiago de Paz.

"Sweetheart," Sandy began, "we're digging up fifteen hundred year old bodies that still have their socks on. If there's a book hidden in that pyramid, it will look no worse than the paperbacks here in the library. Nothing decays here."

"So we're supposed to fund Carafa's book?" Mark Cox, who would be making the computerized site maps, had said nothing until now. A shade past his prime, this job might be his last chance to make a name. It wouldn't hurt the wife's career either, though hers was not as marginal as his own.

"A book in an oak box," Sandy said. "With iron hinges. It could be anywhere."

"A book that the Vatican would not want found," Cox suggested.

"That's right," Sandy said. "The Pope is old. With the right paperwork, the Theatines could make a bargain for one of their own to be next."

"Blackmail," Ben said.

Sandy shrugged.

"Why thirty days?" Bill Field asked.

"We're coming up on the anniversary of Carafa's trip to Santiago de Paz," Sandy said. "500 years."

"Doing the math," Bill noted, "it seems more like about four hundred and forty-eight years ago or somewhere in there."

"I've never been good with math," Sandy said, "and I don't care. I just want to find Carafa's book. This is archaeology, boys. This could be the find of the century. Besides, there's a fucking *El Niño* coming."

● ● ●

Locking the door, Jila found the little spring lock in her bag, and the rubber jamb, and she set them up at the door so that she wouldn't be disturbed. If Ben tried to get in she would just pretend she was asleep.

Outside, the laughter and the chatter were still going. Archaeologists as a rule tend to go to bed only when the bottles are empty, even if they have work the next morning, which in this case they did. She tossed the sheets, checking for the little insects that sometimes hovered or hid, but the light was dim and she had had a few drinks herself. Since no bugs were immediately apparent, she jumped into bed. Despite the crickets outside, and the murmurs from inside the house, she was halfway to sleep when the doorknob shook. She was awake instantly, but didn't make a move. Let Ben just try to get in; her defenses would hold.

The lights off, the shade kept out the glare from the perimeter lights so she couldn't see much. Let Ben think she was still asleep. Make him knock. Then she heard the spring lock snap. The rubber jamb skidded across the floor, and then the key was in the door. "Not bad," Jila said, as Sandy Beckham stepped in.

She sat up in the bed and pulled the sheet close as he came towards her.

"What are you doing here?"

He sat at the edge of the bed. "I didn't have a chance to talk with you." He reached out to touch her hair. "I can't tell you how sorry I was. I should have been there."

"They'd have killed you."

Sandy tucked her hair behind her ear. "I need you for this, or I would never have sent for you. I did my best to make this safe. We've got six guys heavy on the premises, you'll see them if you look around."

"I saw five," Jila said. "Two of them look like they could still be in high school."

"No, they're all ex-military, two inside the walls, two in the back house, and two outside in the cars. It's as safe as we can make it."

"Yeah. You know what? You're a good liar, Sandy. You think your team bought that crap in there? Theatines? I've never heard of a Theatine. Is it even a real word?"

"It's all true," he said, "up to a point."

"Carafa? Is there a Carafa or did you make him up?"

"He's real and he really did become Pope. I made up the rest, but it's a nice story, right?"

Jila shrugged. "It's not bad."

"We're going to excavate that plaza and part of that pyramid, Jila. There is something down there we still need to find."

She worked the covers up around her and held her feet with both hands. "A little ruined church on top of a Moche plaza with just a little something else sandwiched in between the pagans and the holy."

"That's right," he said. "Where are your notes, Jila? The drawings, the photographs? We never found them."

"I don't know, do I? I got shot."

"You don't have them?"

"Yeah, Sandy, I had some intestines that came out from my insides, remember? So with the police already on the scene I spent an hour and a half taking down every page from the walls while trying to stuff my pancreas back into my abdomen."

"You did or you didn't?"

She shook her head. "I didn't. I thought you cleaned up the scene."

"Do you remember any of it?"

She tapped a finger against her temple. "Like it was yesterday," she lied.

"The Ibanez box is out there somewhere," he said quietly.

"And why do we need to find it now? Did your landlady give you an ultimatum? Because it has to be at least a million dollars you're getting, a payroll like this, all the heavy hitters? And this new girl isn't going to work out, I can tell you that much right now."

"It is a lot of money," he said. "But we have a lot of work to do. There are more than a dozen exposed friezes near the top of that pyramid, all of which will be destroyed if we can't consolidate them before the storm comes. And we have a chance to dig now. That's what it's about."

"I'm tired," she said. "I have to be up early.

"Then you're going to stay, right?"

"It would seem so. But listen, if I get so much as a whiff of bullshit, I will disappear."

"Understood. There's just one more thing," he said. "You're going to have a roommate."

"No way. This is a single."

"A single with a bunk bed. You're already in the bottom, so let's put her on top. She was last minute."

Jila put her robe back on when Sandy left. She was tidying her things when Toro came in with the girl's suitcases. Aleza Sabatini came behind him. "Sorry for the intrusion," she said.

Jila lay back in her bed. "Don't mention it. I used the big towel, the yellow one. The little blue one is all yours."

CHAPTER 5

LIMA, PERU

Jimmy Segura parked the rented Toyota on a side street, away from Barranco's bustle and music. Even at four in the afternoon, the music was loud; pan pipes but also mariachis who had no business down on this continent. The neighborhood was first rate, home to expatriates, artists wealthier than their work suggested, and diplomats whose wives wanted a little more authenticity than the condos in Lima could provide. But the street that Edith Heydr lived on was not part of it all.

He walked a block and a half to the decaying mansion, paint peeling off the poured concrete, but a mansion nonetheless. He passed a pair of young girls, Indian girls, not more than five years old selling chunks of goat meat from a homemade barbecue. He nearly passed them right by until the smell of the pepper and the yellow hot sauce made that impossible. He finished his snack, then made his way to the house and rang the bell.

An angry looking old Indian came out to the gate to meet him. You're supposed to refer to them as indigenous, Jimmy remembered from the briefings, but this guy was as Indian as they came, his face worn with age and anger. He wore new blue jeans and a white button down shirt that was perfectly ironed.

"I have an appointment," Jimmy told him.

The man barely acknowledged him, but fit a key into the large padlock and opened the gate just enough so that Jimmy could step through. He saw a curtain move in a first floor window as he followed the man up the walk.

Edith Heydr sat at a rotting oak desk, its surface pocked by the termites or little worms that had been working at it for decades. The woman had to be at least as old as the desk, Jimmy told himself as she pointed to a canvas chair.

"I'm a busy woman," Edith Heydr said.

Jimmy took her in as his eyes adjusted to the low light. No makeup, she had her hair in a long gray braid. She could have been a hundred years old.

"I do some work at the local schools," she said, her bony hands clasped in front of her. "We're always looking for financial support. I expect that's why you're here, to help the children who have suffered while your government looked the other way."

"That's not really why I came," he said, not finding much balance in the rickety chair, and uncomfortable with the damp odor of the room.

"No, it isn't," she said, "but we should start with a donation. You have your checkbook with you, and I have a dozen young prostitutes who need a chance in life. Write me a check."

"I'm here on behalf of the U.S. government," Jimmy answered. "And I have some questions about your work."

"Write me a check and I'll tell you a little. Don't write me a check and I'll tell you a little that won't be of much use."

Jimmy stared into her old face. Why not? he thought, reaching for his wallet. He could comp it. "Will a hundred dollars do?"

She hadn't moved an inch. "The older girls," she said, "those in their teens can make that in a night, four tricks or five. The younger girls can make that in an hour. Write it for a thousand and we'll keep talking."

Jimmy tried to remember what the limit was for something like this. He wrote a check for five hundred dollars and handed it to her. He noticed a small canary sitting on the edge of the desk. He thought it was a doll at first, but then it moved its head back and forth, watching him.

"Thank you," she said, placing the check in the desk drawer, nodding toward the door where her man waited. "You'll have some tea now." It wasn't a question. "What can I do for you, Mr. Segura?"

"I had a question..."

"You are a cultural attaché with the American Embassy," she interrupted. "And I am not an American citizen. You understand that your authority here is limited."

"I'm just following up on what my boss tells me to follow up on." Jimmy leaned forward and brushed a little pink worm from the edge of the desk. "Due to some intricacies of international diplomacy, my government has some limited oversight on Peruvian economic affairs." Another worm crept out of the same hole. "Are these things everywhere?"

"Almost everywhere there are worms."

"You'd think the canary would eat them."

"You would think that."

"You recently took receipt of a very large amount of money," he continued. "Eleven million dollars, minus the exchange commission. Is this for the orphan prostitutes of Lima? Because that would pretty much dwarf my contribution just now."

A small woman maybe half as old as Edith Heydr made her way into the room with a tray, and left quietly.

"I work with a number of charities," she said, not moving an inch. "Please pour yourself some. I've just had tea. The cookies are excellent."

Jimmy poured half a cup. "Eleven million dollars is a lot of money."

Edith Heydr reached into her desk and pulled out a candy, fussed a bit with the wrapper and put it in her mouth. "Did you have a question?"

"Where is the money from, and what is it for?" Jimmy took a sip of tea, found it very hot, very minty, numbingly so.

"The funds were collected by a fellowship of benefactors," she said, sucking on the candy. "They will be utilized to realize the goals of that fellowship."

"Caring for Lima's discarded youth?"

"If you need put it that way, then yes."

"How long have you been in Peru, Ms. Heydr?"

"All my life," she said, her eyes never leaving him. "I was born here."

Jimmy wasn't sure she had even blinked once since he arrived. He took another sip of tea. "I think you're Egyptian. I think you came here in the 1970s, though I can't imagine why you would lie about it."

She sucked on her candy. "Check my papers. I was born here. My parents were school teachers in Ayacucho."

"Then you know I can't check your papers, Ms. Heydr. All government documents in Ayacucho were destroyed by the Shining Path guerrillas when they made it their stronghold."

"Ayacucho always was their stronghold," she said, still not blinking.

Jimmy blew on the tea, still too hot, his mouth numb. "The money came from an Egyptian bank, after a quick laundering in Bermuda. You must be aware that money coming from Islamic sources is scrutinized, perhaps a bit more than is fair, but I'm the scrutinizer here."

She still didn't say a word.

"Is the money for Sandy Beckham?"

A fly landed on her forehead but she didn't move.

"Will you talk to me about this?" he asked.

"I don't think so," she said.

He pulled out his cell phone and punched in a number. "I can freeze your account in five minutes."

She moved quickly, startling the canary, and flipped open a laptop. "I can transfer the money to Buenos Aires in three minutes. Double or nothing on that five hundred dollar check?"

Jimmy thought about it for a moment, wondering if she could do that. The laptop threw him. It had some kind of doily covering it, which is why he hadn't noticed it. Time for a different approach. "Did you know that American consumers don't like using dollar coins?" he asked. "They prefer bills."

"I had heard that on CNN," she said, her fingers hovering over the keyboard.

"Right. We still make them, but they're not common, so recently, the US Treasury gave the Egyptian Finance Ministry a coin stamping press. In return, we got a packet of old documents. Included in that packet was a letter dating to 1863, and addressed to Jefferson Davis, offering a weapons deployment to the Confederate Army. The document never left Egypt, unless it was a duplicate, and you're not going to believe what the Egyptian Pasha wanted in return."

"I can guess," she said. "What could President Jefferson Davis possibly offer except respect? I imagine that was what was requested. May I see that document?"

"I don't have it with me, but I could get my hands on a copy. It was signed by a man named Haj Feyd Heydr, executive secretary to the Pasha."

Edith saw her man coming through the door with his dagger out. She shook her head, and by the time Jimmy turned, the man had turned around.

"If the document you mention is real, it is of enormous historic importance," she said.

"It will be entered into the national archives, and become available for viewing in about twenty-seven years," he said, his lips thick now, the words not coming easily. What kind of tea was that?"

"Coca tea."

"I've had coca tea. This is a little different."

"We brew it special. Maybe we do have something to talk about, after all," she said, getting up unsteadily from her chair. "Tupac will show you out. When you come back, bring the document you mentioned. The original, not a copy. I've seen a great many phony documents in my time. I might answer some questions."

Jimmy sat slumped behind the wheel of the Toyota, his fingers numb. He watched as some kids pried a hubcap from a Volkswagen across the street. He turned the key in the ignition and gave one last look at the house, where he saw the big Indian, Tupac, unroll a mat and kneel down.

Jimmy checked his watch. "Noon."

CHAPTER 6

SANTIAGO DE PAZ, PERU

Here we are again, Jila told herself, stepping into the alluvial dust that for some alchemical reason blew every which way when it was cloudy and cold. And today it was cloudy and cold.

"I thought it was supposed to be hot on the coast," Aleza said. "I've been working mostly in the mountains."

"It will get hot," Jila said, zipping up her polar fleece as the team neared completion of the half-mile hike from Sig's Place to the pyramid, "but it's six in the morning. There isn't a place on the planet that's hot at six in the morning. What do you think of our complex here?"

"It looks like a lunar outpost," Aleza said, taking in the four aging Quonset huts that had been connected and expanded upon with plywood and bamboo to create additional work and storage space.

"Yes," Jila agreed, "except the one on the moon has running water." She raced up ahead, climbing the little dune in a few quick steps and looked out at the alluvial plain, at the sand dunes, the little temple mounds, the ruins of the little church, the Pacific ocean, and towering over everything else, the massive flat-topped pyramid.

Jila had seen it a thousand times, but the pyramid always thrilled her. It was magnificent. Ruined by twelve-hundred years of wind and scouring salt air, it looked like a sand castle gone bad. It was lumpy and uneven, with intact adobe bricks poking out here and there from it steep walls. "You're beautiful," Jila whispered to the pyramid. "And you were loved for so long."

"This is our majestic Pyramid of the Ghosts," Sandy began. "It measures just under twenty-nine meters high. It was built in about AD 250 and it was remodeled at least seven times over the next five hundred and fifty years. For reasons not yet known to us, the Moche abandoned the site around AD 800."

"And how long have you been working here?" Maybach asked.

"I came in 2005," Sandy said, "but by that time, Juan Carlos had already been directing excavations for a decade. He's the guy who discovered the complex of rooms near the top of the pyramid. Each wall is ornately decorated with painted friezes. We'll take you all inside later to have a look."

"It's crazy to think about," Bill Field said, "but all the Moche really had was dirt. So they farmed it to make a living, and then they built something absolutely fantastic out of the very same dirt. We humans are pretty great when we put our minds to something."

Sandy nodded in agreement. "And once they built it, they spent the next five centuries remodeling."

"What are all those little platforms?" Bill asked, pointing to the five smaller structures to the north, each about two meters high. "Are those other pyramids?"

"Those are Moche temple mounds," Sandy said. "We have cleverly named them Temples 1, 2, 3, 4, and 5. Each would have had a ceremonial building on top, but as you can see, the buildings didn't survive, and the temple mounds themselves are in terrible shape. We have not yet gotten around to excavating or consolidating them."

Ben picked up a length of bone from the sand. "Watch where you walk, people. This bone is from a llama, but most of the bones you see on the surface here are human."

"Human?" Aleza asked.

"Yes. These are the remains of the ancient Moche lying all around you. There's a skull right there" he said pointing. "Over there a partial mandible, and most of the others are long bones."

"The preservation is incredible," Bill Field said.

"Yes," said Sandy. "As Dr. Maybach will be briefing you this evening, the north coast of Peru is one of the driest places on earth. Here you can find sixteen hundred year-old skeletons still wrapped in their burial shrouds."

Jila picked up a perfectly intact femur.

"Left or right?" Ben asked her quietly.

"Shut up," she said, smacking him on the thigh with it. "I'm not talking to you."

"Why not?"

"I don't know yet."

"So why are the bones all over the ground?" Mark Cox asked. "How come they're not buried?"

Gordon Maybach took the question as Sandy led them toward the plaza of in front of the great pyramid. "The bones are on the surface because they have been dug up by grave robbers. You see," he began, "this entire site was a holy place. And where there are holy places, people are buried. When Moche lords died, they were wrapped in cotton shrouds and buried with fine ceramic vessels. Even the non-elites, the poor, were buried with what treasure they had, treasure which has grown in value over the centuries. Those vessels are worth a small fortune on the black market. So look around, and you'll see tens of thousands of looted graves, the bones of their former tenants lying broken in the sand, their treasures stolen."

"You're starting to wax there, Gordie," Sandy said quietly.

"You said there were five temple mounds," Bill Field said. "I count three."

Sandy pointed to a pile of bricks covered in sand. "Numbers 4 and 5 were destroyed by looters decades ago. They tore them apart brick by brick."

"Looking for what?" Aleza asked.

Sandy smiled at her. "That is the magic question," he said. "We don't know, maybe a book that was long overdue."

Jila lagged behind as Sandy led the group up to the pyramid. She found a potsherd with a painting of a fish on it.

Aleza peeked. "Nice," she said. "I'm still learning the sequences, but that's pretty diagnostic."

"When does it date to?" Jila asked.

Aleza took the small piece, looked at the fragment of the neck just below the break. "Could be anywhere from 200-500 AD."

Jila nodded. "Not bad."

"I want to ask a question," Aleza said, "but I didn't want to sound stupid. I've been doing mostly Inca ceramics so I'm new to this. There's one thing that I don't get."

"What's that?"

Aleza pointed at the ruined pyramid. "This book we're looking for, it would have been buried out here on the plaza right? Not on the pyramid."

"We don't know. They could have hidden it anywhere."

"But they wouldn't have buried it on the pyramid. I mean, the pyramid was a ruin even then. The Moche were long gone by the time the Spanish arrived."

"I'm not so sure," Jila said, picking another potsherd, this one with no painting on it. She tossed toward it at a little owl sitting on top of a sand dune, just to watch it fly. "The Moche weren't building pyramids anymore, but nobody just disappears. These guys living in Santiago today are very likely the descendants of the people who built this place. So who knows what was going on here five hundred years ago."

"You think we'll find the book?"

Jila shrugged. "If we can crack the code," she said, looking over to where Sandy had the gang lined up on the plaza in front of the ruins of the church. "Come on, or we'll miss being in the photo."

"What code?" Aleza asked, walking after her.

● ● ●

Sandy lined up the team in front of the largest segment of unbroken wall remaining of the Spanish church.

"Reminds me of Poland." Gordon Maybach giggled uncomfortably. "I was a pilot in the Royal Air force. They had me out in this light plane trying to find something, but I got shot down in November of 1942. The Germans lined me up in front of a church wall with a whole bunch of other prisoners. They shot every third man. I was lucky, I spent the rest of the war in a plush POW camp."

"What were you were trying to find?" Bill Field asked

"Rommel," Maybach whispered.

"Rommel wasn't in Poland."

Maybach nodded. "And I'm the guy who helped confirm that."

"Smile," Sandy said, smiling as the driver took a photo. Sandy didn't really want the photo, but group photos were always morale builders, and morale was going to be crucial for the next few weeks.

The tight formation began to pull apart when Aleza rushed forward, brandishing her own little camera. "Just one more, please?"

Sandy grinned; going to be needing that negative. "We are now standing in the nave of the Theatine church," he said, "and for those of us who are not specialists in medieval architecture, the nave is the central part of a church, from the main door to the altar."

"There's not much left of it," Bill pointed out, looking at the remains of the adobe walls, most of which were only a foot or so high, though in places they rose up to nearly two feet. "There are churches in Europe this old that still hold services."

"Yes," Sandy said, "and they are made of stone. What we have here are a few segments of adobe brick wall, some very clear outlines of the architectural footprint, and some fantastic stratigraphy."

"What's so fantastic about the stratigraphy?" Aleza asked.

"Stratigraphy," Sandy answered, "is all about layers. We're standing on the plaza of the Pyramid of the Ghosts, upon which Spanish priests built a church in 1548. So while the Moche may have been cyclical in their construction practices, the Spanish were not. They built a church. It thrived for a short time, and then it died. Now it's covered in sand and we're standing on it.

"Sand on the surface," he continued, "then a Spanish presence. Below that, the Moche, then more sand below, perhaps the remnants of a stray bison that hunter-gatherers took down. Keep digging and there's nothing between you and the molten core."

"So what precisely is our plan?" Maybach asked. "How do we attack this project, Sandy? I'm Anglican myself. I'd kick this Papist structure into dust if I weren't an archaeologist first. But thirty days, pardon my Latin, is fucking nonsense. With this size team, we'd need at least six years."

"Twenty-nine days," Sandy said, wiping the dust from his sunglasses. "This is day one. Twenty-nine days left; you'll be home by Christmas. Get comfy in the sand here, gents and ladies, so Juan Carlos can illuminate you on matters of protocol and tell you about your crews.

Juan Carlos Cortez squatted in the sand. He picked up a llama rib and began drawing lines in the sand.

"Lines in the sand," Maybach whispered to Bill Field. "Reminds me of the month I spent in the Tunisian desert. The women are not as modest as the reports would have you believe."

"Tell me later," Bill said, focusing on Juan Carlos.

"This town, Santiago de Paz, is a sugar cooperative," Juan Carlos began, in heavily accented English. "Most of the men work in the cane or in the distillery. Because this is not high season, we have engaged thirty-eight men, along with two women, to work with us. Most are veteran excavators. As director of archaeological investigations at this site, I will oversee the workforce logistics."

"Let me add," Sandy said, "that most of these men have worked with us in the past, and they are aware of our security concerns. The site will be guarded at all times. Nobody gets near these excavations without our knowing about it. Should the occasional tourist turn up, he will be turned away."

"Unless they are school groups or practitioners of native religions," Juan Carlos added.

"Excuse me?"

"School groups and practitioners or native religions have access," Juan Carlos reminded him. "That is made clear in the permit. This is our national patrimony and some groups are guaranteed access."

Sandy shook his head. "Whatever."

Juan Carlos had four neat lines drawn in the sand in the nave of the Spanish church. "Four teams," he said. "Team One will clear debris and otherwise assist Dr. Bill Field as he conducts a remote sensing survey of the plaza and the pyramid itself. Dr. Field has brought sensitive equipment that can detect metallic elements up to a meter and half below the surface. Am I correct in that statement, Dr. Field?"

"I could find an iron penny in a haystack," Bill said, "given enough time and if a penny is there."

"It's there," Sandy interjected, "but it may be deeper than a meter and a half. So you'll have four men working with you to do your initial sweep, which you noted, would take about twelve days."

"Team Two, the largest team," Juan Carlos continued, drawing a circle with the rib. "Under the guidance of Ben Juarez, will consist of thirty-one excavators to dig the contours of the church and find any burials associated with the church."

"That's a lot of people," said Mark Cox. "If I'm supposed to map this entire delta, I need three people at least. I brought four GPS units and it will take me two days to train my team. So please tell me you're at least giving me three men."

"Three men." Juan Carlos stared at him coldly. "As requested, three men will work with Drs. Mark and Brenda Cox on mapping. The map may lead us to the unexpected, or it might not."

"That leaves only two," said Ben.

"Yes," Sandy said. "We have two ladies, two seasoned ceramic experts who will work with Aleza. If we find late ceramics, we might be getting closer to our goal."

"This, gentlemen," said Juan Carlos, erasing the lines with the rib, "is our team. You will meet them here at six-thirty tomorrow morning when excavations commence. You will also meet, but not have a great deal of contact with, a team of six art conservators who will be working with me on the friezes near the top of the pyramid, friezes that we have discovered over the years. We'll be injecting a plasticine polymer into the stucco so that it can withstand the coming rains. Let's not forget that we have a storm incoming in about a month."

"Let me make one more observation," Sandy said, squinting, looking up at the clear sky, the clouds now receding. "We'll have a normal workday of 6:30 to 4:00. The hours are long but the pay is good. During the course of your studies, you may come across adobe bricks with markings on them. Some of these markings will be of no importance. Some will be maker's marks, indicators of taxation payments by local villages who supplied bricks to the Moche lords here at the pyramid. When you find them, and you will, you will make them known to Jila, who will record them."

Bill Field held up his hand.

"This is not a classroom," Sandy said. "What's your question?"

"I'm still not sure why we care about maker's marks."

"Neither am I," Sandy said, "but Jila has a suspicion that they may be contextual to the architects as well as to the tax collectors. That in building their pyramids, the Moche were constructing a text as well."

"Like you could read the pyramid," Brenda Cox said, following the line of thought.

"Something like that," Jila said. "There is a pattern to how the bricks were used. It wasn't random. And if it had textual undertones then the pyramid has a story to tell."

"It could not have been a very complex notational system," Maybach ventured.

"Computers use only two notational elements, ones and zeros," Jila reminded him, "so the system need not be complex to be effective. It probably doesn't matter anyway - as you can see, most of the architecture is destroyed, so the bricks are out of position. It's like finding a whole pile of those little alphabet blocks kids play with. Little Antonio might be writing the great Peruvian novel, but once he has a tantrum and knocks the blocks down, it's just letters with no context. Anyway, let me know if you see any bricks with marks on them."

Sandy stood up. "Let's all of us keep the goal in mind," he said. "We're looking for a little wooden box. The workers have been informed of a thousand dollar reward for the man who finds it."

Maybach raised his hand.

"Yes, Gordon?"

"What if we don't find it?" he asked. "What if it doesn't exist?"

"It does exist," Sandy said. "I have no doubt of that. If we don't find it, we don't find it, and I'll write another grant next year, but it won't be for this kind of scratch." He checked his watch. "OK, let's go have the requisite tour of the site. This might take a little time because I'm going to show you every last wall segment, every last adobe, every last looter hole, so pay attention. Then we'll head back to the house, have some lunch and swim in the pool, have a good night's drink and some rest. With any luck, we'll find Carafa's box by noon tomorrow."

"Don't be foolish," Maybach said. "You know how excavations work. You never find anything until the last day."

CHAPTER 7

SANTIAGO DE PAZ, PERU

Aleza Sabatini was first in the pool. Jila was half out the door in her black one-piece when she spotted her splashing about in her bikini. The men were more conservative, wearing big long bathing trunks. Though she was neither, Jila felt fat and old. She pulled on a robe and went to sit by the pool.

"It's nice," Aleza said. "You should come in."

Jila smiled. She looked around, spotted the two security men detailed to the inside of the compound, their eyes focused on the bikini. "I would but I'm shy."

Aleza pulled herself out of the pool like a model would, swinging her hair back. She toweled off like a model too, hair first, then sat beside Jila on a plastic chair. "So what's the story with you and Ben?"

"No story."

"Come on." Aleza smiled as Toro brought big goblets of orange juice and vodka.

"Nothing but an old bedtime story," Jila said, slipping quickly out of the robe and jumping into the pool before anyone had a chance to notice.

Then there was Gordon Maybach, eighty-eight years of manhood inching down the ladder. "It's so cold," he whined.

Bill Field cannon-balled in, splashing so much water that Maybach just slid under in surrender.

Aleza lay down on a towel at the edge of the pool. "So tell me," she said.

Jila swam three laps across the little pool, burning approximately two calories. She came up to the edge and folded her arms on the tile. "What do you want to know?"

"You had a thing with him?"

"Why? Do you want him?"

Aleza smiled. "Do you?"

Jila repressed the urge to dive. "No," she said. "Help yourself."

"But you had a thing with him?"

"Yes."

"And it ended badly?" Aleza sat up and rubbed her shoulders with oil that smelled like mango.

"Yes, it ended badly."

"He's cute," Aleza said. "You want him back?"

Jila held her breath and ducked under the surface. She stared at Maybach's little knees, and held her breath for as long as she could before surfacing. "No," she said, climbing out of the pool, grabbing her towel.

Back in the room that was supposed to have been a single, the room that had been Jila's years before and now again, she spent a long while in the shower. She came out naked, towel over her hair and found Margarita working in her suitcase, rolling her socks into balls.

"You look like you did back then." Margarita said, staring at her. "Except for the scars."

Jila grabbed the robe from the hook on back of the door.

"You didn't bring your computer?"

Margarita had been through her stuff.

"Not this time," Jila said.

"Your boyfriend will be coming later, after smoking with the boys."

"Did you check her things?" Jila nodded at Aleza's suitcases, secured by little combination locks.

"I did," Margarita said. "There's nothing of interest except she wears those thong underwears. And she has a little computer."

"Did you turn it on?"

"Yes, but it has a password. You want me to spend some time on it?"

Jila shook her head. "He's not my boyfriend," she said. "And if he comes here, he'll be leaving a moment later."

Margarita shook her head. "He saved your life, little one."

Jila was having none of that. "No. Stand there," she said, shoving her gently towards the door. "Say you're Ben Juarez. You're there by the door when they come in, two guys with guns. There's two more out back but you don't know that yet. What are you going to do?"

Margarita smiled, no stranger to the idea, but the scenario new to her. "I have a weapon," she said, "the little twenty-two I keep in the pocket of my apron."

"Not this time, you've got nothing."

"Then I talk to them like I don't know what's the problem, offer them whatever money I have in my bag."

"That's right," Jila said. "But you see it in their eyes. They're well paid. They'll kill you in a heartbeat. What do you do?"

"I plead with them?"

"No you don't."

"I have no gun, not even a carving knife? With that I could hit one of them in the eye of my choice."

"Nothing." Jila hit the light switch, dark now. "You weren't expecting it, you were sloppy, you don't have so much as a pen in your pocket."

"Then I'd drop to the floor."

"Would you?" Jila asked, drying her hair with the towel. "What if you knew I had two nines?"

Margarita frowned. "It wouldn't matter. If you were there, they wouldn't have the guns just on me, they'd be on you too. If you pulled them out they would shoot you before you had a chance."

"So walk in front of me," Jila said.

"I'd risk getting shot."

"It's not much of a risk. They're not going to leave any witnesses. Walk in front of me." Jila grabbed a brush and bottle of hair mousse from the suitcase and dropped them in her pockets. She motioned to Margarita, urging her to move closer to the door. "Look at them. Talk to them. Just keep moving until you're between me and them."

"I love you baby," she said, "but not that much." Still she stepped in front of the door, the sunlight making a silhouette of her, a little fat from the years in Santiago de Paz. "So what?"

"Turn around."

She did and found Jila pointing the brush and hair mousse at her. "You just covered me. You just gave me time to get to my guns." She aimed the brush over Margarita's shoulder. "I can hit them from here. So if you want to get out alive, you walk in front of me, then you drop to the ground while I kill them."

Margarita shook her head. "That doesn't mean he didn't save your life, baby."

"He saved his own life."

Margarita shook her head. "You blame him for that?"

"No," she said, "I never have, not for a moment. But he saved his own life. He moved correctly into position, and I killed them. It was the only thing that we could have done. We didn't know at the time that there were two more of them."

"He could have sat down." Margarita said, tossing the sock ball at the suitcase, missing it by a long shot.

"It would have been the last thing he did."

• • •

Excavations would start in the morning, but Juan Carlos and Ben had come back out to the site to meet with the men and get organized. Already, eighteen trenches were being mapped out, the strings lining their edges to define them.

Ben knew most of his crew from years past. Carlitos, Nehemias, and Junior had taken a surveying class at the college in Trujillo, so Ben appointed them crew chiefs. Each of the crew chiefs oversaw four or five teams of excavators. The excavators worked in teams of two; one man would do the digging or the troweling while the other carried off the dirt and screened it. The three chiefs would keep the logs for each of the excavation units, bagging and tagging artifacts, and sketching anything interesting. They were also ostensibly responsible for keeping the excavators in the trenches working, instead of socializing and talking about soccer and women, which they did incessantly.

Ben had worked on dozens of excavations, and he knew that some of these men were among the best he had known. But he had learned years ago that the ethic of an underpaid excavator required the immediate cessation of all work the moment a supervisor's eye was averted. It was almost a point of honor.

Ben stared out at the plaza, a great ceremonial space thirteen centuries ago, later a foundation for an intrusive Christianity, and now, a vocational platform for local workers who would screw around now and again but nonetheless provided skilled labor at $9 per day per man.

Juan Carlos seemed to have things in order, so Ben walked around the edges of looter holes. He had intended to climb around the pyramid just to remember it again, but for now, he was just going to walk past the little temple mounds and head down toward the beach.

He stopped now and again to pick up the rags that blended in with the sand, rags that were the burial garments of kings and farmers who died before the birth of Charlemagne, before Europe had a king worth talking about, before Aztecs and Incas and Turks. Some of the rags had interesting designs on them; most did not. Ben reached for a little pot sherd and disturbed a pale sand owl who probably had some eggs or babies in a nest just nearby. Ben watched her as she circled, calling out, warning him. He stepped back, figuring to change his course, and fell into his past.

• • •

On the hot sand of a desert not unlike this, a ten year old Ben Juarez holds an umbrella over his head and passes time by stepping in the footprints of his grandfather who walks in front of him, also holding an umbrella against the harsh New Mexico sun.

Ben's arm is in a cast. He snapped it coming down from the tree he often climbed. He didn't even know exactly how that happened. It didn't even hurt, but it was most clearly broken, the doctor confirmed that. His parents and his sister Anabella had to go. It was picking season and Ben wasn't going to be able to pick much this year, not with that broken arm, so they put him on a bus to stay with the grandpa in his little trailer at the edge of the desert.

Which was really fine with Ben, the bus ride was exciting. A Negro man gave him a warm can of Pepsi, and a young girl across the aisle had only a few teeth and a baby named Theodore who she stuffed with chocolate.

After a week in the trailer, just Grandpa's little black and white TV with one channel, Grandpa's stories getting old, nothing to eat but macaroni and chili and stinky onion rings whose preparation held the old man's attention as if he were splitting an atom, Ben grew so bored he was ready to pluck out one of his own eyes just for novelty. "Can't we go somewhere?" he asked, as Grandpa looked up from his onions. He was crying.

They left in the morning.

"Where are we going?" Ben asked, jumping from footstep to footstep.

"Someplace," the old man answered, moving briskly across a desert that seemed endless.

"Why can't we just wear hats like everyone else? We look stupid holding up these umbrellas."

The old man stopped and spun around. "I look great. You look great. And there is no one here but you and me to see us."

"Where are we going?" They had been out two days, walking quite a bit and making camp in the afternoon in the shade of the mesas. They had brought a great deal of water which Ben was sore from carrying. They ate chili from a can and rattlesnake meat from rattlesnakes that Grandpa blew up with a shotgun. Ben was tired. "Where are we going?" he repeated.

"We're going to look at the paintings the Indians made."

"We've already seen a whole bunch of them. It's boring. It's all just animals and lizards. I'm tired. When can we go home?"

"You want to go home?"

Ben nodded.

"Fine, we can go home when you find a new painting on a rock, one we haven't seen before."

Ben groaned. "That could take days."

And it did. It took two days and the last can of chili. Ben was certain that they were on the verge of starvation. Only one bottle of water left, and the old man still had them far into the desert clambering around a little burnt mesa that was not going to have any paintings on it at all.

Ben walked along the edges, careful to stay away from the low scrub where the snakes hid. Nothing and nothing and nothing. His broken arm was hurting, and the other arm was hurting and he realized he was crying when he saw it. Half hidden, the painting on the inside edge of an irregular boulder meant salvation. He closed the umbrella and dragged its point in the sand, marking a trail back to the campsite where Grandpa sat cross-legged, his glasses on, digging buckshot out of a black snake with his Swiss Army Knife. "I found one," Ben said, elated.

He led him by the hand, it wasn't far, and showed him his prize.

The old man ruffled his hair. "It's beautiful," he said. "What is it?"

Ben frowned. "What do you mean what is it? It's a little bird."

Grandpa nodded. "A little bird." He held an old finger, oily from snake innards, up to Ben's mouth. "Remember those words. There's old Indians that made these paintings, maybe a million years ago. The legend says the paintings have power, and if you find one, you can use that power to move your life closer to where your life needs to be."

"But I don't know where my life needs to be," Ben said, excited but skeptical.

"Of course not," Grandpa said. "You're only about seventeen years old, right?"

Ben frowned. "I'm ten."

"Then hold on to it. Never say the name you gave the painting until you find what you really want, then it will be bound to you forever."

Ben nodded.

They ate snake for dinner and finished the last of the water. In the morning, he followed Grandpa around the edge of the mesa and the trailer was right there, right there. They had been walking most of a circle for days. For dinner they had chili and onion rings which tasted better than anything Ben had known. He fell asleep watching black and white TV and thinking about his painting and the name he had given it, Little Bird.

Since then, the earth had moved around the sun a little more than thirty times. Lives change, Grandpas die, parents and sisters no longer soak their hands after days of picking fruit, and boys grow up to be professors. They do some things right and they make mistakes.

The owl caught the breeze coming off the beach and she flew up over the pyramid until she looked like a little dot. She came down just as fast, gave one last call before diving into an old looter's pit to watch over her eggs.

CHAPTER 8

LIMA, PERU

Jimmy Segura was not prepared for the meeting. It was Saturday for the love of God, and he was off duty. When the car came, when the knock came on the door, he knew it was Montes behind things. That was the way Montes like to do it. Jimmy had no time for a shower so he scrubbed down with a facecloth, trusting that the woman in the bedroom would stay quiet as he had requested. He dressed quickly while the local company boy stood in his foyer, then got into the car and was shuffled to work.

Jimmy felt nothing but regret. Regret that his parents had divorced at a young age; regret that he had once briefly joined a coalition of youths in South Philadelphia that required a series of beatings for disengagement; regret that he had long since given up any illusion of being a poet; and regret that this cleaning woman he had hired, though well into her late forties, had a body to die for, and showed up six mornings a week packing a liter of dry, nutty Nicaraguan rum. And sweet lord help him if she wasn't the best sex of his life. Jimmy finally reported the contact about a month ago, even though he was a little ashamed. The woman had to be ten years older than him and wore only tracksuits.

Jimmy Segura was not prepared for the meeting.

Salvador Montes, head of the anti-terror task force, sat in one of twenty ergonomic chairs that ringed a large opaque glass table. On the table before him lay a pad of paper and a glass of juice.

I'd have sat at the head of the table, Jimmy told himself, *if this was my meeting.*

Montes held the phone to his ear but apparently wasn't getting much out of it. "Local lines," he said, shaking his head. "It's like you want to use the satellite phone for everything, but it gets expensive when all you want to do is call the preschool to find out if the chorus thing is tonight or next week. Do you have children, Jimmy?"

"No sir," Jimmy said, taking a seat. "You and I have known each other for about six years. I was an usher at your wedding. I'd surely have mentioned by now if I had children."

Montes nodded, then put the phone down in disgust. "Nothing. You just have to keep trying." He produced a folder from his briefcase and opened it. "You made an unauthorized request to Document Production. It was sent in the Wednesday diplomatic pouch and is now well on its way toward fulfillment even though it was signed not by me, nor by the head of Consular Affairs, nor by the Ambassador or his deputy, who are the only four people in this country authorized to send work orders to central services."

So that was what this was. Jimmy felt that rush that comes so rarely in life, that feeling like you're out on the edge of the world, like jumping out of an airplane, having sex outdoors, or being called to task for something that was someone else's fault.

"I did make the request," he said. "But I made it to your office, Sal. Things have gotten ever so much easier now that you've color-coded the request forms." Jimmy was starting to feel a great deal more confident. "I can even see the purple form right there in that folder."

Montes leafed through the stack, holding up the purple page, "You mean this one, the one that has your signature on the bottom, authorizing the request."

Jimmy felt his heart sink. "Did I sign on the wrong line?"

"You did, yes, and now we're going to be the proud new owners of a forged Civil War vintage document that was supposedly sent from Cairo. Do you know how much research goes into even figuring out what the stamp is supposed to look like? You requested this to be B Grade? B Grade could fool the Egyptian postmaster general."

"No," Jimmy shook his head. "No, there's no stamp. They misread it if they're think there's a stamp. The letter was never supposed to have been sent, so it doesn't need a stamp, but it has to be B grade minimally, because the intended recipient will have comparables. C Grade is just color matching, language, and ink. Anyone with a light table can tell it's fake. And D Grade, that's just a temp with a quill pen and recycled paper."

"That's not funny."

"It is," Jimmy insisted.

Montes read from the requisition form. "Language specific, vintage to 1863, exploratory tone, two paragraphs. You even wrote out the text and drew a little picture of how you wanted it to look."

"I did, yes," Jimmy said, nodding.

"From Haj Feyd Heydr, secretary to Ismael Pasha, addressed to American General Jefferson Davis, President of the Confederate States of America, offering military hardware in exchange for American tolerance of, and nonaggression toward, an Islamic state in South America."

"That's right," said Jimmy. "It's not asking for much really. They don't even have to give them anything, just recognize the state. It's nice, isn't it?"

"It's a little far fetched," Montes said. "What's this for?"

"Is it far-fetched? We effectively have a semiautonomous Islamic state in South America. You said it yourself in last month's briefing. We've been posting on it for the past year."

Montes leaned back in his chair. "Parana."

"Yes, Parana, that lawless fucking tribal region where Brazil, Paraguay, and Argentina come together; it's like Afghanistan. Nobody knows where the borders are, and nobody is policing them. And it has become a haven for Hezbollah, Islamic Jihad, Al Qaeda, and Shining Crescent. These organizations are involved in terrorist activities all over the continent. Sal, we already have an Islamic state in South America. It's just that they're too busy right now to map out their borders."

"That's a little outside our jurisdiction," Montes countered. "Our job is to investigate links with terrorist cells in Peru."

"Sure, but our mandate extends throughout South America. We had that meeting with the CIA Director. Do you not remember that? He ordered each of us to start having nightmares about Parana so that we would be thinking about it all night as well as all day."

"Have you ever been there? To Parana?"

Jimmy shook his head.

"Wild fucking west. Little Indian guys walking around wearing gun belts and spurs. It's like stepping onto the set of a cowboy movie except everybody speaks Arabic."

"Sounds nice."

"What's the forged letter for, Jimmy?"

"For Edith Heydr. I went to see her about the wire transfer."

"The eleven million."

"Yes. I asked her what it was for and she clammed up. So I threatened to freeze the account."

"We can't freeze the account," Montes said. "If she's holding that kind of money in-country, she's not afraid. That means she has someone at the bank who can move the money if anybody pokes around. But so what, you think she's a terrorist?"

"I would have thought she was just some old lady," Jimmy said drinking his juice. "But there was something about her eyes."

"Her eyes?"

"Yeah, and I think she's lying about her background."

Montes leaned back. "Don't forget that we have operational imperatives not to move heavy on local people just because they're Muslims."

"I know."

"Did you know that Muslims have been in Peru for as long as the Spaniards have?" Montes asked. "Many of the sailors on Spanish ships were Muslims fleeing persecution? Did you know that the wooden balconies you see today on some of the old buildings in Lima are of Muslim design?"

"I did know that," Jimmy said. "I wrote that section of the briefing."

"I thought we were looking to the archaeologist on this, and the old woman was just banking him."

"Right, that's still our position. I have someone working on Sandy Beckham, but I feel there's more to the woman. I want to sweat her with the letter."

"How's that going to work exactly?"

"I don't know. I'm still thinking it through."

Montes shrugged, closed the folder and put it back in his case. "Then I guess we'll tell Document Production to get on it. No stamp."

"No stamp."

"Are you still screwing that maid of yours?"

"Yes, sir."

"Well, good for you," Montes said, standing up.

CHAPTER 9

SANTIAGO DE PAZ, PERU

After dinner, Gordon Maybach nearly killed them all, going on about the history of archaeology in Peru. He started in 1920 and worked his way forward at the rate of about a year an hour until Toro gently pushed them out of the dining room so he could clear the table. Bill Field finally changed the subject.

"What's with the lockdown?" he asked, loudly, bringing in the others into the conversation as they converged on the bar.

"Yeah." Mark Cox added, "I tried to go to go out for a walk earlier and the gate was locked."

"And Toro unlocked it for you, right?" Sandy said.

"Yes, and he went with me into town to the store."

"So what's your complaint?"

"Can we have keys to the gate?" Bill asked, "and use of the car to go into town after work? There are a few bars there I wouldn't mind checking out."

"No."

"Why not?" Aleza was interested now. "I thought it would be nice to walk around in the afternoon. Do we need an escort for that?"

"Is all this security really necessary?" Bill asked.

Sandy said nothing. He just pointed at Ben.

"We feel that it is necessary," Ben said. "As you are all aware, we had an incident two years ago in which Jila and I were assaulted."

"Hold on," said Bill, "Sandy said that was unrelated to the work. I thought it just a robbery attempt."

"And I thought that it didn't even happen here," Aleza added. "Wasn't it up in Chicama?"

"All true," said Ben. "But the incident was never resolved to our satisfaction."

Sandy jumped in. "Let's also note that we have about $100,000 in equipment in a country with an annual per-capita income of about $2,000," he said. "There are no police in Santiago de Paz, and while we enjoy good relations with the residents, there are those who resent foreigners in general."

"I don't want to be locked up," Bill said, shaking his head. "How about getting us some keys to the gate?"

"Sounds fair to me," Mark Cox said. "We're adults. What say we get some keys so we can come and go as we please?"

The mood was heating up. Ben held up his drink. "Why not?" he said. "Why don't we start by having a tour of Santiago tomorrow. I'll show you where the feed shop is, where to go to burn your garbage. There's a town hall and an elementary school, and the distillery. We could arrange a tour of the distillery. There's not much else to see."

Aleza had already joined the enemy ranks. She was standing next to Bill, feeling things out, seeing who had the most juice here. "Still," she said, "it kind of makes me feel like a prisoner. We've got those guards. Anything wrong with just leaving the gate unlocked in the afternoon so we can take a walk or even take the car if we use the buddy system?"

Ben stared at her, waited a moment to see if Sandy wanted to take this one. "Not a chance," he said. "Toro can ferry you into town if you really want to go. Or you could walk and get some exercise. We have lots of friends here, but we're still high profile. So the gate stays locked. If you want to go out, go out. Just ring the bell when you want to get back in. Will that work out for you, Aleza, Bill?"

Bill said it would. Aleza did too.

"If you don't come back, we'll notify the embassy."

"OK then," Sandy said. "Please remember to be careful if you do go out. Last year six excavation teams were working on the north coast. One went down with typhus, and four were robbed at gunpoint. So our security measures are well within normal operational parameters."

"That is an understatement." Gordon Maybach had nodded off briefly but was back on track now. "Back in 1973, there were six of us working up at Recuay. Me, Aldo Cisneros, who now heads the prehistory section of the National Archives, a couple of locals and this little Italian girl who was doing our drawings and photography."

Jila closed her eyes. Twenty-nine more days.

Maybach lit one of his Phillys. "One day, Aldo is down in the village buying food and those chocolates that you used to be able to find everywhere, remember those, Sandy?"

"I do," Sandy said.

"So I'm coming back from the site and I hear noises coming from the house, like the little Italian girl moaning. I figure she's in trouble so I come running in through the door but she wasn't in trouble."

"I didn't see that one coming," Sandy said. "I thought for sure she was going to be in trouble."

"That was my thinking," Maybach agreed.

"Getting a little, was she?"

"No. Turns out I was lost and got the wrong house. They looked very much the same, you see."

"What does that have to do with security measures?" Bill asked.

"Well, they were angry," Maybach said. "The woman began kicking me savagely, and kept at it for what seemed like an hour while the man stole my watch. I was terrified."

"Right." Ben caught Jila's eye and winked at her. "If anybody gets bored, we have a DVD player and a pile of movies. I think there's a Monopoly around here somewhere but it has street names from Lima instead of New York."

"New Jersey," Jila corrected. "And we've got a whole library for anyone who wants to read. Breakfast is as 5:45. If you show up late you don't get any melon."

Aleza chuckled. "We're really starting this thing tomorrow, aren't we?"

"Yes we are," Sandy said. "So let's have some more drinks, then get a good night's sleep tonight. And if you're having difficulty getting to sleep, ask Gordon to tell you another story."

• • •

Starting up an archaeological excavation is not unlike starting up a steam locomotive. Forward motion is possible, but it's going to take some time.

Juan Carlos Cortez had assured that the workers were already milling about when the gringos emerged from Sig's Place and climbed over the dunes. Many of these men had worked with the project for years. Some were new, some were sons and nephews. But forty is a large number of men to draw from a population of seven hundred. Sandy would have preferred to work with a smaller team, maybe eight guys, take a while at it, take a few years. But the deadline he had been given was firm.

Sandy walked over to Gaucho who had worked with him for years. Gaucho smiled, a few less teeth than last time, but the smile was real.

It seemed like Jila had her arms around everyone's shoulders at once. Sandy remembered her first field season. She was an outrageous hit, at first just because she was pretty. Nobody dared hit on her, but any holiday, any birthday, any sorrow, and someone would try to kiss her. Jila would laugh with them and she would drink with them, and she knew the same bad words they did and some they didn't. Sandy shook hands, people were glad to see him. They were glad to see Ben too but some of these grown men were crying when they hugged Jila, crying because they knew she had been hurt in their part of the world.

Sandy motioned to Juan Carlos, who whistled to get everyone's attention, then began introductions and handing out assignments. As each man's name was called, he picked up his tool bag, and the little bucket that held his lunch, his wheelbarrow too if he had one, and stepped forward.

"I'm going to start in the back, right?" Bill Field said, confirming his own understanding of the project.

"That's right," said Ben. "Your equipment should be ready for you in the supply shed. Your team will start with the ground-penetrating radar and move over the pyramid itself until you come to the plaza."

Bill gave him a thumbs up. His Spanish was good but outpaced his confidence in it. He started slowly, meeting the four guys who would be helping with the remote sensing.

Marx Cox didn't speak much Spanish at all, so Sandy had set him up with a few of the younger guys who had some school, who had a little English, and who might enjoy the little GPS computers. Brenda Cox spoke perfect Spanish; she had been doing work on Peruvian fishing economies for much of her career and spoke like a native. She'd get along fine with the men if she could get them to make sense of her. Right now, as she peeled layers of sweater from her body and doused her round shoulders with sunblock, they stared at her as if she were from the moon.

"I think I'm going to need a translator," Mark Cox said nervously, inaccurately assessing the workers' interest in his wife.

Ben shook his head. "Your *curriculum vitae* says you speak Spanish. If you don't speak Spanish, don't say so on your academic resume." Ben waved to his crew, thirty men, thirty-one if you counted Daniel, who was probably as old as Maybach. The man could barely lift a trowel but he was good for morale.

Aleza was surprisingly fluid. The two ceramic analysts were all smiles. They were young girls who had studied in Lima. They spoke a little English, and appeared happy to have the chance to spend some time with a stylish gringa. They led her toward the little lab where they would be working.

Sandy watched as the security men took up flanking positions. "What do you think, J. C.?" he said. "Two days to get set up; that's the quickest start we ever made, I think. Back in 2005, it took us a month just to buy the shovels."

"Progress," said Juan Carlos. "Why did you add the ceramics girl? She doesn't seem to know very much about the Moche. She wasn't on the original list either."

"No, she wasn't, but evidently she has some pull with the Minister of Culture, what's his name?"

Juan Carlos shrugged.

"Whatever," Sandy continued. "Anyway, they asked me to take her on as a favor. I said no, then they said the permits might take awhile, so I said yes."

"She's quite a dish," Juan Carlos said. "Isn't that how you say it? She's a dish."

Sandy nodded. "Yes, maybe in 1950. Does the lab have internet?"

"No." Juan Carlos shook his head. "And no phone lines out here yet. No electricity lines either, that's why the generator."

"No walkie-talkies either, right? You've told everybody."

"Yes. The men were very sad about that. They love the walkie-talkies. The walkie-talkies aren't even powerful enough to reach the edge of the delta, but they're useful to us. What's the problem with the walkie-talkies?"

"You never can tell who's got a receiver. Some fat dude in Hamburg with a goiter spends his whole day listening on the short-wave. He could pick up the signal."

"Could he?"

"I don't know. I'm just paranoid."

"You want to see what we did with the little tomb by Temple 5?"

"I do," Sandy said. He followed Juan Carlos along a route both men knew well, passing the scars of previous excavations.

"That's where you fell in that time," Juan Carlos said, pointing to the lumpy ground, now clearly marked with painted rocks, warning of the danger of collapse, like the collapse that took Sandy and three excavators down two and a half meters through a desiccated cane roof into a tomb that had been looted centuries ago. The discovery had not been worth the back pain.

Sandy walked carefully along the edges of the deep pits ringed by human bones and textiles, the signature of the coastal gravedigger. You had to watch where you walked here. Even though the delta itself was flat, traversing it involved either zigging between looted graves, or walking a straight line and moving up and down. Either way you risked tripping on an old broken bone and maybe breaking one of your own.

Behind the ruins of Temple 5, which had been literally torn apart by treasure hunters, Sandy followed Juan Carlos through a labyrinth of adobe bricks which had been recovered by excavators over the years and meticulously assembled into piles, some two meters high. Each pile was made up of bricks bearing the same maker's mark. Sandy traced an X on a brick from the X pile, then a little wavy line on a brick in the next pile.

"X to wavy line," Juan Carlos told him, "straight ahead to diagonals, then left, immediate right at two circles..."

"I know the way," Sandy snapped. He had walked this path every day for years. He knew the risk. Make a wrong move and nothing happens to you; you find nothing, some bone perhaps, a little bit of cloth or the old fuel drums from past years. Make the right moves and you're somewhere in the middle of the thing, an artifact of archaeology itself, an adobe maze built from ancient bricks that concealed the location of the well behind Temple 5, a well which was long since empty because the aquifer was now several meters lower due to centuries of coastal irrigation.

Sandy remembered when they first dug the well. What a rush, stairs spiraling downward to who knew what, something secret and old and precious. That's not what archaeology is all about, but it can be on a good day. Two months to get to the bottom and you could feel that it was a little damp. It wasn't a tomb or a secret place, just a well where the Moche lords got their water.

They found the tomb a week later when Sandy lit a cigarette six and a half meters down into the well and realized that the smoke was not going up, but going sideways, into the wall. The wall was just a single column of bricks, which they punched through in about an hour. Inside was a tomb. It was enormous. It was empty like they all were, robbed probably a thousand years ago. Just a few bones, some broken pots, the burial shrouds, nothing more, but it was a big room with some ventilation through the foundation cracks in Temple 5's platform.

Sandy followed Juan Carlos down the steps, deep into the well and into the low corridor that led to the tomb, its makeshift door unlocked, its interior now lit with sixty-watt light bulbs. The walls were covered in maps and graphs, and at the far end, Jila sat at a big table with the computers and the monitors and the satellite phone.

"How is it looking?" Sandy asked, leaning his chin on her shoulder, watching the monitor that showed Bill Field sitting, his men crouching in a semicircle around him. Another had Aleza Sabatini's face dead center.

Jila smiled. "I think we're in business."

• • •

Five days into the job, Aleza was feeling more confident as she stared at the piles of ceramics before her on the long table. Mathilda and Loca, the two technicians assigned to her, clearly understood the nature of ceramics sequences far better than she did. And they made that relentlessly known to her as she worked to match the ceramics recovered by the excavators against a sample collection. The sample collection had a known timeline, the product of several decades of experience at several Moche sites. So if you dug up a piece of pottery and matched it against the samples, then you knew where you were in time. It was simple enough in theory, but it was tiring work; not work she was good at. Six teenage girls, happy for the chance to earn a little money, sat outside washing the pot sherds with cloth and brushes, careful not to mar any of the decorative elements.

They listened to music while they did this, and because they worked right outside the lab, the music was heard and appreciated and sung along to by Mathilda and Loca. Both women were pretty sure that Aleza's Spanish was sub-par. They were excited by her and deeply intimidated, and as such, they ridiculed her mercilessly. Mathilda said she was probably a whore, sleeping with the big Doctor Sandy, that's why she got this job here since she didn't know ceramics any better than a baby girl did.

Not that they weren't helpful. Under Mathilda's withering glare, Aleza learned a great deal about Moche pottery, and was daily growing more proficient. She could now easily distinguish between an early Moche potsherd from a late one. The finer distinctions would take some time.

Aleza let them have their secrets. She had hers.

Back in Atlanta, her parents always made a fuss about barbecues, roasting this and that on grills fired hot enough to forge iron. At one such barbecue when she was sixteen years old and well aware that she was considered attractive by men, she came out of the pool to change when she noticed she'd been followed inside by one of her father's friends, a man she had known all her life. He was a gorgeous man who she thought about often, and he walked toward her tentatively, hesitating when a peal of his wife's laughter cut through the house.

Aleza let out a gasp of surprise when she realized that he was here for her, that he was attracted to her. He misinterpreted her reaction, turned to leave but she stopped him. She caught his hand and brought it to her stomach, then grew dizzy as her body began tightening and she understood for the first time how powerful she was.

Years later, a creature of her chosen profession, she had a meeting in Langley, Virginia with a man named Jurgen, a company man. He asked her if she might take a turn in a bed somewhere, if it meant getting a job done, and she said no. The question was never asked again.

She had slept with a number of men, and had boyfriends over the years, but she found them to be almost disturbingly obedient, and their desperation was too often pathetic.

The little stereo was turned up full, but that didn't stop Mathilda and Loca from regularly corrected her ceramic sequencing. Aleza excused herself, took her bag and walked toward the little adobe hut that housed the toilet. She knew her transmission would be noticed so she had to work fast. She held the little computer device between her knees as she sat on the toilet. She didn't have much to report aside from her suspicion that

Sandy Beckham was full of hot wind, and that the business with the Pope was some of that wind. She typed that all in, located an available satellite, and sent a quick eight second burst of message detailing her experiences thus far at the site.

Nervous and a little excited, she walked back into the lab, listened as the women talked of the blonde princess being back. Aleza shook her head which worried them. Then she turned and walked away. She walked past the pyramid, past the five little mounds to the edge of the site, and down off of the ridge into the fields where sugar cane leaves brushed past her face, leaving light red marks. She turned, crouching reflexively as one of the security guards rushed toward her.

"Doctora," he said. "There are rats in here. They might bite you, and the cane will hurt your face. The cane is already hurting your face."

"What's your name?" Aleza asked.

He took his hands away from the military rifle, moved it to his shoulder. "Manuel," he said.

He was gorgeous. She squinted, held a hand over her eyes to block the sun. He looked like Tito Puente at nineteen.

"Come here," she said as she removed her shirt, then her pants.

The boy's eyes widened. "No, Doctora. I am on duty. I don't want the trouble."

Aleza peeled off her panties and hung them on a cane stalk. "I won't ask again."

Manuel fumbled with his rifle, finally laying it down. He smiled as she pulled him down on top of her onto the soft grass between the rows of cane.

"You're a big boy," Aleza said.

His hands were all over her. "I was the biggest boy in my math class."

CHAPTER 10

SANTIAGO DE PAZ, PERU

Sandy Beckham sat in the big chair in the tomb office, working on bits of an omelet he had been curating since breakfast, his attention transfixed by the crossword puzzle. His ex-wife sent them to him, stuffed in with her weekly letters. The crossword was beating him. He stared occasionally at the monitors, thinking of a nine letter word for neglect, certain that a vowel was involved. Jason's craft was an easy one - ARGO, any archaeologist worth his dirt could pencil that one in. Then summer in France - ETE, and underground railway leader - TUBMAN.

He paused and picked up the letter, read of the gossip from Washington and Helen's plans for Rome at Thanksgiving. Would he come and visit? No, Sandy thought, no, he would very likely not. He had spent last Christmas with her in the Seychelles, marveling, after sex with his ex-wife, that life can take strange turns. No, Helen, I'm not going to go to Rome. Sandy didn't mind thinking about the past as long as the part was sufficiently removed from the present. Maybe that was part of the allure of archaeology - you could think about the past all day long without getting too close or too emotional. But get Sandy thinking about more recent events, like his marriages or anything since the Crusades, and he would tense up, start to sweat. The letters from Helen Tower forced him to think not just about her, but about the others.

Sandy was thirty years old when he tied a knot that stayed tied for almost three years. Marlena was a thrill but her thrill waned quickly as she surveyed her world from the parapets of Bowling Green, Kentucky, where Sandy had found employment. 'We could go to Red Lobster,' he begged as she packed her bags.

At thirty-six, associate professor at Columbia University, Sandy had some game now when he married Bronwen, his Scandinavian goddess, a full professor in the history department, a specialist in seventeenth century Irish politics. Bronwen was inordinately excited by his collection of Delta Blues records. The first time he played a Son House record for her, they were eating veal ravioli in his kitchen and she started dancing, tossing off garments every few beats. How could you not love a woman like that? Sandy fed her some of the good wine he maintained for such occasions and took her to bed, bed being the couch that folded out. Even so, it was something else.

She left him seven months later, went with that physics professor, a young guy with a tight shirt. He told her she was elemental.

He was forty-four when he met Helen Tower at the only yoga class he had ever attended. She was smart and bendy. He loved her the moment he saw her stretch. She wore a little blue workout suit that Sandy thought would look really nice on the floor next to his bed. With that image in mind, he offered to make her dinner. Thirty-two months later she was a Senator, and as they sat at the same table eating linguini, she worked him through the finer points of the divorce papers. He was fine until she promised to be his friend forever; that's when he started crying.

Sandy finished off the omelet, wrote ASGARD where the clue Odin's lair suggested he should. He looked up at the monitor and watched as the security guard mounted his ceramic specialist in the cane field. "My goodness," he said.

• • •

Bill Field looked like a tightrope walker. He moved slowly, holding the radar baton parallel to the ground. It was three meters long and weighed eleven pounds, not including the cables which trailed behind him, leading to the equipment in a backpack worn by his support staff, an elderly gent who wore it like a badge of honor.

Bill had designed the system himself, and it was quite possibly the most advanced in the service of archaeology. He had modified an Air Force radar platform that was declassified in the 1970s for the oil industry.

Wearing four-hundred-dollar headphones, Bill Field didn't even need to look at the little LCD screen most of the time. The radar signal was given a tonal signature; large stone features were low and bassy, bricks or even packed adobe registered as a clicking tremolo, while metals gave off high pings. The signal was calibrated along the length of the baton; a subsurface feature identified by the right extremity of the baton registered only in the right headphone speaker. Something directly underfoot would be transmitted to both headphones, and if you trailed off to the right, the sounds would move into the left headphone.

The sensitivity could be significantly enhanced by taking a single Vicodin tablet at least thirty minutes before starting, or forty minutes if you had eaten a sandwich. The apparatus made Bill Field the only human alive who could listen to the architectural past.

In order to calibrate the system, to create a subsurface map, he had laid down a slow backbeat that was timed to his footsteps. As he took a step forward with every fourth beat, the software registered another .72 meters of linear space.

To date, the musical signature of the pyramid involved more blues than rhythm. Bill had been walking the surface of this mangy pyramid for eight days now. The massive adobe core was acoustically monotonous, a steady drum accented by a competent but unremarkable bass guitar. It sounded like Tejano music without the eighty-dollar pianos.

"Move it along," he called to his assistant

The Pyramid of the Ghosts, if you were standing near the top of it, as Bill was, allowed an unequaled view of the entire site. The surf washed slowly across the beach, the cane cutters in the distance cut the cane. And in front, on the pyramid's broad plaza, he watched as Ben Juarez directed his own symphony of excavators working just outside the walls of the ruined church.

Luddites, Bill thought, shaking his head. Still, he had to admit Ben and his team was making quick work, while his own investigations had found nothing much at all.

He began moving forward, listening to the dull bass. This continued for several meters before a tremolo took shape in his left ear, a steady tone suggesting a wall or other linear feature. Then the woodwinds kicked in, something less substantial was below, not more than a meter, maybe wood. Wood was a silent player in his orchestra, but its presence was sometimes indicated by the absence of other tonal qualities. He looked back to be sure his packman was following and that's when he heard the flutes.

The flutes wafted in through the right earphone, very light at first, there might even be a piccolo there but he couldn't be sure, the sound was so faint. The first flutes of the season.

"Sirens of the past," he said out loud. "I think we have some metal here." The signal was weak; the flutes were hesitant and his piccolo was barely producing, but it was there nonetheless. A subsurface wall marked by the absence of heavy bricks and the unmistakable tone of metal suggested that there was a tomb beneath him. It was time to call in the Luddites.

• • •

The next morning, Ben Juarez detailed four teams of excavators to the top of the pyramid where Bill had set his wire flags.

Sandy was excited too. "Four teams is all?" he called out to Ben as he trundled up to the top.

Ben looked irritated. "If it is a tomb," he said, "then it will measure no more than three meters by two. So you put more teams on, they bump into each other."

Sandy drank from his water bottle.

The coordinates had been plotted in record speed and the guide lines were in place. Eight men tore into the structure with little shovels and trowels.

Excavation units were ordinarily approached in the way that most human matings were approached, first with slow caution, followed by hesitant advances and then inevitable abandon. The occasional lunge could at any time be met with resistance. Break something, like a trust or an old pot, and your game was over. If the pyramid was willing, they could move fast. Jila climbed the pyramid as the excavators began digging.

They worked quickly but diligently. Twenty centimeters of dust and debris was cleared in under an hour, revealing a layer of adobe bricks and desiccated straw roofing that had been badly damaged by looters.

"Motherfuckers," Sandy said, lighting a cigarette. "Can we find nothing untouched here?"

"Settle down," Jila said, squatting at the edge of the new pit. "Did you ever wonder if maybe the Moche were doing their own sort of archaeology? Maybe they had guys just like us digging around just to understand their own past?"

"Roofing," Ben called out, holding a handful of dried cane. "This is definitely roofing, and that means that this is definitely a tomb."

As they dug through the morning and into the afternoon, the scope of the looting became apparent. Portions of the adobe brick line that defined the roof edge had been removed in antiquity, and a large section of the cane ceiling had been carelessly disturbed. The workmen groaned with disappointment.

"Just because it's been looted doesn't mean it has no value," Ben reminded everyone. He repeated this in Spanish for the benefit of the excavators. "Looters look for fancy pots and jewels and such. There still might be a lot to find here."

"You're right," Sandy nodded, noting as the workmen began leaving the trenches. End of the workday. Time to eat. "We can come back later. Let's get some flood lights out here and work through the night."

Ben shook his head. "No way," he said. "Come on, Sandy. If we're going to do this, we do it the right way. We post a guard. Then we go home and we look at Bill's sensor arrays and come back tomorrow."

"Archaeology is a beast," Sandy said. "It requires feeding. Feed that beast too much in the way of indigestible data and that beast will become congested. What the beast wants is a lean piece of meat now and again, a nugget here and there worthy of a paper."

"Have you been drinking?" Ben asked.

Sandy nodded. "Yes, quite a lot. The men from the museum came by the house. They were very interested in our findings. But we drank three bottles of Maker's Mark Bourbon."

"Maker's Mark," Ben said, smiling. "How appropriate. We'll be finishing here for the day."

• • •

Back at Sig's place, Bill Field nursed a third tall Scotch as he stood in the pool watching Aleza swim laps. He was feeling quite pleased with himself because the first major find of the season had resulted from his survey. "There's metal down there," he told Aleza as she swam back and forth, traversing the length of the small pool with a few easy strokes. "Get me drunk some time and I'll tell you about this little site on the Nile just by Al-Minya, where I did a metallurgical survey a couple of years back. Do you know much about Egyptian archaeology?"

"No," she said, paying him little attention.

"Well this will interest you then," he said, reaching for the bottle perched on the edge of the pool. "We had this New Kingdom site, and we were living on this old riverboat, and it was just a ball."

"Excuse me," Aleza said, swimming to the edge of the pool, "I don't want to be rude here, but I have the kind of headache that you can feel all the way down to your ass, and I need to take a nap."

Bill watched as she climbed out of the pool.

"I want to hear this," she said, "but later or tomorrow. Would that be okay?"

"Suit yourself."

She wrapped herself in a towel and gathered her things. Toro came up beside her.

"Doctora," he said, "you love the pool more than any other of the guests. It is very nice."

She nodded, unsure what to say.

"Not just the pool," Toro continued. He had a pitcher of something orange in his hand. "We work hard on the garden and we keep the grass cut. Margarita and I have noticed that this pleases you."

"It does," she said, trying to make her way toward her room, toward her bed. "I think you are doing a wonderful job."

Toro stood in front of her. "Would you do something for me?"

She frowned as he poured from the pitcher.

"Would you sit down for just awhile and look at the hummingbirds that play by the roof where the blossoms are fullest?"

Aleza looked toward the roof. She couldn't see the hummingbirds.

"Can you smell the hyacinths?" he asked.

She inhaled obediently, taking in the fragrance of the garden. "Lovely."

"Please sit," Toro continued. "It is my role here to ensure your comfort, and I have prepared this beverage for you. We keep both orange and lemon trees. When you mix the juices with a little of the hyacinth flowers, and put in just a little sugar and some dry milk, this beverage is what is resulting." He handed her the glass, half filled with ice. "Please sit for a moment and enjoy this beverage."

Aleza sat and sipped, not wanting to offend, as Toro withdrew to the doorway.

Inside the room, Jila shook her head. "That was close," she said. "You better hurry up."

Margarita had Aleza's bags open, the little computer laid out on the floor in front of her. "I don't know what this is," she said.

Jila checked to be sure that the door was locked. "It looks like one of those iPads."

Margarita shook her head. "iPads don't have keyboards."

"You can buy them."

Margarita grimaced. "Sure, for eighty dollars. What a waste. If you want a laptop, buy a laptop." She looked at her watch. "Hurry, I have to get back to the kitchen or the roast will burn."

"So what is it?" Jila asked.

"I don't know. Why do you think it's a transmitter?"

"Because it transmits. Because she used it to send a transmission. That was my major clue."

Margarita held up a finger. "Do you know what I do for a living here? I cook and I chase spiders. Sometimes, if I am in a particularly bad mood, I cook the spiders and feed them to the guests. You want something more from me, you have to give me a little time."

"I hear you," Jila said, leaning back. "I'm just frustrated."

"That's because you don't have any sex. I am a relaxed woman because I live with a healthy man. Toro is a like a guinea pig in bed."

Jila closed her eyes. "Yeah, see I have no idea what that means."

"It means he is there with me, then he might leave for a moment, perhaps for a snack or a belt of wine, but then he is back. And then he might leave again for another belt or to eat some lettuce, but then, you know what?"

"Okay." Jila nodded. "I appreciate your metaphor, but we still need to figure this out quickly."

"Why don't you sleep with Señor Ben like you used to?"

Jila groaned. "Because that was a long time ago. You don't just start sleeping with someone again just because he's around."

"You love him."

"I don't know."

"It wasn't a question."

"Just tell me about this little computer, okay?"

Margarita shook her head too. "It's not a commercial product," she said. "The platform is a Dell microcomputer similar to one of those old

PalmPilots but with a keypad. This one has been modified to incorporate a GPS unit and a transmitter."

"Can you get into it?"

Margarita shook her head. "No. It's password protected. I don't know her birthday or the name of her cat, so no. What do you want to do?"

"Disable it," Jila said.

"How?"

"I don't know. It's an electronic thing. Drop it or put it in the tub."

"Dropping leaves scars. Putting it in the tub leaves wetness. Why don't you just ask her about it? Tell her she's not following rules and send her away. I don't like her very much anyway. Toro enjoys her visage."

Jila picked up the little computer. "It's so beautiful, so fragile," she said, slamming it hard on her knee. She did it two more times, then bent it a little, not enough to leave a scar. "Now turn it on."

Margarita hit the little button. Nothing. "I think you killed it."

"Good, now put it back and lock things up. I think Toro has already filled her with as much juice as she can handle."

"Be careful, child," Margarita said, repacking Aleza's bag. "I think that girl can handle more juice than you think."

CHAPTER 11

SANTIAGO DE PAZ, PERU

S andy Beckham took a bath in the only bathtub in a fifty-mile radius. This was Sigmund Klein's bathtub, the centerpiece of an opulent bathroom with two sinks and the only bidet on the north coast.

The heart attack that struck Sigmund Klein, master of a banking empire that sent tendrils further than an Inca road, caught him at his desk in Lima as he signed a document authorizing a transfer of funds from a bauxite mining firm to a bauxite recovery firm. The distinction eluded him even before the documents were placed before him, but became even more insignificant as he felt his chest seize. He pressed the alarm button on his desk as he lost the ability to intake air.

KleinBank's only remaining helicopter whisked him to the emergency room where Sigmund Klein found a moment of truth. He was a rich important man, but in that moment noted for the intrusion of chemicals into his bloodstream, an oxygen mask over his face, he discovered that life was more precious than any bauxite mine. Nine days later he met a young French divorcee and decided to change his ways. It was the year 2000, and it was time for something new.

He had always been interested in archaeology. Just hearing word of these new excavations up at Santiago de Paz, well, he had to go see it, and take his new girl. He met one of the professors at the university who took them to see the ruins. The good man even left him and the girl alone to have sex on top of the pyramid.

Sigmund Klein built a hacienda just half a mile from the pyramid, and when it was finished, he moved the French girl in. All was in order save one signature authorizing the transfer of debt from another bauxite recovery concern to yet another. He had a feeling of deja vu as he signed the papers, felt that pain in his chest, hit the newly installed alarm button, and died at his desk.

Sandy Beckham reclined in the bathtub, wishing he had known the man. Sig's bedroom and private bath were constructed with special attention to security. Though the entire compound was walled, this sanctuary had its own defenses; bars on the windows, and a metal gate that could quickly seal off the door that led to the main living room. Sandy had closed that gate but not locked it. Now he heard it open.

He sunk further beneath the bubbles when Jila walked into the bathroom.

"The anomaly we found yesterday," she said, "it was a transmission." She sat on the toilet seat.

"I saw that on the monitor. I think it might be just the GPS units, they communicate with satellites."

She told him about Aleza's transmitter. "I used my knowledge of electrical engineering to disable it. But we still might have leaks. I think we need to set up the jammers; they'll block any transmissions coming in or out."

Sandy shook his head. "I had my doubts about Aleza."

"I told you she was no good. Besides, I thought no one was allowed cell phones or anything like that. It was in the briefing, right?"

"Yes," he said, "it was in the briefing." He had planned a bubble bath, but he'd been soaking for awhile already and his bubble mass was deteriorating. He began pooling it toward his lower regions. "Alright, set the jammers up in the morning. But that means that nobody's phones will work, even mine. We'll be cut off."

"I like being cut off," Jila said, "makes me feel safe. Hey, didn't you search everyone's luggage?"

"Yes. The first day while we were out at the site doing the briefing, Toro went through everybody's stuff, except Maybach is still trundling around some old British military lockers that open with those tooth keys. Toro couldn't open them. I told him not to bother. More likely than not, the only thing he'd find would be old man underwear and lots of those varicose-vein socks Maybach wears."

"You still have to check it," Jila said, picking up a bottle of cologne from the shelf. "Is this yours?"

"Put it down," he said. "And we did check it. Toro found a skeleton key."

"And? This smells like shit, Sandy. You shouldn't use this. Get some Old Spice or something."

"And inside were neatly folded pairs of old man underwear and those varicose-vein socks, as well as a nice library of vintage porn."

"Porn?"

"Yeah, old stuff, not really old, but the kind of porn that's made to look old. Eastern European, magazines like Volga Vulva and Milkmaids of Bremen. The man has some war-era fetish. And it's nasty stuff too, big girls cradling soldiers between their breasts, or doggy-style while they're churning butter." Sandy sat up quickly in the tub as his penis poked through the bubbles. "Almost dinner time," he said.

"I'm going to see Walter," Jila told him.

Sandy ran the water and poured shampoo directly into the stream to create more bubbles. "No you are not. No way."

"I want to talk to him," she said. "I'm taking the Land Rover."

"Absolutely not." He shook his head. "We have enough to worry about. What we definitely do not need is to involve Walter in any way."

Jila reached over and pulled the stopper chain. "Sandy," she began, as the tub began to drain, "we are well beyond the point where I need your permission." She moved toward the door but he grabbed her arm.

"He might be the one who had you shot," he said.

She pulled away. "I'll ask him."

"At least take Toro with you," he called after her.

"No."

●●●

Toro shook his head sadly and begged, even as he opened the gates to let him take her. "Doctora," he began, he had never called her anything else, even after years of her asking politely, "It is not safe. The roads are dark. And Señor Walter," he shook his head. He knew her too well to think he was going to convince her. He was still shaking his head when she drove off.

Once she passed the little cluster of buildings and the airstrip that Sigmund Klein had built with the idea of flying in his friends for weekends, Jila found herself driving along a packed earth road, an artifact of modernity imposed upon a landscape that had been largely unchanged for hundreds of years. Tall sugarcane on either side and nothing but the headlights to illuminate the path. Every now and again big arc lights cut through the darkness so that crews of men could cut the cane. They were always cutting cane. The distillery worked around the clock, its own generator assuring that the wheels of progress, in the form of sugar and rum, kept rolling.

Jila turned at an unmarked intersection. You had to be careful here. Make a wrong turn and you were going to see nothing but sugar for hours. But she knew the way. Another kilometer and then a quick left. She could have gone right through town, but then she'd have to drive up to the front gate. And it would be locked. Instead, she drove the through the cane, took a short cut, a long cut really, but it led to the workers' entrance.

She drove slowly up the road, toward the lights of the palatial home. It was more ornate, if not any bigger than Sig's Place.

She came around front, drove up onto the circular driveway, and pulled the car right up to the porch, disturbing two short heavy guys playing cards. They were clearly drunk. Pretty shabby security, Jila thought. Each had a gun tucked in his belt, and they stepped forward in unison as she climbed the steps.

Jila pointed her finger at the man on the left. "I've never seen you before," she said, "but you," pointing at the other, "your name is Hector. You're the goalie for the Chimu soccer team."

The man squinted, couldn't quite place her, couldn't quite see her either because she left her headlights on.

"You're not that good. Remember that game some years back when the Piscos tied you 3 to 3? Remember, it went into overtime? That Pisco forward came at you hard, kicked the ball right through your hands. Tragic. I bet money on you and I lost."

The other man moved down the steps and shut off the engine. He turned off the headlights and Hector's eyes began to adjust. A glimmer of recognition.

"I want to see Walter," she said.

Hector rubbed his eyes. "I don't know any Walter."

"I want to see El Morro," Jila repeated.

"He's sleeping."

"Wake him up."

"You have no respect," Hector said. "You make an appointment. I'll bring you the guestbook. You write your name and phone number in the guestbook, e-mail too, if you have it. If Morro wants to see you, you might see Morro."

The periphery was getting noisy. Jila kept her eyes on Hector as a few more hard guys crept from their various lairs to converge on the porch.

"Do you know who I am, Hector?"

He nodded. "You're the girl who got shot."

"That's right. Now tell Walter to get his ass down here. I need to talk to him."

"Drive away now while you can." Now six men hovered on the porch, all nervous, some chuckling, some drunk, most both.

Jila turned and took off her Polar Fleece jacket and laid it on the step, giving everyone a good look at the butterfly holster which sat low on her back. No more chuckling now, the younger men's hands moved toward their weapons. The older men did nothing as she began shouting, "Walter. Get down here. I need to talk to you."

"I'm going to need to ask you for your guns," Hector said, stepping slowly toward her, not sure how to be. If she were a man, she'd be on the ground by now, but a girl, a girl with guns was something you didn't see a lot.

"I know that, Hector," she said, "and I'm glad you asked. But an attractive young lady out on her own, it can get dangerous. I like to be on the safe side. Now go get Walter."

Hector flushed. "He doesn't like it when you call him Walter."

"Listen to me, all of you little assholes. I have come here to meet with Walter. Now go suck your thumbs or something, or I'm going to shoot every last one of you. I mean it."

The men began shaking their heads. It was clear that they felt she was being mean, which was uncalled for. Almost in unison, they shook their heads. The boss was going to have to deal with this one.

Two men went inside. Most of the others retreated off the porch. Hector and his friend returned to their card game as the door opened, and Walter 'El Morro' Ibanez stood before her smoking a pipe.

"Do you get shorter every year?" Jila asked, "or am I growing?" He had to be close to seventy but he looked good.

Walter Ibanez was wearing what looked like a kimono. "In college, "he began, "I was an exchange student in Boston. I learned this expression that I have never forgotten, 'look what the cat has dragged into my home.'"

"Are you wearing a kimono?"

He looked down at the garment. "I believe so."

"Can I come in?" Jila asked.

He puffed on his pipe. "Will you let my soldiers look after your guns?"

"No."

He puffed again. "Are you here to shoot me?"

"No."

"Okay then." He turned, motioned for her to follow, and led her deep into the house, past the colonial era sitting room, past the dining room, and even the drawing room. Toward the rear of the house was a fine study, decked in leather. The surface of his desk was leather as was the chair behind it, in which he sat. "Can I get you a beverage?"

"Yes," she said. "I'd like a Bourbon. No, on second thought, how about some nice Whisky?"

Walter Ibanez grinned. "I'm a rum man myself," he said. "I own the distillery, as you know."

"You have some Johnny Walker Black on hand," Jila ventured. "Drink some with me. I like it neat with a glass of water, too. I think I ate some dust on the drive over."

He waved at a servant, barely visible at the door. "You've got some balls, you know."

"That's probably some kind of compliment," she said.

The drinks were there in an instant, an older man set them on the desk and he was gone before she could get a word in. She tossed hers back. "Tell him to come back and leave the bottle."

"Did you come back to Peru to finish what you almost finished last time?"

"Yes."

"You still think there is something in that pyramid that is going to change the world."

"I still do."

The bottle reappeared and Walter refilled her glass. "Tell me, Jila, will what you find make you sleep better at night?"

"It might."

"What about when you wake up at four in the morning because you have to pee and because those bullet holes ache, and they never really heal? I have two myself. Do you think about that pyramid and the Moche and the Moors, and the fate of the world, and the tiny small insignificant part you play in it? Or do you roll over sometimes, as any sane person would and think about letting it all go?"

"I used to play soccer with the local team," she said. "I wasn't that good so they made me stay in the back court. That was fine, but then I found out that they were letting me play as an extra player, like I wasn't even one of the team. It was such bullshit."

"Why do you discuss it?"

"Because I got to know the players. And two of the guys that are currently working on our excavations wore Chimu Rum jerseys, so I know that you have some people on our team."

Walter shrugged. "Lots of men work for me, almost everyone in the town has at one point or another. I'm not spying on you."

"Yes you are, Walter," she said. "I'm going to ask you a question now and I'm going to be looking at your eyes when I ask it. I've had a great deal of training; you have no idea how much. If you answer dishonestly, I will know." Jila reached for the bottle and topped off their glasses though Walter had barely touched his.

"I read a bulletin," she began. "It said that said ten to fifteen percent of the cocaine that moves from the interior to the north coast passes through your hands at one point or another."

He reached for the drink and gave the matter some thought. "That's probably about right," he said. "It varies of course from month to month."

"I was wondering what you needed all that money for. It has to be a lot of money."

"It really is," he said. "I buy things I don't need. Last year I bought a ski chalet in New Zealand, a little lodge with a hot tub even. I've never been, and I don't ski, but it was for sale on the Internet. You can buy almost anything on the Internet now. You said you had a question for me."

"Chicama," she said.

He downed the Whisky and refilled the glass. "Chicama. That's not a question."

"You know it is."

He shook his head. "It wasn't me. I would have no reason."

She looked deep into his eyes and he felt it.

"I am being honest with you," he said.

"Bullshit, Walter. You have guys all over Puerto Chicama. That's where the coca comes in from the mountains. Nothing happens there without you knowing about it. And Walter," she continued, "wouldn't it be quieter for you to have us gone?"

"Quieter?"

"We're loud. Our excavations bring newspapers in. Getting rid of us would quiet things down."

He fiddled with his pipe. "It wouldn't have been worth it. Killing Americans is always frowned upon; the paperwork alone is overwhelming."

"If it wasn't you, then who was it?"

"I don't know."

"I thought you knew everything that happens there."

"I know," he said. "That's what pissed me off. Whoever took you and Juarez, it wasn't my people." He stood up and began puttering around the room. "Look Jila, you and I have different methods but whatever you want to find in that pyramid, I want to find too. It's a family thing, you understand. And yes, I had some boys there in Puerto Chicama that day. They showed up at your house after the police got the call."

"Not soon enough."

"Not soon enough," he agreed. "And you killed all the gunmen so we couldn't question them. But I have an associate in Chicama who imports vehicles from Los Angeles, vehicles which have been liberated from their previous owners."

"You mean stolen," Jila said.

Walter lowered his head and then looked back at her. "Yes, I mean stolen. Was that meaning not clear to you?"

"Go on."

"Thank you. On the day in question, a Cadillac Escalade went missing from my associate's warehouse. They located it that evening using the GPS. Two guys from Lima had stolen it. Coincidence, I thought, but maybe not. Maybe these guys were working with your shooters, so we went out to where they were being held and we interviewed them."

"So you tortured them?" Jila poured another shot and drank it quickly.

Walter shook his head. "No. It wasn't called for; people talk when the options suggest that talking is good. They were boys from Lima who got recruited by a man they knew nothing about. They were tough boys, hard boys in their forties who had been around long enough but couldn't get good jobs. And this should have been a good job; ten grand apiece, dollars we're talking, plus they were told they could keep the van they drove out in."

"If they had a van, why did they steal the Escalade?"

"Stupid, right? They said they were going to drive back in both vehicles and then chop the Escalade in Lima. The thing is, they didn't know who hired them, couldn't identify him, and they had no further meetings scheduled. This is what we call no useful knowledge of their employers."

"Did you kill them?"

Walter Ibanez looked at her coldly. "You just made me nervous." He motioned imperceptibly, drawing a bodyguard into the room, a large man who moved toward Jila. "You could be wired, sweetheart."

Jila stood. "I'm not. Search me yourself, Walter. I'm not." She lifted up her shirt and flipped off her shoes. She extended a warning glance to the bodyguard who took a step back.

Walter Ibanez came forward but he didn't touch her. He studied her for a moment, then waved his hand and the bodyguard left the room.

Jila breathed deeply. "Be careful, Walter," she said. "I respect you. But you and I are both deadly guys."

El Morro took the message to heart. This girl had a brain made of wire. He retrieved his pipe from the desk, looked at it for a moment, and then discarded it in favor of a cigarette from a leather carton. "Would you like one?"

She shook hear head.

"We did kill them. We killed them both. There were six in all; you got the other four."

Jila closed her eyes.

"You know what troubles me the most?" he asked, lighting his cigarette, moving past her, kicking up a leather carpet to reveal a large floor safe. "What troubles me the most is that you might be incompetent."

He knelt down, moved the carpet next to the desk and then worked the combination on a small safe. He pulled back a little steel door.

Jila looked on in wonder, thinking that this had to be the smallest safe she had ever seen. "Do you keep money in there?"

"I do," he said, removing a thick folder and snapping the lit back shut. "These are the pages you had taped up all over that beach house in Chicama." He tossed the folder at Jila. "I paid $2,000 to a graduate student at Vanderbilt University to make some sense of them. Do you know what he said?"

"I don't," Jila answered, opening the folder, looking at her notes for the first time in two years.

"He said they're called maker's marks, and they have to do with villages supplying the Moche with their tax bricks, nothing more. He said there was patterning, but nothing significant. He took the money and quit school, went back to Shreveport, Louisiana to be with his girlfriend."

"Amateur."

"Have you ever been to Shreveport?"

"I haven't." Jila leafed through the pages, checking to see if they were all there.

"Me neither. I got nervous thinking that maybe this guy was holding out on me, because it's very clear that someone is not telling me everything, so I sent one of my men up to pay a visit, to make sure this ex-student was telling me all there was to tell. My guy finds him and guess what he's doing?"

"I have no clue."

"He's in this barn castrating little bulls. Can you imagine that?"

Jila closed the folder. "You're giving this back to me?"

Walter drew hard on his cigarette. He paced the room, finally kicked back the leather rug over the safe. "Yes, why not?" he said. "In exchange, you leave my workers be. You don't say anything to Sandy Beckham, and if you do find something that belongs to my family there in your little dig, you let me see it first. That's what you call them right, digs?"

"We call them excavations."

He blew a smoke ring. "So if you find my ancestor's gold or diamonds or rubies or deeds to some heavenly kingdom, you be sure I get to see it before it leaves Santiago."

Maybe. Jila nodded as she stood up. "Agreed."

"Before it leaves Santiago," Walter repeated. "We're clear on that? This is between me and you, not Sandy Beckham."

Jila nodded.

Walter Ibanez smiled. "I have a guy works for me named Manuel, not more than four feet tall. You'll find him on the floor of your car behind the seats. He might be under a blanket. When you get to the car, just tell him I said to get out, and he will."

"I'll do that," she said, tucking the folder under her arm. "Thank you, Walter."

CHAPTER 12

SANTIAGO DE PAZ, PERU

The next morning, excavations at the tomb occupied much of the workforce. Those workers not directly assigned to these particular units felt compelled to watch and offer advice, even as Ben coaxed them back into their own trenches. Informal unions had for some decades been ripping a wide trench of their own through the Latin American psyche. Decades of oppressive politics had rendered laborers unreceptive to any type of request perceived as unjust.

"This is our national patrimony," Gilbert said. "These are our ancestors. As such we have a right to understand their unique position in the human cosmology."

Ben agreed. If there was a major discovery, everyone had a right to participate in its unfolding. "However," he told them, "these discoveries are made because of your work. Your work must therefore continue if the discoveries are to continue."

It was agreed that each worker could visit the tomb excavations for a half hour, and would also be alerted to any other major discovery.

Gilbert shuffled his feet, looked up at him shyly, trying hard to find the warrior within him. "We also want breakfast each morning," he said. "Some eggs, perhaps. A little juice."

"You're not getting breakfast," Ben said. "No fucking breakfast. You're being paid well, and you know we give bonuses at the end of the season." Ben looked directly at Gilbert. "Did we not treat you right two years ago?"

Gilbert shrugged. "What's right?" he asked. "You gave us each $300. Is that an appropriate valuation of our labor?"

"Yes," Ben said. "It is. It's above and beyond what any other local employer pays. If you don't like it, go cut cane."

Heels shifted. Murmurs were murmured, but most everyone could live with these conditions. Ben tried to fight off the images of Cesar Chavez that filled his head. His parents would be right on hand, holding hands with these men.

• • •

Ben expanded the excavation unit to pick up any outlying architectural elements that might be associated with the tomb. As currently configured, the unit measured four meters by four. Sixteen square meters, if the math was done correctly, was a massive area by archaeological standards. Mark Cox had set down a laser grid that neatly and visually divided the area into sixteen one-meter segments for the purposes of mapping and plotting artifacts.

They had been working since 6:30 in the morning, all the chiefs here on time today, having finished breakfast on time for once and ready to go with all of their sunscreen and gum and water. Eight excavators methodically ripped into the surface of the pyramid.

They worked with shovels and trowels, alternating between them as the terrain dictated. Any adobes that they encountered were plotted into a grid by Mark Cox who kept a master map on a software system, and by Juan Carlos Cortez, who wielded a more immediately useful sheet of graph paper on which the adobes were mapped. All of the bricks were checked for maker's marks.

After lunch, Jila was down in the pit with the excavators, troweling away.

"Missing the down and dirty, are you?" Sandy asked.

She didn't even respond. She was focused on the silt in front of her.

"Jila?"

She looked up.

"Want to come up and have a chat?"

She troweled away at a layer of sand and found a dark stain underneath. "I've got mad talent, Sandy. I need to be here right now. Have a look at this."

Sandy jumped down into the pit. "What is this?" he asked, getting down on his knees, grabbing a brush and sweeping at the stain.

"Don't know. It could be blood."

He leaned down to smell it. "Smells like dirt."

"We've got loads of llama bones," she said. "I'll bet they're all over."
She called out to the other crews, asking if they were also pulling up llama
bones. Two of the excavators indicated that they were finding them as
well. "I think they sacrificed llamas here," she said.

Sandy rubbed the smooth edges of a llama mandible.

Excavations can be agonizingly slow at times, but they can approach the
speed of sound when conditions suggest that wonderful things are within
reach.

Ben was on his stomach reaching under a partially collapsed section of
adobe ceiling; desiccated cane grazed his back. "Oh my baby, my baby," he
called out, removing the top half of an exquisite Moche pot, alive with
intricate designs.

"Check this out, boss." Ben held the pot. "The looters left it behind
because it's broken, but damn if that is not as fine a depiction of Moche
ceremonial sacrifice as I have ever seen."

One of the workers plotted the coordinates and Ben relayed them in
Spanish and English to Juan Carlos and Mark Cox as Sandy took the
partial vessel.

Jila crouched beside him as he swept away the dirt and crust with a
paintbrush, revealing the complex etching, little by little. It extended
across the neck of the vessel, creeping up into the handle, and ending
sharply at the break where the pot had been broken off from its bottom
half.

Jila grinned. "That's the Sacrifice Ceremony. Oh, there's a paper in this,
Sandy."

"Look," he said, as the excavators and the chiefs gathered around.
"There's our Moche lord." He traced the face of a long forgotten figure.
"Here the warriors are bringing the captives before him. Captives from
some campaign of expansion perhaps. Then here toward the left,"
brushing gently at the dirt, "there's our lord ready to take them. He's a
priest or a king, we don't know, but he holds the tumi in his hand. A tumi
is a copper short sword with a rounded blade designed for only one
purpose, to cut human necks, to spill blood."

Gordon Maybach took the piece from Sandy. "There's more to it, you
see."

"Yes," Sandy agreed. "We have already surmised that this is a fragment
of a pot, and was at one point, part of a larger entity."

"No, no. What I mean to say is that this is a valuable piece that even a grave digger would recognize as such. Therefore, it was very likely broken at the time of its robbery, so the rest of the pot should therefore still be in the tomb."

Tomasino called out, holding up a spout and a bit of the handle.

"Slow down," Ben told him. "Don't be too eager. If you're too eager, it comes across as needy and the graves don't put out as much."

Tomasino nodded, not new to archaeology but still unschooled in sarcasm. "I'll be more gentle," he said.

"It would make me feel more comfortable," Ben said, brushing dirt away, coming down on bone. "I have bone here," he said.

"Think about old nuns," Jila called out.

"A femur," Ben said, ignoring her. "Looks like an intact human skeleton." He jumped out of the unit and called for a couple of guys to brush away the loose sand and some of the hard packed sand that covered the skeleton.

The next five hours or so were among the most interesting. The skeleton had been disturbed in the course of the grave robbery but underneath it, Tomasino and Ben found the tumi.

"There's your copper," Ben told Bill Field. "There's the metal you picked up with your sonar."

"Radar."

"Whatever."

"Can you clear it today?" Sandy asked.

"You bet," said Ben, "but it will take hours." He stared at the tumi. Copper doesn't handle time well. Even when buried, it ages like bone, growing more brittle. "We're working tonight," he said.

"Now look who's in a hurry," Sandy said. "We'll post a guard and come back in the morning. We're already losing the light. And we need to be out of here tonight."

"Excuse me?"

Sandy walked away and Ben followed, climbing quickly down the southern face of the pyramid, catching up to him just as he unzipped his fly.

"A little privacy," Sandy called out.

"What's going on here?" Ben asked.

Sandy held up a hand. "Harmonic convergence," he said, moments later. "The pyramid is being used tonight for other purposes."

Ben was stunned. "For what? By who?"

"By those who are interested in harmonic convergence. Fundamental modes of tonal vibration appear to have some acoustic significance here."

"Is that right? What are we talking about?"

"I'm talking about that fact that we have a limited excavation permit that allows practitioners of indigenous religions to use these facilities during the off-hours."

"What kind of bullshit is that?" Ben asked. "Fundamental modes of tonal vibration have acoustic significance everywhere on earth. You can vibrate a toilet bowl if you try hard enough."

Sandy held up his hands. "The shamans have a voice in local politics, and this pyramid is an organic locus to them. They require its use during any full moon and some Fridays, and the local authorities have concurred."

"You're kidding."

Sandy lit a cigarette. "I wish I was."

"Does Juan Carlos know about this?"

"Juan Carlos's uncle is the shaman."

"Of course he is," Ben said.

• • •

Ben skipped dinner, took his weary self to bed for a needed nap. When he woke past midnight, the house was quiet.

He was hungry but the food had already been taken away. He made his way into the inner sanctum of Sig's Place, into the kitchen, where foreigners rarely tread. He found a bit of chicken and several tomatoes. Kittens sprang out from every crevice in the room; there must have been nine or ten of them, and they came at him relentlessly.

"No, no," he said, gently plucking them off him, pouring a glass of lemonade from the pitcher. He made a sandwich and found his way through the dark quiet house to the main gate that divided Sig's Place from the outside world.

Quietly, he shut the gate behind him. He had a key. He ate his sandwich as he walked slowly in the dark toward the pyramid, where a low light suggested a fire was lit.

Ben stood momentarily in awe. Ruined by time, the pyramid was still majestic in the light of the full moon. It must have been something back in the day, all painted, all gussied up for people to see, for people like him to see. Commoners, that's who this was built for. Just like Stonehenge and Babylon and the pyramids at Giza, built by kings and lords and pashas, but built for common men like Ben Juarez and his kind through time. Built to impress and by impression, to subdue. The trick, Ben Juarez understood now, the antidote to any manifest attempt at social control, is that it is important not be too easily impressed.

He crept over the western edge of the pyramid, crawling the last few meters to the ridge so he wouldn't be seen. Drumming, low singing, and a lot of smoke confirmed that an event was underway. He had the binoculars with him, night-vision goggles that Sandy got from Sharper Image. Ben nestled in behind a low rim of adobe wall and trained the binoculars on the events before him.

The shaman sat beside the fire holding a drum. He wore a wool poncho onto which coins had been sewn. It looked like some kind of armor. He rocked back and forth, drumming while a woman moved through the crowd, ladling a beverage from a large gourd, refilling the cups of the congregation. Tangy Copal incense filled the night air. Perhaps fifty people were present; Ben watched as they held up their cups. It was hard to make out faces but he was sure he saw Tomasino and Rafael, and there was Juan Carlos front center.

Ben had tasted the beverage before. It was the fruity extract of the San Pedro cactus, mescaline, mixed with homegrown corn moonshine. He had sampled it on two occasions. The first time, he fell right asleep. He didn't remember what happened the second time, but he woke up in bed with a German woman who owned an Internet cafe.

It might have been like this eighteen hundred years ago, Ben imagined, except for the fact that this was a commercial production intended for American and European New Age spiritualists. A mid-sized tour bus in the parking area bore a placard reading, 'Spirit Vision: Reconnecting with Your Inner Shaman.'

The shaman himself wore a microphone which snaked across his face.

"And when we lose sight of our connection to the past," Ben heard the shaman say, "we lose our own connection to the spirit world."

Pausing to beat on the drum, the shaman continued, "And this is how our lives become senseless. We toil each day to make money and we disregard the divine in each of us. Find the jaguar. Find the jaguar inside you and set him free."

Ben groaned. The Moche didn't have much exposure to jaguars.

"We come here tonight to give honor to our spiritual ancestors," the shaman continued, pausing to drink from his cup. "To those who built this magnificent monument to the spirit world." The drumming became more intense.

"We give honor to the Moche gods. We give honor to Inti, the Inca god who took hand here when the Moche fell. We give honor to Allah, who took hand here as the Inca fell, and to the Christian god who is the same god but more vigilant. We give honor to life and divinity." The shaman lifted his cup and drank as the congregation followed.

Now that was unexpected, Ben noted. Local lore alluded to the mere possibility that Muslims were present on the north coast before the Spanish Catholics came, yet this was already solidified in the changing and ever-accepting world of shamanic spirituality. Why are they first to accept new visions of the past while the scientific community waits for proof?

Maybe, he imagined, because these are precisely the complementary roles that religion and science play in managing the human psyche. Religion can afford to be at once unyielding and inviting, whereas science is unholy, eternally vigilant, and unforgiving.

"The archaeologists who work here," the shaman continued, "have their own understanding of this sacred structure, an understanding which must be honored. They will tell you of blood and of sacrifice. They will unbury the dead. But tonight we will reconsecrate this sacred space. We will dedicate our ceremony to the Moche priests who negotiated a difficult path between political structure and spiritual need. And if the pyramid dripped with blood from time to time, we will forgive her tonight. The Moche gods watched over an ancient world which we cannot truly comprehend."

He paused to dip his fingers into his cup and pinched the flame of a candle before him. The drumming stopped.

That's not half bad, Ben thought. Forty-five minutes of rhythmic drumming later, he was half thinking about joining them.

"Divinity must favor us all," the shaman said softly, "or it favors none of us."

A low murmur signaled agreement with this premise.

"Tonight," he said, lifting his cup, "we celebrate the presence of the Moche priests. We celebrate. And we forgive."

Ben jumped back as the image faded in his binoculars. The little LCD screen indicated the batteries were dying. The event was concluding and people began milling about. It was time to get back in the bus. Ben trained his binoculars toward the northern edge of the pyramid where a single figure sat transfixed even as the crowd milled about. "Jila," he said. She had paint on her face and a vacant look in her eyes. Maybe nobody else might notice that but Ben understood her eyes.

CHAPTER 13

LIMA, PERU

"**W**hat? Why are you touching me?"

"I think you are a good man," Flor said. "I'm touching you because I'm your lover. Will you take me to breakfast at the Italian place at LarcoMar? I like the little pizzas with pineapple."

Jimmy Segura turned away. "Italians don't eat pizzas with pineapple," he said. "The restaurant is a fraud."

"But the food is good. Take me there."

"I can't," he said. "I have to go to work."

Flor caressed his his back, nurturing compliance.

Jimmy Segura coughed. He was hung over and had smoked too many cigarettes the night before at the Casino New York where he had tried to work the little confidential assistant from the French embassy. Dinner went fine. At that point he still had a chance; the French girl wanted to see where the locals went so he took her to the casino, but she drank heavily at Blackjack and Jimmy knew just watching her that this was going to be her way out. She might have enjoyed the dinner, maybe even his company, but it was going nowhere after that.

He helped her to a cab owned by the casino so she wouldn't be messed with, and then went back to the tables. An hour later, playing well, he was up about ninety bucks and left, taking one of the street cabs back home. Flor was there. Flor was asleep in his bed, which was not part of the job description. Jimmy bit her toe to wake her up and she woke up simmering.

She was still simmering in the morning.

"I have to go to work," he told her.

"Make love to me before you go."

Too tired, Jimmy jumped out of bed and into the shower. She stayed in the bed while he dressed. "Let's have a baby," she called out, a familiar taunt. Jimmy groaned.

"We could have a fat little baby and take him for walks in a carriage. They make them with big tires now so when you go over the bumps, the baby doesn't even know about the bumps."

"I have to go." Jimmy didn't know what else to say. He got himself combed and gelled and detailed quickly.

"A baby," she said from the doorway, still naked as he made his way toward the elevator. "We could call him Baltazar or Raul."

He groaned as the elevator doors opened. He pressed the button quickly but it seemed like an hour before the doors closed.

He drove quickly to the annex, three blocks from the embassy, where he hung his hat on a peg in a little office with no window.

"New things," said the new girl at work. There was always a new girl. Jimmy had never figured out the whole security thing, never understood why there was always a new girl. She might be an intern. He himself was a cultural attaché, nothing more or less, and given the current budget crisis, interns were all the rage. The last one was cute; this one looked like his own mother.

Jimmy logged on to his secure account. He was pleased with the information from Aleza Sabatini, from the excavations at Santiago de Paz. He had never heard the word Theatine before, but relayed the communication to his unit supervisor in Langley.

E-mail had changed the world, even the intelligence world. No more code phones, no more safe rooms for conversations.

He scanned his In-Box for the reply:

To: James Segura, Deputy Counsel for Cultural Affairs
From: Project Station Violet, Operator #216
Re: Theatine Order

Message: Don't know what to make of it, Jimmy. Theatine sounds like a breakfast drink. Is it nutty or more of a chocolate thing? Just a joke. We contacted the Giovanni Carafa archive outside Naples. They don't have e-mail, so they sent an actual telegram. I haven't seen a telegram since 1972. They use the word 'stop' a lot to end a sentence. Don't let that get to you. I had it scanned. Here it is:

"Thank you for odd note. Stop. I review His Eminence's journals for the time you inquired of, 1553, and also for several years before and after. Stop. Carafa is in Spain or Italy the entire time. Stop. In 1553, Carafa is 77 years old, too old to get on a sailing boat and did not travel to Peru. Stop. Entire Theatine budget last year is $2.32 million American, this to pay for six missions in Sumatra and one in United States. Stop. Mission in United States invested in stock market, lost almost all money because of Bernie Madoff, so no millions to pay for non-existing book of importance. Stop. God bless. Stop."

Jimmy leaned back in his chair. "Yeah, it did sound far-fetched. So Sandy Beckham is cooking up a story, telling his people that the money came from a theological society when it really came from Jibrail Holding of Cairo, via Twinberries Hamilton of Bermuda. Sandy doesn't trust his team.

"You've got mail," said the new girl, sounding just like the computer did, tossing the sealed packet onto his desk.

He opened it quickly, cutting the seal with a letter opener shaped like a little copper Moche sword. He leafed through the paperwork to find the document, the forged Civil War letter. It looked good. It even had a wax seal with the Pasha's name on it. Nice touch. He put it in his briefcase. What was most explicitly not allowed, was to remove this kind of thing from the premises without permission from Langley, or at least from Salvador Montes, but that was too bad. Jimmy had to take it home and see how it compared to the original. And Montes didn't know about the original. Nobody knew about that.

CHAPTER 14

SANTIAGO DE PAZ, PERU

Late in the morning, under a brutal sun, they cleared the area around the tumi. Careful troweling and brushing revealed the outlines of the copper weapon. It would be a thrill to pick up, but it could not be picked up until it was properly drawn, plotted, and photographed, which took most of the morning. Finally, as the cloud cover increased and the wind picked up, Sandy and Ben squirreled into the pit to gently lift the ceremonial object.

"Careful," Sandy said.

Ben's trowel nudged the top of the tumi free from the soil matrix. "I'm glad you said that, because I was just going to rip it out."

Together, they gently freed the tumi and placed it on the edge of the trench. It was magnificent, a ceremonial short sword measuring about a foot and a half long, thin at one end near the grip and flaring to a curved convex blade at the other end. "How about that." Sandy pressed gently, testing the structural integrity of the blade, and finding it solid and intact, he held it high. "Tumi," he said.

Gordon Maybach stepped down into the trench. "It's beautiful." He traced a finger down the length of the blade. "This is not a battle weapon, as you know. This is a ceremonial implement."

"It's what we're seeing on the pot," Bill Field added.

"It is," Maybach agreed. "This blade was used by high priests to bleed and decapitate sacrificial prisoners. Its presence would suggest that our deceased friend here was in fact a Moche high priest."

Juan Carlos clapped his hands. "We've been waiting for our own señor here for some time, and now we have him."

"Agreed," Sandy said. "The burial has been looted, but enough remains of it to reconstruct an understanding of his death and perhaps his station in life."

"But it's not the burial were looking for," Jila said. She had been quiet all morning.

Ben stared at her. She didn't look right. "Where's your hat?" he asked.

"I think I lost it. I mean, it's a nice burial, right, but it's not what we're looking for."

"This is a more-or-less intact high-status Moche burial," Sandy said. "We're pretty happy with it, in case you haven't noticed."

"But it's not what we're looking for," she repeated, her eyes not quite working together.

Ben grabbed her arm. Her pulse was quick. He put his hand on her forehead. "You're burning up, sweetheart."

"I'm fine," she said, pulling away. "I just don't know why we give a shit about this burial, that's all. This whole project is a mess. We could get killed out here. And for what, for some fucking box that nobody has cared about for five hundred years? And now we find this little copper sword that has nothing whatsoever to do with the box, or the Cordoba papers, and we're acting like we just found the Holy Grail."

Ben closed his eyes.

Murmuring in the back now, Aleza raised her hand but Gordon Maybach beat her to it. "Might I ask the obvious question?"

● ● ●

She was shivering by the time Ben got her back into the room. He took off her fleece and helped her into bed. Then he moved beside her, pulled the blanket up, and held her tightly.

"I'm sorry," she said.

He kissed the back of her head. "It's all right. I think you have sunstroke, which is coming down hard on all the mescaline you drank last night. Also, you're dehydrated."

"I'm sorry," she said, wiggling around to face him. "You're mad because I went to the ceremony."

"No, but you could have brought me with you."

"I think I understand the maker's marks," she said. "They were making sense to me last night. I was having a breakthrough."

"That's great."

"But then this morning I couldn't remember anything." Jila threw her head back into the pillow. "Sandy's going to be mad. I wasn't thinking, then I just blurt out Cordoba papers. Shit. I know it's a secret. This is going to be hard to spin, Ben."

"Yeah. Maybe we can try a brave new tactic and just come clean about it."

"Tell the truth?"

"Yes."

"You think?"

Ben smiled until she smiled back. "No," he said. "I was just messing with you."

Jila laughed until she wept. "You know, in my current state, I might respond favorably to an advance on your behalf."

"That's good to know," he said, climbing out of the bed.

"Bastard."

Ben leaned over and kissed her. "Sweetheart," he said, "I want you sober, and with both of your eyes pointing in the same direction. But right now you need to drink a liter of electrolytes, so I'm going to the kitchen to stir that up for you. Then you're going to take a Valium and go to sleep, and I'm going to hang out with Sandy and plot our spin."

"I want to go, too."

"And then tomorrow or the next day, we can continue where we left off here. Okay?"

"You'll be back," she said.

"I just said I'd be back. I'm bringing electrolytes and Valium."

"They always come back," Jila called after him.

• • •

Sandy was in rare form. He tore across the cane field roads in fifth gear, the Land Rover bouncing like a top. He held up a hand just as Ben was about to protest. "This is the whole point of having a four-wheel-drive vehicle. It's not like we're going to drive through a hurricane, or run foul of a bear, so the only reason to buy a vehicle like this is to negotiate difficult terrain."

Ben rolled the window down. "What does run foul of a bear mean?"

"Like you're driving along and the road takes you between a mother bear and a yearling cub. That would be running foul of a bear."

"So the bear would be mad?" Ben asked.

"I imagine."

"And this would validate having a four-wheel-drive vehicle?"

"It would," Sandy said.

Ben shrugged. "It still might be possible to drive less than seventy through the cane fields. It's dangerous. Didn't you see Children of the Corn?"

"I was terrified," Sandy said, nodding. "I'm thankful that we're not anywhere near corn. There are no Children of the Cane."

"You're sure about that?"

"Quite sure." Sandy slowed finally, and turned onto the road that led to the bars catering to distillery workers.

Molasses, the smell wafted in as they drove down the main street. The sugar refinery and distillery worked around the clock, washing the residents of Santiago in a perpetual sugar bath. The first shift ended at two in the afternoon, so the few bars were getting set up.

Sandy parked in front of Betty Snow's pub, paying a moped-taxi driver three dollars to vacate the spot. The place smelled like ammonia when they walked in. A local girl was mopping. She paused to give them the finger; they were too early.

"Is there going to be any service here?" Sandy asked, taking a seat at the bar.

The girl set down the mop and turned on the lights. "I'm going to go get the boss," she said.

"Let her sleep, okay. Just bring us a couple of beers." She did, and left quickly.

Ben waved the glass away and drank from the bottle. "We're going to have to produce the documents."

"No, we say they're undergoing archival work."

"We'd have photocopies."

"We didn't have time to make photocopies," Sandy suggested, lighting a cigarette.

"Right, we've been planning this project for years but haven't had a minute to make photocopies? No, Maybach is going to have a fit. Bill Field, Mark Cox too. We're in trouble. We could just show them the manuscripts."

Sandy shook his head. "No, we can't."

"No, you can't," Betty Snow called from the hallway as she trundled into the room. She was heavy and moved slowly.

"We can handle this," Ben said, as she moved behind the bar and popped the cap from a bottle of soda water.

"No, you can't," she said. "That's why you're here." She ran her hands through her thick gray hair and caught it in the back with a little clip. "Who screwed up? Let me guess, Jila?"

"It wasn't a screw up," Ben said.

"It's always a screw up," she said. "What's the exposure?"

"Not much," Ben said. "She mentioned the words 'Cordoba papers.'"

She stared at him. "That's nothing. You boys are pussies. Tell them about the document, just don't mention the box."

Sandy shook his head. "It shouldn't have come to this."

"This much is clear," said Betty. "And this is on top of the transmissions coming out of Sig's Place. Were you able to determine the source?"

"We have." Sandy told her about Aleza.

"This is getting heavier faster than we thought," she said. "Are you getting too old for this, Sandy?"

He looked up from his beer and gave it a moment of thought. "No," he said. "Not yet."

Betty Snow leaned over the bar and took Sandy's cigarette from his hand. "Keep it together, boys. Because I'd hate to have to tell Mrs. Heydr that her investment is being wasted."

"So we lie about it?" Sandy asked.

Betty exhaled what seemed like six lungs of smoke into his face. "Of course you fucking lie about it. Couple of whiners, I should come out from behind this bar and spank the both of you."

"I always hated this bar," Ben said. "There's no ambiance."

"Honey," Betty said, leaning toward him. "Half an hour from now a whistle will blow at the distillery and shortly thereafter my bar will fill with happy men. And none of them will complain about my ambiance. They like the nudie posters in the men's room."

● ● ●

They stayed a while longer, drinking more than they needed to. By the time they got back to Sig's Place, dinner had been waiting an hour. Margarita wouldn't think of serving it without Sandy present.

"The old man is angry," Toro said when Sandy came through the kitchen door. "He has the young woman ready to be mad with him. But Dr. Field and the other man are calmer."

"That's good news," Ben said. "Where's Jila?"

"She's still sleeping."

Maybach looked up when Sandy stepped into the room. "Where have you been, captain?" he asked. "We missed you all afternoon."

"Like I told you, Gordon, we went to Santiago to fill up the fuel tanks for the water heater. You like those hot showers, don't you?" Sandy turned to the bar and poured a tall Scotch.

"Can we eat dinner now?" Aleza asked.

"Of course. You needn't have waited for us."

The room was silent as Toro brought out bowls of cream of asparagus soup. Sandy added a little salt to his. "Gordon, have you ever made this kind of money before working on an excavation?"

Gordon Maybach put down his spoon and shook his head.

"I thought not," Sandy continued. "You might have noticed that is not a normal project. We have security measures and information firewalls that are preconditions to our funding. Is it okay with you then, Gordon, if I don't share every last detail with you?"

Maybach shook his head again. "I'm not certain I trust you, Sandy."

"How about if I tell you about the Cordoba papers?"

Everyone at the table looked to Maybach. It was clear that this was a duel, and duels have an internal logic apart from the conditions that necessitated them.

"You'll probably just lie."

"I won't, so hear me out." Sandy stirred his soup. "This is more interesting than you suspect."

Bill Field folded his arms over his chest. "Let's just have out with it, okay?"

"Okay," Sandy began. "About nine years ago, I received an inquiry from an antiquities broker in Cordoba, Spain, who said he had a set of documents he wanted authenticated. I sent him a list of specialists but he asked if I myself would come to Spain to read the documents to see if I could shed any light on their contents. He indicated his client would pay $10,000 plus expenses, so I went."

"What city did you fly into?" Maybach asked.

"Madrid."

"What month was it?"

Sandy thought for a moment. "August."

Maybach smiled. "A pleasant time of year in Madrid; I can still remember the cool breeze."

"Nope, nope," Sandy said, "Madrid is a furnace in August. People visit saunas for relief from the heat."

Maybach nodded "You traveled on the bullet train to Seville, getting off at Cordoba. It would have been the fastest way."

"It would have been, but I drove. I rented a car."

"How much did the car cost, in Euros?"

"Pesetas," Sandy corrected him. "This was before the Euro. And I don't remember how much it cost."

"Proceed."

"I met the client at a law firm in Cordoba, and I spent about three hours with the documents. They were handwritten accounts of purchases and preparations for outfitting an expedition to Peru, dating to 1542."

"It was typed, was it?" Maybach asked.

Sandy ignored him. "Three ships and a great many armaments with a destination some four or five hundred miles north of Lima."

"Why did they contact you?" Maybach asked.

"Oddly enough, my landlady set it up," Sandy said. "She was a family friend of the client in Cordoba. The client wanted the confidential advice of a trusted archaeologist. So here we are."

"You said purchase and preparations, right?" Maybach asked.

Sandy nodded.

"Does that include permits?"

"Yes, there was a license from the House of Trade in Seville."

"And a permit from the Council of the Indies."

"No," Sandy shook his head. "No there was no permit, at least not in the documents I saw, but come on. It's been five centuries. Stuff gets misplaced."

"You can't sail to the New World without permission from the Council of the Indies."

"I know that," Sandy said. "And I told them as much. They half expected the expedition was illegal, but they were interested in learning if it had come to any fruition. The document was discovered in the archives of a very prominent family who was not eager to have their name be known. I told them I was already planning to excavate in the region, and they offered matching funds with the understanding that they would be alerted if any connection could be made to their ancestor."

Maybach put down his spoon and clapped. "That's very good. Now you said three ships, and you read the trade licenses. Tell me the names of the ships."

"I can't remember," Sandy said. "I'm not playing games with you, Gordon. I've told you what I know. They made it clear that this was a secret. It doesn't impact our work here at all, but it would provide a bonus if we were to find some evidence."

"Does anyone have a pair of pliers?" Maybach asked.

Everyone stared at him.

"I worked information extraction for three months in Marseilles. You can get a lot of information with pliers. Get me some pliers and I'm going to rip out one of your teeth, Sandy. Then I'm going to ask you the names of the ships again and then rip out another tooth if you don't tell me. Nobody forgets the names of ships."

"I don't remember their names. And if you threaten me again, I'll send you packing."

Maybach glared at him. "What kind of ships were they? How big?"

Sandy shook his head. "Sloops, converted revenue cutters, maybe forty tons."

"No sloops," Maybach said. "Too early for sloops, and nobody was building revenue cutters in 1542."

"Then the nature of the ships was lost in my translation," Sandy said. "I've told you everything except the names of the principals involved. And I am not at liberty to reveal that information. Is that going to be okay with you, Gordon?"

"So there is no wooden box to be found, Sandy? Buried somewhere out there?"

Sandy hesitated. "I'm afraid not."

Maybach slammed his fist on the table. "I think I might have mentioned that I did some information extraction in Marseilles some decades back. What that means, Sandy, is that I have some experience coaxing truth from people unwilling to part with it. Lying in so much more complex than telling the truth. It leaves telltale signs on the face, in the drawing of breath, in posture, in the darting of eyes. I just asked you a question, Sandy, and you lied to me. There most certainly is a box."

Sandy leaned in. "I've shared with you all I intend to share with you, Gordon. If you don't like it, we can have you on the next airport run."

Aleza jumped in. "Are our lives in danger here because of this, Sandy?"

"Why do you ask?"

"Because we did a little surveying this afternoon, Gordon, Bill, and I. We found a couple of items in the laundry area that were quite disturbing."

"Sandy's boxer shorts are full of holes," Ben said. "We're all aware of the problem and are working to resolve it."

Nobody even looked at him.

Bill Field cracked his knuckles loudly. "You have two machine guns in there, Sandy, behind the ironing board. Israeli light installation guns. Are you thinking we might need those? Because that was not part of the briefing."

Sandy went back to his soup which had cooled considerably. "I told you already," he said. "We've had trouble before. Jila and Ben were attacked by a well-armed and well-trained group of assailants. The weapons are here to ensure our protection. Is that a problem?"

"No it is not," Bill said. "But it makes me worry that the risks might be greater than we were led to believe."

"Again," Sandy said. "We have no reason to believe that there is any need for concern. I just want to be certain that we remain safe."

"It would have been better if we had been alerted up front," Bill said.

"You would have been interested in knowing about all of the security features?" Sandy asked.

"Yes." Bill nodded. Maybach nodded too, as did Aleza.

Sandy looked to Ben just as Toro began clearing the soup bowls as he brought in steaming plates of goat meat with rice and mashed potatoes.

"There's not much more to tell," Ben said. "The razor wire on top of the compound walls is electrified. Our six Peruvian guards are trained counterinsurgency soldiers. And we can have two helicopters here in an hour. We're running a tight ship here. Let's eat more and bitch less."

Bill nodded slowly. He appeared convinced.

Gordon Maybach said nothing as he cut into the strips of goat meat.

CHAPTER 15

SANTIAGO DE PAZ, PERU

Over the next few days, Jila began taking long walks in the morning, working a patterned circuit. She would begin at pyramid. Now that the skeleton and the tumi had been dug up and sent to the lab, the excavations were finding very little except for the odd bit of pottery and llama bone.

She would check in early at the command center in the tomb to have a look at the surveillance files, but nothing much ever transpired during the night. Young couples regularly visited the pyramid to have sex, recorded for posterity by the night vision cameras. And now and again, looters dug furtively for pots at the edges of the archaeological zone, away from the gaze of the site guards.

Jila would spend about an hour in the surveillance tomb and then walk a quick path behind the temple mounds toward the beach where she waded for a short while and then came back to look over the excavations.

She was concerned by her lack of progress on the issue of maker's marks. What seemed clear some nights ago under the influence of the San Pedro cactus was now more elusive. She knew she had to sit down with the material, and she would one of these days. Maybe tomorrow.

Mark Cox had made great headway on the mapping, noting every last surviving structure, though he admitted concern about the fact that he was consistently rebuffed when he tried to get near the piles of adobes behind Temple 5. Juan Carlos had told him not to worry, they were not significant to the study. So Mark focused more on the pyramid, and on the plaza where Ben's team had moved literally tons of dirt and uncovered three intact skeletons.

The skeletons were arranged in a row, but they had clearly been disturbed by looters at some point in the past. The weathered burial shrouds had been ripped open in several places, presumably in the process of looking for grave goods. But the fact that the skeletons were still in a row suggested that the looters didn't find much if anything, which was odd. Everybody was buried with something, rich or poor, you don't just send someone off into the unknown empty-handed. No, something was different about these skeletons.

Ben detailed his excavators to dig up much of the plaza and part of the central nave of the colonial church. He spent much of his time recording the adobe church walls. This would have been one of the earliest churches on the continent. Fifty years after the Catholics were praying in their first New World cathedral in Santo Domingo, the influence of the Christian god would be felt on the South American continent.

But the skeletons held his attention. It wasn't a tomb; archaeologists studying the Moche made a hard distinction between a tomb and a burial. Both involved skeletons and assorted grave goods, and both could provide a wealth of information about ancient lives, but tombs were structures, whereas burials were often little more than holes that bodies were placed in. Furthermore, tombs were rare, while on the north coast, burials were everywhere. You might uncover a new one before lunch and another after, but three skeletons in a row was unusual. Something about them was bothering Ben. They were all at the same level, about seventy centimeters down. They were probably the remains of three men who died at the same time and were buried together.

Gordon Maybach was overseeing the recovery and photography of the burials. It became clear to Ben, watching him, that even though the man was old, he was masterful. He treated each burial like a treasure.

Ben reached into his pack for sunscreen and was delighted to find a granola bar. Suddenly Maybach was in his face. "Where did you get that? I didn't see any granola bars at breakfast"

"I think it was from the flight over," Ben said, chewing.

"Give me half of it," Maybach demanded. "I'm accustomed to sweets. We've had no sweets at breakfast."

Ben smiled and bit into it. "I've eaten half of it already, but I will give you a bite," he said, breaking off a small portion.

Maybach grabbed the larger part and quickly stuffed it in his mouth.

"You've got to be quick to succeed," he mumbled, chewing.

"Bastard."

"This is supposed to be a collaborative effort," Maybach said. "You don't hold back."

Ben thought about hitting him. He might have if the man wasn't a walking fossil.

Maybach fussed and stepped back into the excavation pit to poke around the burials, measuring bones and taking notes. Then he sat next to the open pit for more than an hour, watching as the men meticulously cleared away the sand and debris that had accumulated over the centuries.

Ben figured it was time to make peace. "You're liking these burials," he said.

Maybach grinned. "Not half as much as I liked that granola bar. Nutty, yet it had a hint of blueberry. My family made a vacation to Maine when I was a young boy. There were blueberries everywhere. I would collect them in a basket. Everyone did. One day I saw a pretty girl, and she had a basket too, but it wasn't nearly as full as mine. I told her I'd give her all my berries if she kissed me. Don't you think that would be a bargain?"

"For you or for her?"

"Good question. In any case, she kicked me and ran away and told her parents. They told my parents. I wasn't allowed to eat blueberries all summer, that was my punishment. But of course I did continue to eat blueberries all summer. You can't really prohibit behavior if it is conducive to basic human urges, can you?"

"I don't know," Ben said. "Why are you liking these burials?"

Maybach scratched his bottom and sat back on the pile of adobes that had been his perch all morning as he watched the excavators work. "They're special," he said. "I can say more once I get them on a lab table but they're already special to me. They might be what you're looking for."

"Why do you say that?"

Maybach pulled a bottle of sunblock from his pack. "Would you mind putting some of this on my neck please? I think I am burning."

Ben squirted some of the lotion in his hand and began rubbing it onto Gordon's neck, not at all pleased to be doing so. What strange times we live in, he thought, when an old man smells like coconut oil.

He stared at the skeletons, tall skeletons with bits of cloth clinging to them, partially ripped away by grave robbers. Ben looked at the skulls, the thin rib cages. We look so small, he thought, without all the meat.

Maybach reached into the artifact bag next to him, the bag where the workers had been collecting the fragments of pottery associated with the burials. "This is late," he said, holding up a thin potsherd. Then reaching for another. "This is early. I think they are souvenirs."

"What do you mean?" Ben asked.

"I mean that these grave goods are souvenirs. They don't date to the time of the burials."

"What gives you that impression?" Ben asked.

Maybach smiled. "Several things," he said. "Whoever buried them made use of several cultural cues. Look at the patterning. They are all three of them facing in the same direction."

Ben shook his head. "The context is disturbed. These skeletons were moved when their graves were robbed."

"Yes they were," Maybach said, "but not significantly. Looters want treasure, and whatever treasures these men took to their graves were taken, but I don't think they were moved much. Now, look at the cloth, the burial shrouds." He motioned to one of the men who put down his shovel and handed Gordon a piece of cloth about the size of a facecloth. "This is part of the shroud, right?"

Ben took the little piece of cloth and rubbed it between his fingers. "Yes," he said. "But this stuff is all over the place. Centuries of grave robbing means that we have this type of cloth blowing around all over the place. The workers use it when they run out of toilet paper."

Maybach shook his head. "No, not this type of cloth. Feel it. I got meningitis after the Korean War and spent a month and a half in a hospital. I needed a hobby so I decided I would learn about cloth."

"You weren't in the Korean War," Ben said.

"I didn't say I was in it. I said after it."

"So?"

"So that's canvas you have there in your hand. It's sail cloth, of European manufacture. We'll need some tests to prove it but you'll find I'm right. These are colonial burials, men wrapped in old sail cloth as shrouds."

"Son of a bitch." Ben stared at the cloth. "You're sure about this?"

"Quite sure," Maybach said. He reached into the artifact bag and pulled out a small disk of metal. "This is a button. It's made of zinc. I have no idea why anyone would make a zinc button but it surely is not native to Peru.

And look at the skeletons. I'll do some work on them in a few days when their excavations are complete, but don't they look a little tall? Aren't the heads a little different from the others you've found so far? Rounder at the temple? These are European men."

Ben's heart raced. "I have to find Sandy."

"Yes you do," Maybach said, catching his arm, "but stay with me for a moment. They are sootier than most of the skeletons we've seen so far, aren't they. Why are the bones darker, Ben? Touch them and the soot rubs off on your fingers like greasepaint."

Ben kept staring at the skeletons; they were a little darker. He noticed that before but attributed it to the sand, thinking they would clean them up in the lab. But looking at them now, it was clear they were different.

"How does a skeleton get sooty, Juarez? Can you think of a way?"

"They burned them," he said softly.

"That's right. These men were burned, very likely burned alive. What's more, someone who cared about them took care to bury them. Look at the placement of the burials. Do you see a pattern?" Note that the bodies were aligned so that the heads pointed in one direction."

"This is not a primary context," Ben insisted, his heart beating fast. "The position of the skeletons has been altered by the grave robbers. This much is clear."

"Even so," Maybach continued. "We must assume that looters would approach their goal with the same measure of efficiency."

"Right."

"So I doubt that they moved the skeletons much. They merely dug through the sand, took whatever there was to take, and then left. Am I not right?"

"That sounds about right," Ben agreed, unwilling to give away any more than he had to. "So what's your point?"

"My point," Maybach said, "is that these skeletons are more or less articulated in their primary burial positions."

"So what?"

"So what?" Maybach stood, annoyed. "So we are a remarkably inventive species, Ben. A hundred years ago we didn't even have space flight and recently, your government sent John Glenn to the moon for the second time."

Ben shook his head. "John Glenn never went to the moon. They just sent him back into orbit."

"Even so, my point is that human culture changes rapidly along almost every front with the exception of burial ritual. We might buy new computers every year but we don't change the way we bury people. Caskets are made of metal now but they're not so different from the wooden ones used for centuries. We still fold the hands, lay them flat."

Ben nodded.

Maybach drank from his water bottle. "Do you have another one of those granola bars?"

"I don't."

"Do you have a compass?"

"Yes."

"Good, then get down into that trench and give me a compass coordinate toward where the heads of those gentlemen are pointing."

The workers moved aside as Ben stepped down into the trench. He moved gently around the skeletons. They did seem to line up. Roughly then, you could make a calculation as to their orientation even though they had been moved. Ben took out his compass. "They're facing east," he said.

"Brilliant," Maybach said. "I would never have guessed before you told me that those heads were facing east."

Ben looked over at him, would have flipped him off if he weren't now holding the pocket transit with both hands. "What do you want, exact degrees?"

"That will come in time," Maybach answered. "We'll have Mr. Cox do an accurate mapping, but just give me your best guess. To what or where are these skeletons oriented?"

Ben looked up, looked east. "To the sunrise, maybe," he said. "Maybe to the sunrise?"

"A little oblique. They're oriented a few too many degrees north for that. Don't you think? To Spain maybe? Do you think that their heads are pointed toward Spain?"

Ben shook his head. "I don't have a GPS unit on me, and I don't have a map."

Maybach smiled. "But it's between Spain and the rising sun, wouldn't you agree?"

Ben fiddled with the compass. "Maybe."

"So tell me what's out there, professor? What's between Spain and the rising sun?"

Ben let the compass drop on its lanyard. "You and I are both part of a collaborative effort," he said. "If you know something, you share it. This is not a geography contest."

Maybach took another drink from his water bottle. "You're right. Information should be shared, though I'm not certain that's happening. I don't have a map either," he snapped, "but I know the shape of our world. From here, what's between Spain and the rising sun is a lot of Brazil, then ocean, then a great deal of Africa, then Saudi Arabia. Do you find any of that significant?"

Ben looked at him, didn't know what to say.

"Do you know who faces Saudi Arabia when they're dead, Ben?"

"Mecca." Ben stared at him. "You think they're facing Mecca."

"I do."

CHAPTER 16

LIMA, PERU

Jimmy Segura couldn't sleep. He lay in bed listening to Flor snore, and placed a hand on his heart to see if he could determine how fast it was beating. He had a lot to worry about. Some years back when the notion of Islamic terrorism was not yet budding in the minds of most, Jimmy Segura had been assigned to a special unit and detailed to Alexandria, Egypt, joining with a small group of men who were being trained in the same line of inquiry.

Jimmy hated Alexandria from the first day, and he didn't especially like his cohorts. He hated the food. They had a Kentucky Fried Chicken, not that this was a special thing or anything, but it was nice to see it sometimes. Things worked differently in Alexandria. It was hotter than hell, even with the ocean breeze, and while he learned Arabic quite effectively in a short while, he made few friends.

He was dark enough to pass when he tried, and he did try as assigned. And after a year, he could speak with an almost flawless accent, fluidly too, so long as the conversation kept to narrow canals. But ask him about a colander or a sauté pan, or talk about too many different bird species and you would lose him.

No shame here, Jimmy would tell you if you asked, but he began spending some time with the prostitutes of Alexandria for the same reason that men of all stripes spend time with the prostitutes of Alexandria. He was lonely and he wasn't meeting available women.

Dalia told him she was twenty-four. He guessed about nineteen. She was a Bedouin whose family disowned her because she had a child before being married. Now she lived in a little studio with a balcony overlooking the beach. She was thin and lovely and would hold him when he cried because he was lonely. She was lonely too.

Raisa had found life in Russia depressing, the men depressing, the food depressing. She got a visa from a cousin who worked at the Egyptian embassy and bought a little condo in a building with a doorman and a balcony that overlooked the beach. She was always smoking, sometimes during sex too, which Jimmy found disconcerting.

Lety was something else, and Jimmy fell quite in love with her. She was older than the others, a thin woman you wanted to hold when the wind blew, just to keep her safe and near, and she always seemed a little sad. Cheer up, he would tell her. You cheer up, she'd answer, I'm the whore.

Unlike the others, Lety never told him anything about her life. She cried so much one night that Jimmy didn't know what to do. He held her tight on the balcony as they looked out at the ocean. I'll do whatever you want, he told her. If you want me to marry you, I will. She clung a little tighter to him, but she was still crying. The next day she showed him the first document.

"This is my cousin Herman," she said, gesturing with her cigarette to a young Egyptian man seated on a cushion. "It's okay we will call him Herman?"

"Yes," said Jimmy.

"It is not the name his father gave him, I tell you in truth."

"I suspected as much."

"Herman has something he wants you to buy," she said, indicating a crisp manila folder on the dresser. "He works at the museum in Cairo and he stole this from their storage place. You must understand, Jimmy, that I am being completely honest with you so I tell you right now, even as Herman wanted me not to, that this is a stolen thing."

Jimmy opened the folder and looked at the single page inside, a stock certificate confirming majority ownership of shares in a French silver mine in Turkey, dated 1897, and deeded to a Mr. Ali Heydr.

"And why are you giving this to me?" Jimmy asked.

"He is not," Lety said. "He is offering it for you to buy. For $100 US."

"Why would I want it?" He took her out onto the balcony. "I'll give you $100," he said. "But I don't need a souvenir."

Lety shook her head. "Herman has a girl he wants to marry. To do so, he must pay her father a sum of money."

Jimmy took five twenty dollar bills from his wallet and placed them on the leather ottoman in front of Herman. "I wish you well with your wedding plans."

The money vanished into Herman's robes. He pointed to the document. "A nice frame perhaps; it will look lovely."

"Perhaps." Jimmy would report the contact in the morning and turn in the document. Maybe, it was a small thing.

A week later, that folder still rested on his little desk, nestled comfortably amid a stack of papers, and he never quite got around to reporting it. There would be complications, having to admit things about yourself that were not quite admirable.

Two more purchases followed; Herman was an industrious thief. Jimmy didn't mind since it put Lety in a most receptive mood. The second document was a map of the proposed Suez Canal, signed by its architect, Ferdinand deLesseps, with a note, wishing good will to a Mr. Hassan Heydr of Asuncion, Paraguay. This one was $150. The next, valued conservatively by Herman at $200 was a letter addressed to Mr. Jefferson Davis, Montgomery, Alabama. Jimmy squinted. He scanned down to the signature line. Feyd Heydr, secretary to Ismail Pasha.

"I can't remember who Ismail Pasha was," he said.

Lety shrugged.

Herman popped a date into his mouth and spoke up. "He is the one we call Khedive Ismail," he said. "He built the canal. You know, Suez."

Jimmy peeled off ten twenty dollar bills and a month later found himself in Virginia.

CHAPTER 17

SANTIAGO DE PAZ, PERU

Ben Juarez drank from the bottle of fizzy water, which he had grabbed by accident instead of regular water. Yuck. He was wandering. He spotted Jila over the dune, so he climbed. What was she looking at?

"Go away," she said. "Peeing."

Ben sat down on the windward side of the dune, found the bottle of sunscreen in his pack and rubbed it on. You had to do it two or three times a day or the sun would imprint your tee-shirt logo on your back.

"Good poo?" he asked when she sat down next to him.

Jila grabbed his sunscreen and went to work. "Good pee. I have to walk half a mile each time. The guys have a bet that I never urinate. Sandy told them that if they get a picture it will make the cover of National Geographic."

"That's funny," Ben said. "How's work coming?"

"It's not," she said. "You're the only one getting anything done. Bill Field's big radar wand isn't finding anything else even worth excavating."

"I know the feeling. Back in Mississippi, there was like an eight month period where my big radar wand couldn't find anything worth excavating either. I felt like a monk."

"You're a pig."

"Will you kiss me?"

"I don't even want to start with that," she said, rubbing her face with sunscreen. "And Cox isn't doing any better."

Ben opened his mouth to respond but Jila held up a finger.

"I walked right into that," she said. "But really, all this security, all this fuss for one little box. There's about a billion cubic meters of sand here and it could be anywhere. We won't find it just by digging."

"Then we go back to the notes, and we figure out the code. We'll spend a couple days in the surveillance tomb, just you and me. What do you think?"

She looked up at him.

"We'll bring some cookies and some wine and go to work. It will be just like Chicama only without the shooting." And that's where he lost it. He felt her pull away. Bits of burial shroud tumbled past them in the wind.

"What do you think they were like, the Moche?"

"What do you mean?"

"I mean as people. What do you think they were like?"

Ben reached into his pack for a granola bar and gave her half. "I think they were assholes," he said.

"Why?"

"Why, because when the opportunity comes around, most humans who have the opportunity become assholes."

"You're just jaded because you don't get laid."

"Maybe, but look at this landscape eighteen hundred years ago, just when the Moche came into play. What do you see?"

Jila squinted, looked out at the ocean, taking in the fertile land. "I've read the same books you have, so let's say nice villages, maybe a chief who takes some measure of taxation in labor or corn or cotton. What are you getting at?"

Ben pointed to the coast. "Nowhere else on God's earth did any group of people ever have a better chance to build a perfect world."

"Anchovies." Jila said. "Here you could live like kings without having to be them, or endure them. You could build adobe villages and fill them with people who lived like lords, and spend your evenings weaving cloth and telling tales to the children."

"Until the Moche got their act together," Ben said, removing the plastic from a little cigar.

"Where did you get that from?" Jila asked.

Ben smiled. "Gordon gave it to me last night. It's a Philly, a blunt."

"How nice for you."

He lit it and pulled deeply. "It's got marijuana in it. Want some?"

Jila gave it a try, coughing at first. "The Moche didn't come out of nowhere," she said. "They were here all along, just getting organized."

"Yeah," Ben said, taking the blunt from her. "I like to think of it as a casino game."

"A casino game," Jila repeated, letting the air out slowly.

"You have your coastal villages, happy with their cotton crops, their corn crops, and their anchovy harvest. Like a couple of guys playing poker, everybody wins a little some nights and everybody loses on other nights. But in the end, it's just nickels."

Jila shook dirt from her boot. "Until some asshole comes along and says he's your lord."

Ben shook his head. "No. Like you said, the assholes were here all along. They just got more ambitious. Now the card game becomes a bigger event."

Jila nodded. "I know what you're getting at, but pretend I'm one of your Mississippi freshman lasses." She leaned against his shoulder.

"Okay. Back in Tupelo, they had a casino training program. Lots of opportunities at the houses in Biloxi and New Orleans. So the guy that taught the course once won ninety grand at roulette, then lost eighty-nine within the next thirty minutes. Wise man, he was."

"That counts as wise?"

"It does. The house always wins. He told the girls, and they were all girls, that they would sooner or later play, so play smart, never hit the slots at the end of the aisle. Learn the rules and you can almost even out the odds. If you don't learn the rules, you'll be tossing quarters into a hole for the rest of your life, sometimes getting some back, but never realizing that you're never getting ahead. And just for a rainy day, practice how to count a six deck shoe. It's against the rules, but sometimes it's important to break the rules."

Jila picked up a partial fibula from the sand. "You think any of those girls ever got rich?"

Ben shook his head. "No. And I think the local inhabitants of this delta we call Santiago de Paz fell under the thumb of some local boy, the first Moche wiseguy to put together a six deck shoe. And after that, these people were nothing better than sharecroppers. They pop in their quarters, spin the wheel, but they better understand that the Moche lord runs the house. Start bitching, and the house cuts your head off."

"Did you just make that up?"

Ben coughed up a lungful of smoke. "Are you nuts? Have you not been following my career at all? I just recited to you, nearly word for word, my paper at the archaeology meetings three years ago."

"And then the Spaniards came and they're bigger wiseguys," Jila said, following the line of thought.

"No, they were just better organized and disease-ridden." Ben stood up and looked over at the plaza. "They had been running casinos since Rome. They understood how to shake down the local talent here, so busy fighting each other for millennia they never bothered to tell someone to invent a musket."

They stared out at the ocean for a time, passing the blunt back and forth.

"What's happening over on the plaza?" Jila asked.

"I think," he said, "that Maybach might not be as far gone into dementia as we thought."

"Why? What's up?"

He told her about the burnt skeletons looking toward a point between Spain and the rising sun.

CHAPTER 18

LIMA, PERU

Edith Heydr's car arrived at the embassy's consular offices promptly at 10:30 in the morning. Jimmy had requested one of the smaller receiving rooms for the occasion. Her car was checked perfunctorily by a Marine who expressed admiration for the nearly pristine 1981 Chrysler LeBaron. Her driver opened the door and helped her out, and she was photographed several times on her way into the building. She wore a dark purple dress, of a style not seen in the United States in decades, and not in Peru for nearly four years, and her hair had been set in some bluish pompadour. She had not been happy about the conditions of the meeting when Jimmy phoned her, but he explained that the document was of enormous historical value and could not be removed from embassy premises.

"You took my picture," she said. One of the aides brought her a cup of tea and she sat alone now with Jimmy before an ornate hardwood table on which the initial meeting between Pizarro and the Inca Emperor Atahualpa had been carved.

"Yes," he said. "It's procedure when anyone enters the premises."

"What if I don't appear on film?" she asked, her face expressionless.

"Then we will have no picture of you." Jimmy produced the leather folder and opened it, revealing the forged letter signed by Feyd Heydr, secretary to the Pasha. He made a point of putting a pair of cotton gloves on his hands. "I've been instructed to ask you not to touch it. And on a personal note, I would ask you to respect the fact that I had to go through a great deal of trouble to bring this here for your inspection."

Edith Heydr drank her tea. "This is quite a table you have here. This meeting, do you know the date of this meeting, Mr. Segura?"

Jimmy closed his eyes, trying to drum up the date. "1533. I'm required to ask that you please keep your beverage away from the table. You understand."

"1532," she said. "November 16. This moment marks the definitive end of a native empire in the Americas. Is that cause for celebration?"

"I should think not," Jimmy said. "From a historical perspective, it is a momentous day. Nothing to celebrate."

"So you wouldn't put such a table in your home?"

"No, I wouldn't."

"That's comforting to know." She hadn't yet looked at the document. "And why would you go to the trouble to bring this document here to me?"

"Because I want some information from you," he said. "And when last we met, you indicated that you might be willing to speak with me if I showed it to you."

She set the cup down on the carved table and picked up the document, holding it close as she read it. When she put it down, she was smiling.

"What amuses you?" Jimmy asked.

She shook her head. "Feyd so very much wanted to be remembered by history. Do you want that, Mr. Segura?"

Jimmy sat back. "I don't know," he said. "I don't have too many expectations of posterity."

Edith Heydr removed her eyeglasses. "Feyd did. He was passionate, you see, and passion by necessity keeps desperation quite close at hand. You might know from your readings of history that his employer, Pasha Khedive Ismail, lost control of his country after only a few years. The bankers in Europe called in Egypt's loans which he could not pay. He was forced to sign over his country to English bankers by 1867. Perhaps dear Feyd was looking for a way out. Perhaps he saw the future and thought to move the seat of Islam to South America."

Jimmy sat still for a few moments. "As I understand it," he said, "the political seat of Islam was still rooted firmly in Istanbul. Egypt was just an outpost."

"Very true," she countered, "but Istanbul was always an embarrassment to those who believed. Istanbul was more European, even more Christian than it was Muslim. Holy men prayed in linen shirts held tight by French buttons. Kneeling they thought first of the creases in their Italian shoes.

Islam needed a new holy land, and had been needing one for some time. This was before the oil, you see. The oil didn't become known in Arabia until the 1930s. Before then, those who clung to our way of life clung by their fingernails."

"Are you a Muslim, Ms. Heydr?"

"I am," she said. "But I've noticed that as I've grown older, I think less about aspects of faith. I had anticipated that as one walked nearer toward death that faith would become more prominent, but that has not been my experience. Has it been yours?"

Jimmy laughed nervously. "I think I've never really seen myself walking toward death, but no, I don't find myself becoming more reflective or spiritual as I age."

"How sad for both of us."

"Perhaps. Why do you think Feyd Heydr sent a letter to Jefferson Davis and not maybe to Abraham Lincoln or to other heads of state all over the world?"

"But of course he did," she said. "Of course he did."

"He did?"

"Yes. My boarder, a man who lives in an apartment in my home, Dr. Sandy Beckham, told me something about scientific discovery. He told me that you can never use negative evidence as evidence. That means in this particular case, that simply because you do not possess a letter to Abraham Lincoln, you should not immediately conclude that none was sent."

Jimmy nodded. It was a good point. "Ms. Heydr, eleven million dollars is a great deal of money.

"It is," she said, not missing a beat. "You are about a GS13 and with living allowances, you might be taking in eighty-six, five."

Jimmy felt his pulse quicken. That was actually pretty close.

"Is our conversation being recorded?" she asked.

"No. This is a general meeting room, nothing more. You can feel safe that anything we discuss will not be recorded."

"Are you certain? I ask this for your protection, not for mine." She drank her tea. "I'm going to tell you something that will put your mind at ease," she said. "And then I'm going to tell you another thing that will fill you with fear. I want you to know that this fear has no genuine basis and will dissipate in time."

Jimmy reached under the table and switched off the recorder. "You certainly do have my attention," he said.

"The thing that will put your mind to ease is that I have no connection, financial, emotional, or otherwise, with anything involving Islamic terrorism. You can trust me."

Jimmy folded his hands over his chest and leaned back. "That's quite reassuring," he said flatly.

"And now we have to talk about this document," she said, setting her cup down roughly on it, spilling tea which soaked quickly into the parchment, blurring some of the letters.

Jimmy jumped from his seat. "Oh, Christ," he said. "Oh, Christ." He wiped at the letter with a napkin, making it worse.

"I would expect the guards will be here in a moment, a letter of such value."

He stared at her, holding up the dripping document. "What?"

"It might have been worth forty thousand dollars if it were real."

Jimmy figured he was blown but not sure how, so he laid the page flat and dabbed at it with a napkin. Even so, it was bleeding badly.

"You should have been posted to Paraguay," she said. "Look at Parana, that's where the terrorists are. Parana is nearly their own country now, Jimmy. Or what about Colombia? It's quite cosmopolitan; a man with your coloring could sit anywhere unnoticed. But you'd never pass muster in Arabia or North Africa because you don't speak or look enough like part of that. Peru would be the third most likely place for a man with your talents and limitations; it's quite cozy these days with the American government."

Jimmy stared at her, giving up on the document.

She smiled at him and reached her hand across the table. Jimmy didn't reach back.

"It doesn't even look like the original," she said, "though the text is much the same. I know therefore that you did not report the original to your employers, which I understand is grounds for termination and prosecution for someone in your position. Even so, you might be pleased to know that the original is also a forgery. Had you been posted to Paraguay or Colombia, you would still have figured out a way to use that document you bought years ago in Alexandria."

Jimmy stared, bewildered. He wondered if there was a microphone somewhere in the room broadcasting this turn of events into a big hairy ear connected to Salvador Montes, which would be the end of his career. Back in Philadelphia. Jimmy's Uncle Ernesto had recently bought a Red Lobster franchise. Maybe he could wait tables if he avoided jail time for treason.

Edith Heydr gestured for him to sit down. "Don't be upset," she said. "Had you been posted to Paraguay or Colombia, you would have met someone much like myself, someone else named Heydr, someone else who had been sleeping for a long time, stepping closer each day toward death. But you chose me, Jimmy Segura, and I'm ready to work with you to make a better world."

"I can't even begin to imagine what you're talking about," he said, shaking his head.

"This document was my calling card, Jimmy." She stood and moved across the table, taking a seat next to him, putting her hand on his back. "I'll be requiring some information from you before long," she said. "You don't have to do anything right now, but I will soon be asking you details about field strength, that means human resources, finances, command structure, and military hardware estimates, of each of the following Parana cells," she paused to count them out on her fingers. "Shining Crescent, Hezbollah, and Al Qaeda, and any of the new more independent cells."

Jimmy was certain, hopeful even, that he would be dispatched momentarily by an embolism sent by some merciful god. "Why not Islamic Jihad?" he asked sarcastically.

"They're no longer active in the region," Edith Heydr said, standing up. "See, we can help each other with information. It's as if I were your agent. I can make you a star." She kissed the top of his head and walked to the door. "I've forgotten my manners," she said, her hand on the doorknob. "Lety sends her love. She has a little baby now and a sailboat called Corniche."

CHAPTER 19

SANTIAGO DE PAZ, PERU

Jila had lost her favorite pair of sunglasses. She retraced her steps many times but was unable to recover them. Sitting cross-legged, watching the work on the plaza in front of the pyramid, she adjusted the old Gargoyle sunglasses that Ben had lent her, the ones she had made fun of for years. He had relented, bought thinner, more modern ones, but the Gargoyles resurfaced, and now rested on the bridge of her nose. Sometimes, discarded things find new lives under the gaze of new people.

She had been assisting Bill Field for the last few days, trying to master the radar imaging, which was more complicated than she expected. She watched Bill move back and forth across the interior of the ruined church. The radar baton was so large, she was thankful that what remained of the church walls was no more than a foot high in most places, otherwise he'd be bumping into them. He was moving slowly, staring over the low wall fragments at the deep excavation pits where Ben's skeletons were found. The pits were empty now; the skeletons had been taken to the lab three days ago. Jila checked her field notes; Bill had already been over this area before. "What gives?" she asked when he passed nearby, earphones clamped to his ears, the long pole gripped firmly in his hands.

He looked up.

"What gives?" she repeated.

Bill removed the earphones. "What's that you're saying?"

"You've been walking back and forth over this one area. What's that about?"

"Something is bothering me."

"Do tell."

"Listen," he said, placing the earphones on her head. "You're going to have to walk right next to me."

She nodded, removing the Gargoyles to fit the headset over her ears. Static, like trying to get NPR in Rio Amador, but there were some instruments making noise. She followed Bill as he ran the wand over a section of nave in front of what would have been the altar.

She heard the same noise still, not a very pleasant noise, but it was only in her right earphone. Lots of bass guitar and drums nothing more.

"What do you make of it?" he asked.

"I don't know." She handed him back the headset. "The band sucks but other than that, I have no idea. But the signal is clearly localized. There's something right beneath us."

"That's right," he said. "I think it's adobe."

"Wow, you went out on a limb with that one. There are adobes everywhere."

"No, no. It's patterned. I think it's a platform."

"How deep?"

"It's hard to tell from the signal, but I'd guess about sixty or seventy centimeters. It's under the church. I think it might be just above the level of the plaza."

Jila took off to find Ben, and quickly got a team together to begin excavating through the puddled adobe floor of the church. Within two hours, down 56 centimeters, the first contours of the platform became apparent.

They spent the rest of the afternoon digging. Ben took pictures of a single layer of high quality adobe bricks, a tiny platform. He jumped out of the excavation unit and used a thin metal rod to poke through the sand to determine the contours of the platform. We'll have to open up some adjacent pits," he said, "but I'm guessing this is going to measure about two and a half meters on each side, assuming it's square, which it seems to be."

As the excavators dusted off the surface of the adobe bricks, it became apparent that each one was marked with a light impression of a circle with a single dot inside - maker's marks.

"What do you think?" Ben asked.

Bill shrugged. "I don't know."

"Floor of the church?"

"No. It's too deep. It's just above plaza level. The church is up another forty centimeters, but this is a floor, Ben."

"What about the ceramics?"

"There aren't any."

Ben made a quick survey of the area, talking to each of the site recorders, noting their empty bags. No ceramics. "I hadn't even thought about that."

"It's a late construction," Jila said. "There are no ceramics because whatever this was, it was built long after the Moche abandoned their pyramid."

"After the Moche, before the church?" Bill asked.

"It has an adobe brick floor," Jila pointed out excitedly. "The Moche made their floors out of puddled adobe, functional mud. And the Spanish only built one church so this is something in between."

Ben grinned.

Jila held up one of the many river cobbles that the excavators dug up. "What do you make of these?"

"They're just cobbles," Ben said.

"Yeah, and why are they here?"

"I don't know. No archaeologist has ever made sense of cobbles. If a stone wall falls down, you have a fallen wall. If an adobe wall falls down, you have a fallen wall. If a cobble wall falls down, you have a pile of rocks."

"True," she said. "But where have we found these before?"

"In context, only around wells, and this is not a well."

"Very true."

"So what do you make of it?"

"Patterned construction." She asked Bill to sweep the area a few meters north of the church to see if there were any other platforms.

"You think that's going to turn up anything?" Ben asked.

"I don't," she said. "He won't find anything. Then you'll put a team there, and you'll find a few more of these bricks at the same level, mostly broken ones, bricks with circles and dots."

Aleza's head appeared over the edge of the plaza, followed by her torso and then her legs. "I have to be the last to know everything?" she complained.

"Have a look." Ben said. "It's just a floor, not much to look at. Besides, there's nothing here for you."

"Let me see the ceramics bags before you say that."

"There are no bags."

"There are always bags," she said. "I see empty bags. Where are the ceramics?"

"There are no ceramics," Ben told her. "That should be obvious."

Aleza shook her head. "Come on. You both look like you just got into the cookie jar. You hid the ceramics from me?"

Jila didn't have time for this. "You have to be joking, Aleza. Talk to the excavators, see if just one of them has any recollection of ceramics."

"Then why are there no ceramics?"

"Think." Jila took off the sunglasses and stared at her.

"Because they didn't bury anyone there so they didn't bury any pots with them."

"Okay."

"So what is that adobe floor? It looks too deep to be the floor of the church."

"It is too deep."

"So what is it?"

"I don't know," Jila lied. "What are those fifteen or sixteen little walls out there for? Who knows? All we have are little bits of floor and wall here and there."

"So what is it?"

Jila shrugged. "I don't know."

• • •

"Share," Ben said.

"Take a walk with me." Jila led him off the plaza and into the adobe maze behind Temple 5 near the entrance to the surveillance tomb. As they walked, she pointed to the columns of adobe bricks that the archaeologists had erected over the years, not so much as monuments to their work, though they were that nonetheless, but as temporary storage for bricks that might be used in the eventual reconstruction of the site.

"Single dots," she said, tapping the first column. Then moving along, "Xs, double dots, single diagonal lines, moons, hearts, clovers."

"There are no clovers," Ben reminder her.

Jila hung her head. "There are no clovers. But look," moving along, "this column is two horizontal lines, this one two vertical lines. This one looks like the letter U, and this one almost looks like an S."

"I know about this, you know," Ben said. "Each mark represents labor supplied by the local communities. You need to tell me something new here or I'm going to take my sunglasses back."

Jila led him through the maze and began walking down the stairway leading to the surveillance tomb. She paused halfway, turning as Ben almost bumped into her.

"Be careful," he said. "It's like seven or eight meters still to the bottom."

"Remarkable engineering isn't it?" she said.

Ben stared at her, knew her game from years past. "What?"

"How many of these wells are there out here?"

"I don't know." He shifted on the small stair, looking up at the circle of light above and the tiny pool below that still absorbed dirty groundwater. "I think about five or six, but this is the deepest."

"It's pretty cool, isn't it?"

He cocked his head and grabbed onto the wall for support.

"What's that you're holding onto?" she asked.

"It's a rock. A beach cobble, and yes it's like the beach cobbles that we found today." He stared at his hand again and frowned. "That wasn't a well we found today."

"No it wasn't. Why do you think they used cobbles in their wells?"

"Beach cobbles are part of the normal geological makeup of this delta," he said.

"Yes they are," she admitted, "but they are not found in large numbers except in certain architectural features."

"I'm not following you."

"And I'm not happy about that," she said. "Watch your foot, Ben. It's very close to the edge of this step. If you make a wrong step you could fall to your death."

"You care?"

"My point is this - why are you so comfortable standing so close to the edge of a fifteen-hundred-year-old step?"

"OK," he said. "I trust the step because I trust Moche engineering skills. The steps are laid in stone, stone cobbles, yes. The cobbles gave the steps some form."

"Why?"

"Give me a break," he said. Then he saw it. "They consolidated the steps with river cobbles."

"Why did they do that, do you think?"

Ben nodded. "Because in a land of dirt and dirt bricks, you trust cobbles for your stairs."

"That's right."

"You can't make an abode stairway."

"You can't make an adobe stairway," she repeated.

Ben thought this through. "OK. The Moche built most everything out of adobes, but when they needed to reinforce something, they used wood if they could find it, but wood was rare on the coast. It's only in the wells that they used stone cobbles because the wells had stairways."

Jila took him by the hand and led him into the tomb. The monitors flickered, revealing a powerful workforce on full throttle. "Look," she said, "out there we have one of the most talented excavation teams ever assembled. Bill Field is walking a tightrope."

In another screen, Sandy was applying duct tape to the main mast of a kite shaped like a pirate ship. Gordon Maybach was urinating while looking at his compass.

"He's multitasking," Ben said.

Juan Carlos sat eating salted fish with the teenage girls from the ceramics lab, his intentions obvious. Mark and Brenda Cox had stolen away and now sat on the caldera of a particularly large looter hole behind the pyramid doing what married couples often do, having an argument. Even without sound, the argument was apparent, exaggerated like an old time movie.

"I'm tired of you wearing my underwear," Jila narrated, trying to get into Brenda's groove.

"Oh yeah?" Ben countered, settling into a chair, watching as Mark gesticulated. "We'll, I've had it up to here with you and the pool boy."

Jila smiled. "At least the pool boy listens."

"Oh does he? Does he just listen or is there more to it? How come every time I try to swim, I have leaves in my face? What does the pool boy do exactly?"

On-screen, the Coxes continued their animated discussion.

"He makes me laugh," Jila said.

"He's 78 years old."

"But he's spry. What about you and the chambermaid? I've seen you watching her, the way she moves as she dusts my numerous trophies."

"Marta makes me feel alive," he said. "When I come home from work, she has my paper right there, a double Scotch, a little sandwich."

"My pool man might be old, but he pleasures me, and afterward, turns on the TV before leaving to bring his mother, our chambermaid, back to the hospice."

Ben winced as Brenda Cox smacked her husband's face. "She might be old, very old," he said, "but after a long day of work, I welcome the attentions of woman who has a century of experience."

"You're a pig," Jila said, rolling her chair away from him.

Ben pushed after her. He caught her from behind and kissed the back of her head.

"It would be like that for us one day," she said. "Do you really want to go there with me?"

"It won't be like that," he whispered. Losing her now. Needed to keep her together. "The river cobbles are not necessarily indicative necessarily of wells, but of stairways, right?"

She nodded.

"Adobe bricks don't make good stairways, so the quantity of cobbles that we found today suggests a stairway in the absence of a well."

"That's right," she said.

Ben felt her coming back.

"I'm complex," she said, "Not in a good way." She sat in his lap, and put her hand on his face. "You better be sure about this."

"I'm sure."

She kissed him and caught site of Sandy Beckham in the monitor. He had taped up the main mast but the kite was listing dangerously.

"Don't look," Ben said. "It's an issue of twine, nothing more."

"Twine," she repeated. "Strands of living fiber coming together."

"They built a staircase," Ben said.

"Yes. I think it was a minaret."

CHAPTER 20

SANTIAGO DE PAZ, PERU

At first, Ben didn't know where he was. A surge of adrenaline followed the discovery of his strange surroundings. A surge of pleasure-inducing neurotransmitters followed, washing though his brain when he discovered Jila curled up next to him.

The light was dim. Ten trickle-fed marine batteries assured that the surveillance tomb was never without power, and the monitors flickered with nondescript night-vision images. Ben adjusted his pillow, discovering with alarm that it consisted of a bunched up length of Moche burial shroud. "Sacrilege," he said, but it wasn't.

Because the tomb also served as an emergency bunker, Sandy had laid in some provisions that were utilized throughout the previous evenings. The sleeping bags provided a comfortable bed. Vacuum-packed brie, and crackers from a tin, tasted good, as did the three pints of Jim Beam they had polished off during their two-day semi-romantic, working holiday.

Ben was happier than he had been in years. He stared up at the screens which showed largely static images of the pyramid, itself a celebration of a sense of order many years past.

"Rub me," Jila said, half asleep.

He did, thinking about the marks on the adobes they had found today. He felt certain now that Jila's notion was correct, that the adobe platform they found under the church was the base of a small mosque with a cobble-reinforced minaret. It would have been Diego Ibanez's first order of business in the New World. Excavations would bear that out over the next few days. He was certain too that excavations would find similar bricks and cobbles off the side of the plaza, representing the tearing down of the mosque by the Spaniards who came to dominate the region.

Ibanez would have hired local labor to build his mosque in the most efficient way possible, by tearing bricks from the pyramid. And because the pyramid aggregated over time, became larger and finer over the centuries, the finest adobes would have been the later ones, the ones on the surface, closest to hand. And because the pyramid was considerably larger than the mosque, Ibanez had more bricks than he needed, so he would have taken the ones from the east face because it abutted the plaza. East face adobes bore inscriptions of circles and dots, Ben remembered. So the mosque would have been made of circle and dot adobes.

"Rub me," Jila whispered.

"I'm rubbing you," he said.

"Rub me."

Ibanez's second job, once the mosque was complete, would be to build his house. It would not have been right next to the mosque. It would not be on the plaza; it would not therefore, be built from adobes from the east face of the pyramid. So find the circles and dot adobes and you are not in the place where Diego Ibanez slept and hid his box.

Maybach was very likely correct in identifying the three skeletons as Muslims. One of them might have been Ibanez himself, Ben guessed. The Spanish military commander who heard tell of Ibanez's mosque would have moved quickly to tear it down. Although the military and the priests enjoyed an uneasy relationship in colonial Peru, they would have cast their differences aside here. They would have come by ship, soldiers and Inquisitors united against this new threat. Diego Ibanez must have seen this coming, must have trained his men and his converts for this inevitability, but no training would allow an adequate response to Spanish might. Ibanez had only three ships. They would have been well armed, but the Viceroy in Lima had nearly the full attention of the Spanish crown.

How it went down, if even a battle was fought, Ben doubted he would ever know. Whatever battles or negotiations ensued were lost to the wind and beyond even the most alchemical of archaeological techniques. What is certain is that the mosque was destroyed. Diego Ibanez lost his battle. The inquisitors would have made a fast judgment and the soldiers would have been sent scrambling, looking for any stick of wood, anything flammable at all that could be used to burn the heretics.

Jila stirred.

"Hello sweetheart," Ben said as she opened her eyes.

Jila rubbed her eyes. "I had a dream," she said. "I dreamed about Diego Ibanez."

Ben stared. "I was just thinking about him."

"I dreamed he was standing in the minaret when he saw the Spanish ships come for him. He had to know it was over but he was smiling even as he watched the ships near."

"He had a few good years," Ben suggested. "It was probably hopeless from the onset, but I think I know how we can find his house, find his box."

She sat up.

"In Chicama, I think we were on the right track with the maker's marks. We're going to need the notes you got back from Walter to understand the patterning. We need to run them against the field log books from back when the archaeologists first started making those piles of maker's mark adobes. We'll identify the most prominent of the late period marks that do not feature circles and dots. Then we hunt for them using your notes as a guide. This will lead us to Diego Ibanez's house."

Jila hugged him. "I like the way you think," she said. "Double horizontals, two dots, hearts, diagonals, and clovers," she said. "That's what we're looking for tomorrow."

"There are no clovers," Ben countered, holding her tightly.

• • •

Jila frowned when she realized the desk was inadequate. It was morning, and she was sitting in the tomb revisiting her data from some years earlier. The notebooks she recovered from Walter Ibanez had been rearranged, no doubt copied, and many of the pages now evidenced the touch of hands unaccustomed to the care and respect generally enjoyed by scientific documents. Still, she had to admit, they were complete. She laid them out on the floor in an attempt to reorder them. She had paid scant attention to maker's marks since the incident at Chicama. She told herself she would never give them another thought, yet here she was, and now she needed to remember what she said she couldn't, and resolve what she had been quite adamant not to resolve.

The desk she culled from the ceramics lab had three metal legs and one made of plastic tubing, but the surface was the worst part. Once she had stripped off the worn and oddly aromatic plastic covering, she found very little of substance, only a thin particle board surface that had spent too much time in the sun. Rather than concentrate on the work, she began her project by scraping away at the surface in an attempt to render it mostly horizontal. So much of life transpires in the moments of mundane activity.

She heard a beep and looked up at the monitors. The perimeter alert revealed a car, a little minibus to be precise, heading for the ruins. Nothing new there, buses had been coming daily, mostly school children on field trips, which must be accommodated under the terms of their permit. Three of the four guards currently on duty had moved to high points to assess the situation while the other went with Juan Carlos to meet the intruder. Jila watched as the minibus was stopped and a man stepped out. The picture conveyed little of the detail, but it was clear that the man was not leaving anytime soon, as most uninvited men were required to do. She watched as Juan Carlos trotted off toward the lab, no doubt to find Sandy.

Juan Carlos Cortez entered the lab nervously. "Visitor," he said. Sandy was photographing the three skeletons, which despite any force of his will, were now being called the Mecca skeletons. One of the lab technicians assisted as Gordon Maybach measured the long bones.

"No time for visitors," Sandy said sharply.

"It's a gringo," Juan Carlos added. "Very white. A gringo who says you'll want to meet him."

"Tell him to go away."

"I did," Juan Carlos said, shaking his head. "He said he declined to leave, and if we were interested in removing him we would be welcome to do that."

Sandy looked up from his camera. "Who is he?"

Juan Carlos handed him a business card. "Ned Peterman, Archival Consultant."

"What the hell does that mean?" Sandy asked, staring at the card. He handed it back to Juan Carlos. "Tell him this is a secured government property." He turned back to his camera and nodded to Maybach to continue.

"One thing more," Juan Carlos said nervously. "He said he wants to talk about the Pope."

"The Pope?" Even Maybach stopped what he was doing now.

Sandy frowned. He followed Juan Carlos toward the car park.

"I put on a sweater this morning," Ned Peterman began as Sandy approached, "but it gets quite hot by midday. You must be Professor Beckham."

Sandy walked toward him, not smiling. The man looked to be about fifty years old. Fit and muscular with white hair. "You're an albino," Sandy said.

"I am," Ned Peterman responded. "I've been told that archaeologists are quite observant, and so far I've not been disappointed. I'm certain you are a source of inspiration to your students. I wonder if there is a place we could chat away from the ravages of the sun."

Sandy led him to their first line of diplomatic defense, a small adobe reception hut near the labs. It featured only a desk, two chairs and a water cooler. Sandy motioned for him to sit. "What can I do for you?" he asked.

Ned Peterman eyed the water cooler, raising his eyebrows. Juan Carlos pointed to a bag of cups. "I'm interested in your project," he began, filling a cup. "I want to become part of your team."

Sandy shook his head. "I'm afraid we are at capacity."

Peterman took a drink.

Sandy stared at him. "You're a priest, aren't you?"

Peterman nearly spit up. "Is it that obvious?"

"The sunburn on your neck is more profound that the rest of your sunburn," Sandy noted. "You normally wear a collar."

"Well done," Peterman said. "I never was very good at this undercover business. I am a priest."

"So what can I do for you, Father?"

"Yes," Peterman began. "Yes, let's get to the point." He leaned forward and clasped his hands together. "I live in Assisi, in Italy. Have you been?"

"I have," Sandy answered. "Lovely."

"Yes. Prior to that, I spent a number of years in Panama where I worked as a missionary. And while I benefited greatly from the experience, my constitution is not well met by the tropics. I have already undergone two operations to remove skin cancers, and if I spend much more time here, I worry that I might have to endure another."

"I'm sorry to hear."

"Nonetheless," Peterman continued. "I professed to do the Lord's work.

And to be honest, I'm not cut out for parish work either, so I find myself being called upon now and again to resolve problems for the Church."

"I can't imagine what that means for us," Sandy said. "We are excavating a colonial church, a Theatine church."

"A Franciscan church," Peterman corrected him. "I'm quite sure of that."

"It might be Theatine," Sandy countered. "They established seven on the continent, most right about here. Are you a Franciscan priest?"

"I am. Yes."

"Do you have some opposition to our work here?"

Peterman shook his head. "I do not. In fact, I welcome it, which is why I came here to become part of your team."

"We have common areas of interest," Sandy told him. "Unfortunately, we are under a great deal of pressure to complete our investigation, so I regret that I will not be able to include you in our project."

"Oh, but you must," Peterman interrupted. "You must include me in every aspect of your work. And there's this." He pulled an envelope from his jacket pocket. "You can't say no."

Sandy stared at the envelope. "Are you going to open it, or do I just say no?"

He held the letter out to Sandy. "This letter is addressed to the Papal Nuncio in Lima, the Pope's ambassador to Peru, from His Holiness Pope Benedict. It authorizes me to become part of your team. Should you feel disinclined to comply, the letter advises that the Archbishop of Lima, in concert with the Papal Nuncio, request that federal authorities shut down your project. We can't have you desecrating a Catholic cemetery, can we?"

Sandy read the letter. It said just that.

"I have a satellite phone," Peterman said, pointing to the duffel at his feet. "I met with the Papal Nuncio just last week in Lima. Today, he is in Iquitos for a ceremony marking the opening of a farming cooperative. He will be accompanied tomorrow by the President of Peru. If you like, I can relay your regrets, but in a country that is 90% Roman Catholic, I think you would find it difficult to proceed with your investigations."

Sandy read the letter again. Pontiff, the seals, the language, the Pope.

"I'm excited about this," Peterman said. "I've always wanted to be on a dig. That's what you call them, right?"

"We call them excavations." Sandy stuffed the letter back in the envelope. "Why is the Pope interested in this project?"

Peterman shook his head. "I have no idea, nor do I question the judgment of Christ's representative on earth. I brought a tent. Can I pitch it in your yard, maybe by the pool? I like to go swimming at night when there's no sun. Otherwise I burn."

CHAPTER 21

SANTIAGO DE PAZ, PERU

Toro rubbed out his cigarette in an ashtray shaped like a llama. Never an effective pacer, he puttered around the kitchen.

"You're making me nervous," Margarita said, frying strips of fragrant goat meat in the large iron skillet that Jila called a Wok. "You shouldn't smoke so much. You'll get the heart attack. I'll have to shock you back to life like on TV, except we don't have that machine. I could try with the waffle iron."

"He's a priest," Toro said, scooping up one of the kittens. "Professor tells me to mistrust a priest. How can I do that?"

Margarita stirred the meat and turned to cut the carrots that would be required for the meal. "Now you don't trust Doctor Sandy?"

Toro held the kitten over his head and tickled its stomach. He watched as it jumped then, and scurried back to its mother. "I don't know. A priest, Margarita."

"And Doctor Sandy," she said, holding the carrot in one hand, the knife in the other. "This man once woke up a judge to pull you out of jail. He has always been honest with us."

"You trust him?"

Margarita shrugged, turned back to the skillet. "I trust you, that's all, and maybe Jila. So what, so Sandy says to check out the priest? You think priests can't be bad? Some of them like the young boys, just like that Michael Jordan fellow in California."

"Michael Jackson," Toro corrected her. He lit another cigarette and reached for another kitten but it bolted through the open doorway.

"Him too?"

"Remember the priest at our wedding? Padre Rogelio, I think he died in the fighting. Someone shot him, remember? Who would shoot a priest?"

"Maybe someone who was being shot at by a priest," she said, adding a stick of margarine to the skillet. "Rogelio believed in the struggle. He used to say that God helps those who help themselves. I remember the clicking noises during my confessions. He would use that time to clean the carbines."

Toro waved that thought away, inconsequential, who wouldn't do two things at once if two things needed to be done. "I think I wouldn't lie to a priest."

"You told Padre Rogelio I was 16, when in fact I was 15."

Toro stared at the floor. "It's true. So maybe I will burn in hell for that. You said you were a virgin."

Margarita chuckled. "So at least we'll be together."

"I talked to the priest today," Toro said. "He's called Padre Ned. He put up a tent between the pool and the tomatoes. I told him we could find him a bunk but he said no. He didn't bring much, just a bag with some clothes and toothbrush and skin cream. He must have a Bible. He had a telephone with a big antenna but Sandy made him leave it at the lab. Sandy said I should find out if he was really a priest. How could I?"

"Just ask him."

Toro blew smoke rings at the plastic kitchen chandelier. "I did. He just nodded his head, so I said to him this. I said, what is the fourth book of the Old Testament? He said Numbers. I asked him who wrote Acts, and he said Luke. I think that's right. Is that right?"

Margarita peeled three bullion cubes from their wrappers. "Amor," she said, "I really don't remember."

Toro nodded. "Makes me nervous."

• • •

Dinner would be interesting.

Ben found Sandy in his lair, in the inner sanctum of Sig's Place, sprawled on the bed smoking a cigarette. He had an ashtray propped on his belly and it bobbed up and down with each breath.

"He's a fake," Ben said.

"Maybe, maybe not," Sandy said. "He's got a letter from the Pope."

"You have a pen? Because if you do, I'll have my own letter from the Pope."

"Why don't we hear what he has to say?"

"Because he's a fake," Ben said, irritated at the situation. "It's too much of a coincidence. You think a priest just turns up when things get interesting?"

Sandy shrugged.

Ben pulled back the curtain and looked out at the pool just as Aleza Sabatini emerged and leaned over to look into the tent that had been set up on the lawn. "You have to see this," he said.

Sandy moved the ashtray and stepped over to the window. "If I wasn't married," he muttered.

"You're not married."

Sandy stared as Aleza got down on her hands and knees and peeked into the tent. "I know," he said. "But I've grown used to saying that."

"Do you think she and the priest are working together?"

Sandy's head bobbed up and down, keeping in time with the movements of the girl's rear. "No, I don't."

"That's a tiny thong," Ben observed. "Why didn't you just tell him to get lost?"

"I want to know who he is. We'll find out soon enough."

"How do you figure?"

Sandy smiled as Aleza stood up, shook the water from her hair. "Did you ever go hunting for quail or ducks?"

"No."

"Me neither," Sandy said, letting the curtains fall back into place. "I don't like hunting birds. I prefer to hire people to hunt them for me. Let's just sit back and let Maybach tear him a new asshole."

Margarita had not been anticipating a guest and had not prepared one of her specialties. A little goat meat and a lot of rice. It was still going to be wonderful, she had determined, a meal fit for a priest.

Sandy caught hold of Jila as they moved to sit down for dinner. Ned Peterman engaged the team with adventure stories from his work in Panama, but now dinner was about to start, and dinner was when the knives came out. "Did you get pictures of him?" Sandy asked.

Jila nodded. "Seventeen, but only from two cameras."

"Any good?"

"Yes."

"Send them to Betty."

"First thing in the morning," she said.

"No. Tonight, after dinner."

Jila nodded.

Toro was serving the corn chowder so they took their seats quickly.

"I thank you for the warm welcome," Ned Peterman began. "And I wonder if you would indulge me, let me lead you in a prayer of grace this evening."

All hands went out, indicating no objection. Peterman asked if Toro and Margarita could appear and they did, and he bowed his head and delivered an inspired prayer.

Then there was the soup.

"I'm anxious to learn of your discoveries," Peterman said. "But first I must ask about these place mats. Is this not the Hindenburg zeppelin depicted?"

Juan Carlos chuckled. "Yes, our benefactor, Dr. Klein had two passions, archaeology and the Hindenburg. You'll see that many things around the hacienda are decorated with blimps or Moche art."

"It's quite disconcerting," Maybach added. "One doesn't know whether to daydream about pyramids or airships."

"Professor Maybach was alive during the heyday of both," Sandy added. No laughter.

"Lovely," Peterman said. "This is quite an adventure for me."

"As it has been for all of us," Maybach agreed. "I'm wondering if you could tell us how the Pope himself grew interested in our project."

Peterman nodded. "A fascinating story," he said. "His Holiness maintains a strong bond with Peru. And when he learned of your project, he apparently expressed an interest in learning more about the activities of the Church in its early years in the Americas."

Gordon Maybach matched him spoonful for spoonful. "Fascinating," he said. "What about the Theatine connection?"

"I don't know anything about that," Peterman said. "I don't know much about colonial Theatine missions. In fact, much of what I know about history in general comes from the Discovery Channel."

Brenda Cox lit up. "I did a program for the Discovery Chanel last year," she said. "I filmed an ethnography of one of the villages that make the reed boats that the fishermen still use. My husband and I spent three months on site. It was called, 'Los Caballitos.' Did you happen to see it?"

"No." Peterman shook his head. "I'm afraid I didn't."

Maybach stirred his soup. "I remember my last visit to Assisi, the birthplace of St. Francis, the founder of your order, a good Catholic, wasn't he?"

Peterman reached for the salt. "As a point of fact, St. Francis wasn't even Catholic. It wasn't until after his death in 1226 that the Church began acquiring him. He was canonized two years later, made a saint."

"Did you study in Assisi?" Maybach asked.

"I did."

"What do you make of that theater complex they're building? A major theatrical production about the life and times of a saint, isn't it a little gaudy?"

Peterman took a drink of wine. "I've not been back recently, but several attempts have been made to make the work of our saint more appealing to the MTV generation."

"MTV," Maybach repeated.

"It sounds so silly," Peterman repeated. "I'd never watched cable TV until I visited Colorado recently. I have a close friend who is, in fact, a Theatine monk. I found lodging in a Best Western hotel and enjoyed quite a lot of good television. It can be intoxicating, don't you think?"

Sandy laughed. "It sure can. I love 'Sex in the City.'"

"I'm sure many do," Peterman said. "But some of us have taken the vow."

"It's a TV show."

"I only stayed at the Best Western for two nights," Peterman continued, "and then I was invited to stay at the Theatine monastery. They don't have cable TV."

Bill Field jumped in. "Their vows don't let them watch TV?"

Peterman laughed. "No, of course they can watch TV. But one of the younger brothers lamented that the cable provider cut the link for nonpayment. I spent an afternoon hiking through the desert with Brother Franklin and I must tell you, he was quite eager to learn of the recent antics of a family called Soprano."

"I thought they were rich," Mark Cox said.

Toro trundled in silently with the main course, the rice and lamb.

"Rich?" Peterman said, shrugging. "It looked to me like they were barely hanging on."

Gordon Maybach clicked his teeth audibly. "From what I understand, the Theatines are as rich as Borgia popes."

Peterman didn't miss a beat. "I was not at their monastery long," he said, holding up his spoon. "And I'm not an expert on Theatine finances but I can tell you that I was present when two men come with a flatbed to repossess a tractor that had not been paid for. So if these gentlemen are rich, they are hiding their wealth."

"Then who's paying for this?" Maybach asked.

Sandy frowned.

"I don't understand the question," Peterman said, sifting through his rice.

Maybach smiled. "Sometimes I just talk too much," he said, lifting his wine glass, encouraging others around them to do the same. "A toast to a reversal of Theatine fortunes. May they drink from the goblets of capitalism."

Sandy raised his glass.

"Here here," Peterman said.

CHAPTER 22

SANTIAGO DE PAZ, PERU

Later, sitting in front of the good desk in the surveillance tomb, Jila picked the best shots of Ned Peterman that the cameras had picked up. They weren't especially clear. Only one camera faced the reception area, and it was far away. And Ned Peterman kept his head low, one hand over the other to ward off the sun. "You're not a priest," she said aloud as she sent the images up the antenna to a satellite that hovered three thousand miles above Peru, to be relayed to Betty Snow's receiver not two miles away. "But I can't imagine there are too many albino spies or secret agents out there, so I don't know who you are."

The console beeped, and Jila looked up at the little monitor bolted to the wall which showed two figures making their way down the stairs.

"Welcome to my humble tomb," she said, as Sandy and Ben entered the room.

Sandy fished out a cigarette. "What say..."

"What say we don't smoke," Jila told him. "This room is nine meters underground. You light that and you'll stink it up for months."

Sandy tried to stuff the cigarette back into the pack, breaking it in the process. "Did you send the images?"

"I did," she said. "Did you ask Maybach what he thought?"

"I did. Maybach says the man is bogus. He offered to share more if we were willing to share more."

Jila swiveled in the chair, making a full circle. "Well maybe he's on to something, Sandy. Maybe it's time we all came cleaner here."

"What do you mean?" Sandy sank into a low canvas chair that had seen better days.

Jila looked up at Ben, waited for him to nod. "What I mean, Sandy, is that I don't feel as informed as I want to be. What's with those big guns? We haven't had much opportunity to talk about that, but those are big artillery machine guns. And absolutely explicit in our understanding," she said, wheeling her chair over until she was knee to knee with him. "Absolutely explicit in our understanding, was that there would be no secrets. So why didn't you tell me about those big machine guns?"

Sandy took the cigarette back out and fiddled with it. "I didn't know about the guns," he said.

"How's that?" Ben asked.

"I didn't know about them?"

Jila's brow tightened. "You're the boss here. And you're telling me you didn't know about the guns?"

"That's right. Toro told me they came in cartons addressed to me."

"Who sent them?" Jila and Ben asked almost in unison.

Sandy looked up. "Mrs. Heydr."

Ben rubbed at his eyes while Jila swiveled in the chair.

"I figured she was taking extra precautions," Sandy said.

"Extra precautions?" Jila said. "Sandy, guns like that are not precautions. They're for taking out something heavy, like a truck or a helicopter."

Ben paced the little room. "Something isn't adding up. I thought we were here to find the box."

"We are here to find the box," Sandy assured him.

"To be clear," Ben said, "the box is the box that Tomas Ibanez gave to his son in 1542. Not some Theatine nonsense that you probably made up on the plane, right?"

Sandy grinned. "It was good nonsense though, wasn't it? We even got the Pope on board."

"Answer the question, Sandy," Jila said.

"I'm telling you as much as I know. So yes, I'm talking about the Ibanez box, the one mentioned in the documents that we have been referring to as the Cordoba papers. Tomas Ibanez gave his son a box, a very important box that is worth many millions."

Jila took the cigarette from his hand. "We're going to find the box, Sandy, I can taste it. What do you think is in the box?"

"We've been over this," he said. "I don't know. Some relic. A piece of Mohammed's coffin, a snip of his beard, a handwritten letter."

"Or a little genie lamp," Ben said.

Sandy shook his head. "There are no little lamps."

"There are thousands of little lamps," Jila said.

"Maybe so." Sandy snatched the cigarette back and lit it. "But not a single one has ever produced a genie."

"A jinn," Ben corrected him. "They're called jinns, revenants of scorched fire, aspects of thermal energy that can whisper to us in our dreams. They're all over the Islamic world. If you catch one, you can compel it to do your wishes."

"There's not a magic lamp in the box," Sandy said firmly. "There are no jinns."

"There doesn't need to be a lamp," Jila said. "How about just a jinn in a box?"

"Jinns can alter brain waves," Ben noted. "They can haunt houses or pyramids. A captured jinn in a little box could have allowed Diego Ibanez to take hold of a continent, subdue it perhaps, and defeat the Spaniards."

"Then they had a crappy jinn," Sandy said. "I'm fairly sure that those skeletons out there are Ibanez and his lieutenants who were burned at the stake for heresy."

"Maybe not so crappy a jinn," Ben suggested. "We know this much for sure; Islam took hold, at least for a short while. It wasn't the Spanish who buried those men facing Mecca, according to Islamic law. It was the Peruvians, Ibanez's converts. With a jinn watching over them, keeping them safe."

"Jinns are timeless," Jila added. "Maybe the time wasn't right for Islam to prosper. Maybe they have their own jinn agenda."

"Stop with the jinns," Sandy said firmly.

Ben rested his elbows on the table. "I don't think it was about jinns either," he said. "But I also don't think it's one of Mohammed's whiskers. When we find this box I think we're going to be disappointed. It won't be worth it."

"I agree," Jila said. "We're not in the loop here, Sandy. Some bank is going to front more than a million dollars on the off-chance that there is a box out here with someone's petrified left nut in it? Nobody even questions that Muslims came on the early voyage. They were here with some of the first ships, probably with the Pizarro brothers. And Muslims don't really go in for relics. They don't even make statues. Why is the box important?"

"I don't know," Sandy said. He was frustrated now. "And I don't think we're going to know until we find it."

"No, no," Jila said. "We're going to need to know before that. Ben and I can find the box, but before we do that, I want to know why we want to find it. And maybe also why people out of nowhere shot us, and why our housekeeper is now equipped to repel Blackhawk helicopters." She rolled the chair around Sandy as she spoke.

"You're making me dizzy," he said.

"You're getting a little bit bald on the back," she said. "We now have possibly two operatives on our team, Aleza and the priest. This is heating up fast, and we need some more information."

Sandy looked down at the floor.

"I think I know what's in the box, Sandy. You want to know what I think is in the box?"

"What?"

"I think there's a jinn in the box," she said. "I really do. Think about it, jinns whisper suggestions into the minds of mortals. They whisper things."

"You're kidding, right?"

She shook her head. "I'm not kidding at all. This box has been whispering for almost five hundred years, only now it's whispering a little louder."

"I'm not buying into any supernatural bullshit."

"Neither am I," she said. "I don't think there's anything supernatural about it. And that's what disturbs me. Something in this box has value, and that value is whispering to someone. That jinn has been dormant too long, and someone wants it out. This means that it does have the power to change the flow of energy. And in our world, energy is money."

"Money," Sandy repeated. "I think we've established that the contents of the box are worth a great deal."

"How much, Sandy? How much is Mrs. Heydr fronting for this?"

Sandy nodded. "It's difficult to pin down, but ultimately about a million and a half."

Ben whistled. "That's a lot of money," he said. "And if she's going to pay that much, it must be worth a whole lot more than that."

Jila shook her head. "Something here is worth killing and dying for, but not to me."

"I agree," Sandy said. "So what do you want me to do about it?"

Ben grabbed the back of Jila's chair to stop her. "Please," he said. "The sound of the wheels is driving me crazy. I think we need to meet with Mrs. Heydr."

"No," Sandy said. "If we leave now and go to Lima, it will look suspicious."

"I have no intention of going to Lima," Jila said. "I think it's time Mrs. Heydr paid us a visit."

Sandy shook his head. "She won't do that."

"Yes she will," Jila said. "I sent an invitation with the photos I sent to Betty. I told her I knew where the box was but I needed to talk with her before we dug it up. Hopefully she will respond soon so we can plan ahead, maybe get a cake."

"Do you know where the box is?" Sandy asked.

She shook her head. "Not yet. Not a clue, but my brain is working on it night and day. It's percolating, Sandy. It's percolating."

● ● ●

"We're only about halfway through," Juan Carlos said. "We have a lot of work to do before the storm comes." After lunch Sandy led them single file up the pyramid. There, near the top, in a series of small rooms that had been discovered a decade ago, the ancient Moche lords made paintings of their gods and their world.

Ned Peterman gasped. "My heavens," he said. "I had no idea."

Jila had been helping out all morning, injecting the German plastic compound into the delicate clay. You had to use just the right amount. Stick the syringe in about half a centimeter and then squeeze until the paint appears moist. Too little and you've not really injected enough and erosion might still take its toll. Too much and bits of stucco and clay would fall off. Yesterday she had injected too much and lost a prisoner's toe. The head conservator frowned and spent forty minutes building a shunt to set the toe back in place.

Juan Carlos smiled. This was the part of the job he liked the most, the friezes, working with the artwork. In total, in a little more than a decade, Juan Carlos had discovered thirty distinct friezes on the pyramid. The discovery part was easy; the preservation part was not. It was slow work with thin dental picks and brushes that had fewer hairs than a woman had eyelashes. But if you worked carefully, you could peel back a layer of the pyramid and see a little bit of what the Moche thought about when they painted their world.

"These must be worth a fortune," Peterman observed.

Juan Carlos frowned.

"I mean they are of value, are they not?"

"They are," Sandy said. "A da Vinci painting could sell for more than fifty million dollars. Some of these paintings are eight hundred years older. In terms of art alone, you could value this pyramid at about nine billion dollars."

"How did you come up with that?" Jila asked.

"I couldn't sleep one night," Sandy said. "So I did the math, cubic feet of paintings times the average insured value of Renaissance paintings."

"Not bad."

Six conservators from the university in Lima worked diligently with their brushes and syringes. Sandy shook his head. "You're not going to make it," he said.

"No," Juan Carlos agreed. "Not if the storm comes on schedule. We'll still have two entire walls unfinished."

"Work faster."

Juan Carlos smiled faintly.

Maybach lit a cigar and Ben pulled it from his mouth. "You're going to regret you did that," Maybach said.

"Have a little respect," Ben said. "You're in a holy place. What do you see on these walls?"

"What do you see?" Ned Peterman added. "What are these drawings?"

"They're paintings," Ben said.

"They're friezes, technically," Sandy said. "A frieze is a three dimensional painting - a painting with some relief. They used stucco and mud plaster to accentuate their paintings."

"Then what are these friezes?" Peterman asked. "This looks like a line of people being tied up."

Jila had seen this particular frieze hundreds of times but it always gave her a chill. Twelve naked men stood in a line, tied with a rope around their necks.

"They are going to kill them, aren't they?" Peterman asked.

"Yes, they are going to kill them," Maybach said. "These men are captives, part of a sacred Moche ritual in which captives were marched into a little room, much like this, perhaps this room. There they were received by a high priest, a Moche lord, who asked them questions."

"What kinds of questions?" Peterman asked.

"Questions about the future," Maybach said, "questions about the afterlife. It was believed that those close to a divine death could speak of issues that they were on the verge of knowing."

"Gordon is exceeding his evidence by a long margin," Sandy added. "We don't know what the priests were saying to the prisoners, or if they said anything at all. What we do know is that these men were soon sacrificed, their throats cut with a tumi, their blood drained and drank."

"Godless," Peterman said, crossing himself.

"Not godless," Maybach corrected. "It was done for god. A different god perhaps, but it was not godless."

"But these men died nonetheless," Peterman said.

"Yes," Sandy answered.

"And this scene over here?" Peterman asked, pointing to the frieze behind him.

Five kings wearing four pointed crowns held hands, smiling. "Are they indeed kings?"

"It's not clear," Maybach said. "Interpretations vary, but they are minimally lords, men of importance. What really is a king? Was King Arthur a king? Very likely not. Perhaps these lords oversaw the ritual, bore witness to the final questioning, maybe learned something about god as they cut their captives' throats and dispatched them to the afterlife."

"Once again," Sandy interjected, "Professor Maybach is walking a thematic line that exceeds his evidence."

"Come on, Sandy," Maybach countered, fiddling with a new cigar. "Don't you think you learn something right there on the edge of death? Don't you think this was all about that? The Aztecs played the same game. The Grand Inquisitors did too. Don't you think they asked questions as their heretics burned, half already in the company of our Lord?"

Peterman glared at him. "No modern cleric will defend the actions of those men charged with carrying out the work of the Inquisition, but can you really make a parallel between men who tried to bring the word of Christ and those who would cut the throats of naked prisoners?"

"Why not?" Maybach asked.

"It works for me," Jila said.

"Me too," Sandy added. "If you're killing for god, does it really matter what you name your god?"

Peterman shook his head.

"Professor," Juan Carlos said, getting Sandy's attention, waving his hand at the six conservators who stood watching as the debate wound to a disagreeable halt. "We have work to do. We're not going to make it as it is. Can we get back to it?"

Sandy nodded. "Of course," he said, leading the group out of the rooms, back into the harsh daylight and down the narrow path off the pyramid.

"Diabolical," Peterman said as they neared the ground.

"No," Sandy said. "No, it's not."

CHAPTER 23

URUBAMBA VALLEY, PERU

The sun was directly overhead, illuminating the high mountains as the train cut its slow path through the Urubamba Valley. Jimmy Segura sat back in his puffy first-class seat and drank a Cuzqueña beer from a bottle that he had been exchanging every half an hour or so for a full one, courtesy of a young man with a cart who made his way up and down between the rows. Jimmy stared at the snow-capped mountains. He remembered reading that the railroad had been constructed alongside an old Inca road, but right now he didn't care much.

He was a day behind schedule. He had intended to take last night's train, but after landing in Cuzco, he was overtaken by seroche, the altitude sickness that greets nearly every visitor to the Inca capital, 12,000 feet high in the Andes. He spent nearly an hour at the airport cafe eating plain rice and drinking coca tea. The rice was important because you needed to have something in your stomach, and the tea, which had only the mildest narcotic properties, was essential to adjusting to the altitude and the paucity of oxygen. Then he spent the night in a hotel and slept heavily.

Catching the morning train, he planted himself in an empty compartment. Like Jimmy, most of the tourists were bound for Machu Picchu, the royal Inca estate which had long been the most popular archaeological site on the South American continent. But most of them were backpackers or hippies or both, and they didn't go in for first-class seats. So when the train began moving and nobody else had joined him in the compartment, Jimmy put his feet up, opened his case, and pulled out a wheel of strong cheese and a couple of thick sausages he purchased in Lima. He ate slowly as the train climbed out of the Cuzco Valley before beginning its descent to Machu Picchu.

With the exception of last night, Jimmy not been sleeping well at all. The day after the incident, as he now referred to it, the incident in which Edith Heydr drove a fork through his career, Jimmy made two visits, the first to a pharmacist known for his liberal prescription policies, and the second, which necessarily had to transpire after the ingestion of some anxiety pills obtained from the first visit, to Salvador Montes' office.

He had resolved to tell Montes everything. Jimmy estimated that the downward slope that his career was about to take was probably not too steep. His crimes were not great when weighed against the alternate course of action, which was to not report the meeting with Edith Heydr and the proposal she had made. How much trouble was he in now? He should have reported the contacts in Egypt. That was the rule. In his line of work, sexual contacts had to be reported within twenty-four hours. No mistakes. If it was a Friday night, you reported it on Saturday. A Saturday night, you called in to a secure server on Sunday morning. No hassles, nobody gave you even a sideways look.

Sexual contacts with foreign nationals were a different sort of thing entirely. You report it just the same, but phone calls are made. Computer terminals blink. Failure to report is grounds for disciplinary action or termination of employ. Add to this the illegal purchase and smuggling of culturally significant documents that were almost certainly procured by a foreign operative, and termination of employ was almost certain. But at least he wouldn't be checking in to a military prison for twenty to life if he came clean now.

Montes had been waiting for him, frowning.

So, it was over. Montes had apparently heard the entire conversation, which was going to make things a whole lot easier, really.

"Do you know why I've asked you here?" Salvador Montes asked sadly, sitting on the edge of his desk.

"I was not aware you had asked me here," Jimmy said. "I haven't been to my office yet. I came directly to see you."

"You have some idea, though."

"I do."

"Quite a meeting you had there, wasn't it?"

"It was, yes. That's what I came here to talk to you about."

"Do you know how I learned about your meeting?" Montes asked, shaking his head sadly.

"I can imagine."

"Have you met the ambassador's wife?"

Jimmy squinted. "I believe so, why?"

"She came to see me yesterday and she was quite upset. Do you know why?"

"No, I'm not certain I do," Jimmy answered carefully.

"Did you know that she did the interior decorating for the public rooms in the consular section?"

"I did not."

"Well, I got an earful this morning because you stained her Atahualpa."

"I did what?"

Montes spread his arms wide. "That was my question. She was having new blinds installed in the meeting room, and she noticed that the Atahualpa table she had installed in the room had been stained. Not only was it stained, but only Atahualpa was stained. His whole head. She dragged me down to look at it, and it's a mess, Jimmy. Pizarro looks great, but Atahualpa has a big dark stain covering his face. You stained the table, didn't you?"

Jimmy's mouth opened slightly, allowing about fifteen percent more air to enter his lungs, and via his bloodstream, travel to his brain. "It was an accident with the tea."

"We follow protocols here," Montes reminded him. "If there's a spill, you call housekeeping. If you don't follow the protocol, then housekeeping does not get called, stains set, and Atahualpas are ruined."

"I'm sorry," Jimmy said. "I'll pay for the table."

Montes shook his head. "It's not about the money; it's about procedure. Mrs. Ambassador checked the bookings log for the room and found your name. She demanded that a reprimand be included in your personnel file."

"You're joking."

Montes produced a sheet of paper from the desk. "You have a right to see your file. I need you to read this reprimand and sign it."

Jimmy read the document, incredulous. He could not believe this was happening. He picked up a pen and signed the paper.

"I'm sorry about this, Jimmy," Montes called after him as he walked towards the door. "You should have been more careful."

Jimmy held up his middle finger when he reached the door and found it locked. "Open the fucking door, Sal."

"I'm not trying to be the heavy here," Montes said. "And I still need to hear about the meeting. Did you develop any relevant information from your meeting with this Edith Heydr?"

"I'll write you a briefing," Jimmy said. "Now open the fucking door, Sal."

He did, from a switch on his desk, and that was that.

Jimmy left. Forget about the other thing.

"Otra cerveza?" the boy asked, poking his head into first class compartment.

"You bet." Jimmy fished out a couple of coins from his pocket.

Several backpackers got out when the train came to a squeaky stop by Ollantaytambo, one of the Inca safe houses, one of the many places the Inca royalty hid as the Spaniards pursued them, promising to burn them if they didn't surrender. It was a cruel threat, even crueler then it sounded. An Inca needed his mummy to assure eternity, so the threat of burning was to end not only this life but his life in the hereafter as well.

About twenty minutes later the train came to a lurching halt in the middle of a lush clearing.

"I'm good," Jimmy said as the beer boy poked his head back into the compartment. He held up the bottle to indicate it was not yet empty.

"You get off here," the boy said.

"No, I'm going to Machu Picchu."

"The man outside says you go with him."

"What man?"

"Look."

Jimmy turned to the window and saw nothing but Andes and green.

"Look down."

Jimmy jumped back startled. Right under the window was an old Indian wearing a bright woven llama wool cap staring at him. Next to him stood the llama that very likely provided the wool. "Who the hell is that?" he asked but the boy was gone.

In no mood to go trekking on the Inca trail, Jimmy sat back down and waited for the train to leave. When he peeked out the window again, the man was still there, standing under his window looking up. He was holding a sheet of paper.

"This is your stop, Mr. Segura," it read. Edith Heydr's name was embossed on the page.

Jimmy grabbed his case and jumped down just as the train started to move. In seconds he was alone at the edge of the track with only the old man and the llama for company.

The man carefully folded the letter and tucked it into his shirt. He took Jimmy's case and secured it on top of the llama. Then without saying a word, he led the llama along a worn footpath into the mountain forest. Jimmy followed.

It was quiet, just a few birds and the snorting of the llama. Jimmy pet the soft fur, but the animal gave him no notice. The old man was chewing something, probably a wad of coca leaves as was custom in the high mountains.

Jimmy felt lightheaded. He thought about writing a letter to his mother. "Dear Mom,'" it might start, "I'm in the mountains following this old Inca, who I swear is wearing the same snow cap I had when I was a kid, to meet a hundred-year-old Muslim woman who works with some people who got me laid back in Egypt." The letter wasn't working out.

At least he wasn't huffing and puffing. Jimmy was finding the hike quite pleasant, even after they left the main path and veered onto a narrower one. Twenty minutes later, he could hear voices as they came out into a clearing where several houses clustered around a plaza. The old man waved to the heads that peeked from every window and doorway as he led his caravan of two beasts through the plaza and down a wide path, past more houses, and stopped, pointing to a path paved in flat stones that had been fitted together like pieces in a jigsaw puzzle.

The man pointed again, removed Jimmy's case from the llama's back, then walked away. Jimmy stood alone at the foot of the path half expecting a poison dart to come out of somewhere. The path was only about fifty meters long and ended in front of what was quite obviously a mosque.

• • •

It was a small mosque, maybe ten meters along the front. The foundation was stone, rough cut, but the building itself was made entirely of wood, even the dome, and the minaret which rose high into the crisp mountain air. Jimmy watched as a man climbed the minaret and began calling out in Quechua, the language of the Andean Indians, making the call to afternoon prayer.

He heard the footsteps before he saw anyone. Then the clearing filled with Indians in their colorful ponchos and pointy knot caps, Incas making their way to the mosque.

Hundreds of men, they were moving slowly; old men, teenagers, even little ones. And just as suddenly, they were gone, hidden away inside the mosque. The doors closed and it could have been a dream except for the neat rows of leather slippers that lined the edge of the building.

How about that! Jimmy sat on a stone bench at the edge of the path and wondered what would be next. A leprechaun?

"You must be thirsty." The voice came from just behind and startled him off the bench.

"Christ," he said, turning around.

"Christ is a prophet of Islam," the young man said.

Jimmy was confused. "You speak English."

"Yes, we learn English in school."

"You live here?"

"Yes. I've been here a little over a year now." He held out a water bottle which Jimmy took gratefully. "I was getting into trouble in Trujillo, so my father sent me here to clean up."

"That's what this place is for?"

"No. No," he said. "This place is for worship, for people who want to live close to the land and worship God. Very few of us are from outside the valley."

"How long has this all been here?"

"Forever if you ask some. This mosque is new," he said, "but there was another before it and one before that, all the way back to the 1860s."

"1860s? That's a long time ago."

"That when the movement started, when the Pasha entrusted Feyd Heydr to bring Islam to the Americas."

Jimmy folded his arms across his chest. "You're kidding, right?"

"Come on," the young man called out. "You have to keep walking. The jaguars come out in the afternoon."

"There aren't any jaguars left in the Andes," Jimmy said. "What's your name?"

"Cesar Ibanez," he said. "And there are thousands of jaguars in the

Andes. Now, you're supposed to follow me to Mrs. Heydr's house."

"She's not in the mosque praying?"

"No. Men and women do not pray together. What's more, she doesn't pray at the mosque at all."

"Why not?"

"Ask her," he said, leading Jimmy down a path behind the mosque that descended further into the valley. The sound of the prayers grew fainter in the distance.

"You're looking well," Mrs. Heydr said from behind a large wooden desk.

Jimmy sat down on a bench inside the small wooden bungalow that smelled like pine. Across from him, a fire burned in an iron stove. "What is all this?"

"A special place that I wanted you to see." She made notes in a ledger with a fountain pen as she spoke. "Are you tired, or hungry?"

"I'm good."

"There is a guest house you can stay in."

"I'm fine, thank you," he said. "Why did you ask me here?"

She walked around the desk and sat beside him. "To show you this place, a seed we planted a long time ago. That seed grew into a town, and that town has been nurtured but has not yet matured. I wanted to show you what I want for this world, what I am working for."

"A bunch of indians praying to Allah in Quechua? It's a little incongruous, don't you think?"

"Do you know much about Islam, Mr. Segura?" She poured him a cup of coca tea from a thermos.

Jimmy sipped the fragrant beverage which warmed him instantly. "I do, of course. You know that I do. I have deep respect for some of the core belief sets, but as for some of the rest of it...."

"I would agree," she said sadly, looking down at her hands. "I don't believe in it quite like I used to. But some days it moves me. Mostly the tenacity of it."

Jimmy pulled off his shoes to rub the cold from his feet. "So you want to turn Peru into an Islamic state?"

"No," she said. "A Caliphate, not a state. And not Peru; South America."

He said nothing, rubbed his feet for a while longer.

"Plans were laid out almost five hundred years ago, but there were some difficulties. And then the faithless began to act in the name of faith. These terror groups that operate in so many countries are no more Muslim than those Spanish Inquisitors were Christian. God is tolerant. Were he not, I would have no use for him."

Jimmy wrapped a wool blanket around his shoulders and sat on the floor by the stove. It was colder inside than it was outside. "So your plan is to get rid of the bad Muslims so the good Muslims can take over."

"Yes," she said. "That's quite well said. What I want, what I work for, is more or less just what you've articulated."

"Why bother?" he asked, poking at the fire. "Why not just leave Peru alone? These people would be just as fine without your interference."

"Or your interference? Why are you in Peru? Why does your government have to interfere in Peru?"

"Good point, but we're not trying to take over, to totally redefine a nation."

"Then I find your ambitions wanting. This was once the richest most powerful nation on earth. Now it's violent. You dare not walk the streets of Lima after dusk. And the drugs, the drugs, Jimmy. They are ripping the country apart."

He nodded. "I don't know what to tell you," he said. "You have a nice village here but I don't see it spreading all over Peru."

"There are dozens of villages like this in the mountains. It will spread, trust me with that end. Tenacity, remember. I want you to stay here for a day or so. Talk to people. And I want you to do another thing for me."

Jimmy stared at the fire as she stood beside him, handing him a photo. "I want you to tell me who this is," she said.

"Sandy Beckham," he said. "You know that." The photo was grainy as if taken by a long lens or a surveillance camera.

"The gentleman he is talking to?"

Jimmy squinted, felt his pulse quicken. Can't be. He looked up just as she handed him the magnifying glass. "Is this the only photograph you have?"

"No," she said, handing him a half dozen more. "But this is the best."

Jimmy scanned each photo with the magnifying glass. The shots weren't great, but good enough for him to make an identification.

"Is he one of yours?"

"No," he said. "Does he have very light skin?"

"I'm told he does. He claims to be a priest."

"He's not." Jimmy opened his case and brought out the heavy satellite telephone. It would take a few moments to set up and orient. "His name is Hugh Holland. He's been high on the watch list for about four years."

"Who does he work for?"

Jimmy took the phone outside to get a signal. Edith Heydr followed.

"He was Special Forces but he went AWOL after Desert Storm. Then he turned up on a surveillance photo of a Hamas training camp in Syria. He is believed to have the rank of commander. He does a specific sort of counterintelligence; he moves in quickly and kills fast. What name is he using?"

"Ned Peterman."

It took nearly ten minutes to find a signal; Jimmy made the call to Langley, Virginia, and then via relay, to the Lima Service which would alert Salvador Montes within ninety seconds. "I have no direct contact with my agent in Santiago," he said. "Holland does counterintelligence work. He's not a closer, so he won't be there long. If he is able to identify operative personnel, he will kill them to control information flow, then he'll disappear. Do you have any means of contacting Sandy Beckham?"

"Not directly. There was a problem, so Sandy switched on his cell phone jammers. There's an old landline in the kitchen at their hacienda, but it doesn't normally work." She dialed the number on Jimmy's phone, then shook her head. "But I have a backup plan." She called Betty Snow and told her about Hugh Holland.

"I need to get back to Lima," Jimmy said.

"There's no train back to Cuzco until this evening."

Jimmy sat on the ground, feeling useless. He turned off the satellite phone and folded its big antenna. "Why is there a Hamas commander in Santiago, Mrs. Heydr?"

"That will take some time," she said, moving back into the house.

"We have until evening, I guess."

"Come inside," she said. "You have information to share with me, a packet of resources"

Jimmy followed her inside and sat by the fire. "I don't know what you mean by a packet of resources."

Edith Heydr draped an alpaca-wool blanket around her shoulders. "Sandy Beckham told me that resources can be understood in terms of packets. The Inca could never have consolidated rule by force alone, he said. They did it by controlling packets of resources. Llamas, potatoes, maize, guinea pigs, fish. That amounted to a packet of resources and intelligence is another such packet. We have work to do, you and I, and you came here to deliver a packet of resources."

Jimmy shook his head. "I will probably be fired for this."

"Nonsense."

"Sharing intelligence with a foreign national? They'll incarcerate me."

"You wouldn't do well in prison," she said. "Peruvian prisons are chilly."

"That's not what I'm most worried about."

She laughed. "You needn't worry at all. I have so much money it would make you cry. There's no prison for you, Jimmy. You're family to me now."

"Comforting," he said, rubbing his hands, taking the documents from his breast pocket and handing them to her.

She held the envelope in her hands. "Is this what I asked for?"

"Yes," he said. "Field strength. What you're holding is the current CIA assessment of the relative field strength of the various terror organizations operating in the Parana administrative region. Both Al Qaeda and Shining Crescent are growing, recruiting dozens of new members each month. You have the names of the leaders and their political allies, as well as those of Hezbollah and some local orders. This intelligence spans the jurisdiction of four sovereign nations: Brazil, Paraguay, Argentina, and by way of interference, the United States."

"It will be most helpful," Edith Heydr said.

"For what?" Jimmy asked. "You cannot imagine the risks I took to bring you this information. Is it worth it?"

"It is," she said sternly. "It is. Your government won't stop these organizations, but I will. I have no worries about jurisdiction or borders. And I will bring withering fire to bear on my enemies. Give me a couple of months to take care of these terror cells in Parana. It will take me no longer than that, Jimmy. I will live to see a secular nonviolent Islamic Caliphate in South America."

CHAPTER 24

SANTIAGO DE PAZ, PERU

Aleza was organizing potsherds into discrete typological piles when Ned Peterman entered the lab. She looked up and smiled briefly. She was finding the work very difficult. Moche ceramic styles changed dramatically over time, and so it was possible to date the ceramics, more or less, by paying attention to details such as spout length, and the degree of flare at the mouth. With a chart like the one she had propped up in front of her, and a great deal of practice, it became almost second nature. But the sheer quantity of ceramics unearthed each day by the excavation crew made for a never-ending task.

"Interesting," Peterman said, peering over her shoulder. "What is it you hope to learn from these fragments?"

Aleza smiled. "Hopefully they will allow us a sense of time. The more we learn from the ceramics, the better we can tell what years we're digging through."

"I had no idea," Peterman said, picking up a small spout handle. "It's really quite interesting, not so tedious as it at first appears. Do you enjoy it?"

"I do."

"You don't mind staying in here and missing all the excitement?"

"No," she said. "They'll let me know if they find something."

"So you know about the tomb this morning down by the beach?"

Aleza spun around.

Peterman picked up another sherd. "This one has a bit of red paint on it."

"They found a tomb?"

"Yes," he said. "An undisturbed one, I'm told. That means it has not been looted. They've been down there for hours. Have you any idea what could be inside?"

Aleza stormed out the door. Several teams of excavators were at work on the plaza, but she couldn't spot Sandy or the others. "Bastards," she said.

"Can I show you the way?" Peterman asked, already walking down the road toward the beach, confident that she was following as they left the archaeological zone.

"I didn't even know they were working out here," Aleza said when he turned off the road and climbed over the remnants of old looter holes.

"Just over behind that one," he said, pointing to a large sand dune.

"I don't hear anything," she said, following. The wind was high today and it whistled loudly between the dunes.

"I think they were trying to keep it quiet."

Aleza took a few more steps before she realized it was all wrong. Adrenaline poured through her. She dove left and rolled out, coming up with a collapsible baton in her hand. She flicked her wrist and the baton extended like an antenna.

"Wow," Peterman exclaimed. He was ten feet away from her, holding a hand up to shade his eyes. "Is that some kind of walking stick?"

She stood there facing him, her heart racing. "There's nobody out here."

Peterman shook his head and moved toward her.

Aleza sank into a low crouch, hands up in front, the baton heavy in her right. "What do you want?"

"I can't imagine what you're referring to," he said, moving closer.

"Stop or I'll hurt you. What do you want?"

"Just you, baby," he said, closing.

"It's not going to happen."

"I just need to know who you work for, what you know, that sort of thing."

"Back off," she yelled.

When he came, he came in fast. Aleza raised the baton in her right hand but surprised him with a left jab to the throat. He doubled over, and she swept his legs with the baton. "You should have brought company," she said.

Peterman struggled to his knees, but she cracked the baton over his back, snapping a rib. "I underestimated you," he rasped, catching his breath. "Do they teach you this in archaeology school?"

"They do. Who are you?"

"Someone looking for some answers," he said, not yet daring to get up.

"You're not an archaeologist."

"Neither are you."

She shifted her weight back and forth on her legs, breathing deeply. "Who do you work for?"

"If I tell you, will you tell me?"

"No, but I'll beat you less." She moved closer and smacked the baton across the back of his legs.

He screamed and sprung up at her, two quick punches to her face, dropping her before she could swing again. She fell back and rolled. He came in low and dove at her legs, took a blow to the back but he had her down. He punched her hard in the stomach, driving the air out of her lungs. "That fucking hurt," he wheezed. He grabbed her hair, pulling her head up. "You are U.S. intelligence, aren't you?"

"Yes," she said.

"What's your assignment here?"

Aleza coughed and threw up. "Infiltrate and find out what's in some old box."

"So what's in the old box?"

"A letter from the Pope, I'm told. I don't know, they didn't find the box yet. Who do you work for?"

Peterman wrapped his arm around her throat and squeezed. "What's in the box?"

Aleza tried not to panic but it wasn't working. Just as she was about to pass out, he let up the pressure. "I don't know what's in the box," she said, coughing. "Why don't you strangle someone who does?"

"Already did." He squeezed her neck again. "Jila, Sandy, Ben. They weren't willing to talk either so I had to kill them. You better come up with a better answer. Second question, how do you communicate with your handlers?"

Aleza felt like she was going to throw up and pass out at the same time. This one was getting too close. "I don't," she said after coughing and taking in air. "I had a transmitter but they broke it."

"They know about you?"

"Yes."

"Are there other operatives here on the project?"

"Yes,"

"Who?"

"I won't tell you until you tell me who you work for."

Peterman began squeezing again. "I can't do that."

"Okay," Aleza managed to squeak out and he let up.

"Ready to talk?"

She nodded. "I can't do this anymore. Shoot him," she said.

"There's nobody here but you and me," Peterman said. The shot rang out and caught him in the side of the neck, not a clean shot. He jumped up, his hand clamped to his neck to stop the blood flow. He spun around to face the security guard and shook his head. "The guards never come down here," he said, gurgling.

Aleza stood up and rubbed her neck. "They do if you fuck them," she said. "We have time; you'll bleed out slowly. Who do you work for?"

Peterman stared at the guard as the blood seeped through his fingers.

"Is it worth your life?" She took the gun from Manuel and held it out in front of her.

Peterman turned slowly. Aleza would have missed it but the harsh Moche sunlight caught on the knife he pulled from his boot, and she shot him twice in the chest.

Manuel, the security guard, took the gun from her. "I followed you. I kept my eye on you, like you told me. But I did it because I love you, not because you told me to."

Aleza pressed her forehead to his shoulder. "Thank you, sweetheart."

CHAPTER 25

SANTIAGO DE PAZ, PERU

Mark and Brenda Cox left that afternoon, after calling ahead to confirm a flight back to Lima.

"I'm sorry," Sandy said, standing next to the Land Rover. One of the guards would drive them in.

"Me too," Mark said. "We'd stay, Sandy, but this is too screwed up."

"I understand."

Brenda Cox held up her middle finger.

Sandy nodded to the driver as he pulled out of the driveway, moving onto the side of the road as a jeep moved in fast, leaving a plume of sand in its wake. Sandy moved back behind the wall and looked up at the guards, two of whom had drawn their guns. The jeep came to a halt just in front of the gate and Betty Snow jumped out.

The guards looked to Sandy. He held up his hands and they withdrew.

"We've got trouble," Betty said, jogging up to the gate. "Peterman, the man in the photos, he's not a priest. He's very dangerous."

"You think?" He told her what had happened and she told him what she had learned from Mrs. Heydr. "I think I need to shut this down," he said. "Too many surprises. We just lost two people. Maybach will probably leave, and I don't think Aleza's going to be sticking around."

"You still want her around?"

Sandy shrugged. "She's getting really good at the ceramics."

"Mrs. Heydr is on her way. Can you keep things together until she gets here?"

Sandy looked up at artillery gun that the security men had positioned on the wall. "I'm getting creeped out," he said. "For all we know there's a team of ninjas landing on the beach tonight."

"Settle down, Sandy. How's the rest of the crew?"

"Stunned or pissed off. Ben is stunned. Bill Field is stunned, Maybach is pissed off. I don't know what Jila is. I think pissed off or maybe stunned."

"Where's the body?"

"In the lab with the textiles. We have some exposure here. Some of the workers heard the gunshots, and Juan Carlos saw the body as did Toro and Margarita."

"We trust these people, right?"

Sandy sneezed. "I'm having a hard time trusting anyone now. I don't even trust the Pope. I especially don't trust the Pope."

"Do you want me to take care of the body?" she asked.

"Yes, please."

Gordon Maybach sat quietly, alone in the big room when Sandy came in. He had a copy of Moche Lords open on his lap. "I was just reading my dedication," he said. "Listen here, 'To Monica, who left Swansea, Wales for Boston just to take a chance on me.' What do you think of that, Beckham?"

"Lovely."

"God, I'm old. I wrote this book forty years ago."

"Monica was your first wife?"

"Yes."

"What happened to her?"

Maybach took off his glasses. "She went back to Swansea after the divorce. Looking back, it occurs to me that I was not very kind to her. And some of those graduate students, they were so pretty."

Sandy found the bottle of Maker's Mark and the bar and poured a drink. "Can I refill you there?"

"Yes, thank you," Maybach said. "I think we need to talk."

Sandy downed the liquor and poured another. "Where is everyone?"

"I believe Ben is still at the lab with the dear departed Father. Dr. Field is drinking beer in the pool. Toro has taken up position on the wall out back. He's packing a gun now and wearing a bandolier. He looks like Pancho Villa. Jila and Aleza are in their room."

"Then let's get Bill in here."

"Sandy, let's be clear. Our departed friend, whoever he is, did not try to rape her. Aleza can say so all she wants but that story isn't going to hold water. It would appear that the man wasn't really a priest, but you'd have to be one eager sporting rapist to go to this kind of fuss. So you need to come up with a better story or I'll become very mad, and I'm too old and tired to become very mad."

"Alright." He went out onto the patio and walked over to the pool. "You okay, Bill?"

"Peachy." Bill Field had several empties lined on one side of the pool, and a pail of bottles on ice on the other side. "I've been swimming back and forth every few minutes."

"I can see that."

"I'm thinking about leaving, Sandy. I might go tomorrow."

"I might go with you." Sandy crouched at the side of the pool. "Will you come inside and talk with Gordon and me?"

He shook his head. "I feel safer here."

"Come inside, Bill."

"Okay."

• • •

"I'm fine," Aleza said, standing in front of the mirror, admiring the bruises on her neck.

Jila opened her hand, revealing three pills.

"What are they?"

"Two ibuprofen and a Valium."

"Perfect." She took the pills and drank from the faucet to wash them down.

Jila held out a bottle of water. "You're not supposed to drink from the tap."

"Crap," Aleza said. "Now I'm going be up all night shitting."

"Did you get in some punches?"

"I sure did."

"Did he say who he was working with?"

"No."

"Did you ask?"

"Of course I did." Aleza brushed her hair. "You know, I really am an archaeologist. I have a degree but that's not why I'm here."

"I know."

"And you broke my transmitter, right?"

"That's right."

"So then you know that I asked him who he was working for and he didn't tell me."

"Would you tell me if he did?"

Aleza put down the brush and stared at her bruises in the mirror. "I think at this point I would," she said. "But I don't know any more than you do; I'm just tracking some $11 million wire transfer to Sandy Beckham's concubine, or whatever she is."

"Is that right?" Jila sat on the edge of the bed. "Eleven million?"

"Yeah, eleven million. So can you tell me what this is all about? I'm having a hard time believing that you guys are Islamic terrorists."

"I never saw myself as such," Jila said.

"Will you tell me what this is all about?"

"It's supposed to be a secret. And the whole point of a secret is to not leak it to spies."

Aleza sat next to her. "Look, I don't know much about you, but I think you have some experience doing the kind of work I do, right?"

Jila didn't respond.

"So you know that I'm here to find answers. And if I don't get answers, I'm going to shut down your whole project."

"I'd disappear like the wind," Jila said, blowing on her fingers. "I'll come back in three years and find the box myself."

"So there really is a box? What's in the box?"

"A letter from the Pope," Jila said, giggling. "No, I'm just fucking with you. I don't know what's in the box, I haven't found it yet. There were some Muslims came over from Spain about five hundred years ago. We have the paperwork on their expedition."

"What does the document say about the box?"

"Not much. Just that it whatever it contained was supposed to be kept hidden. That means it's valuable. Let's go talk to Sandy about it."

• • •

Toro moved silently around the big room, setting plates of toasted sandwiches on the end tables. He had taken off the bandolier but still wore the pistol low under his dinner jacket. No real dinner tonight as Margarita had gone to bed feeling ill.

Nobody touched the sandwiches. They sipped their Scotches quietly as Sandy opened the blue plastic box that held the pages.

"These are photocopies," he said, "of a diary entry that was written in Alexandria, Egypt in 1544 by a woman named Aminah Ibanez. It's four pages long."

"This is the original document?" Bill Field asked.

Sandy stared at him. "These are white 8 1/2 x 11 sheets of copy paper, Bill. That's the second clue that this is not the original document. The first clue was me saying that these are photocopies."

"It's written in Spanish," Maybach noted. "And yet you say it's from Egypt."

"Correct," Sandy said. "Aminah Ibanez was the wife of Diego Ibanez, the leader of a secret and illegal expedition that set sail from Cadiz, Spain in 1542. The rest of the Ibanez family, fearing retribution, sailed for Egypt."

"This is very difficult to read," Bill said, holding the page close to his face.

Sandy held up a single typed sheet. "Here's a transcript. I've made copies for everyone to look at."

"How did you come by this document in the first place?" Bill asked.

Ben paced back and forth by the door and caught sight of Jila leading Aleza toward the big house. "Heads up," he said, gesturing to the open door.

"Oh shit," Sandy said, snatching up the documents.

Maybach held onto his sheet. "No more secrets, Sandy."

"No," Sandy said, agitated. "You don't understand, she's. . . .."

"Who is. . . .?" Maybach asked.

"Aleza. She's CIA."

"Really," Maybach said. "Is she working for the Pope as well?"

"I don't know," Sandy said. "Can we just put this away for now?"

Maybach shrugged. Sandy took all the paperwork and hid it under the big Moche Lords volume as Jila entered the room.

Everyone stood as Aleza followed her to the couch. She was wearing a shirt buttoned up to the neck. Her eye had swelled up.

Toro was behind her in an instant with ice cubes wrapped in a linen napkin.

"How are you, dear?" Maybach asked.

"I'm okay, thank you."

"We were just talking about Peterman," Sandy said.

Jila popped the cap off a liter of the local beer. Toro held out a glass but she shook her head and drank from the bottle. "I told her," she said.

"Excuse me?" Sandy said.

"I told her about Ibanez."

"Really! Somehow I thought that was going to be my call."

"I did too," Jila said. "I also thought there wasn't going to be any more shooting."

"Fine," Sandy said. "Well, I told everyone she was a spy."

Aleza threw her head back on the sofa and groaned.

"Is this true?" Maybach asked.

"Yes," she said. "I work for the Central Intelligence Agency."

"A spy," Maybach said.

"Yes. I've been keeping an eye on all of you. Sandy smokes in bed and sleeps cuddled up with a little sock doll."

"It's not a doll," Sandy said. "They're socks, in case I have to get up at night. The floor is cold."

Aleza shrugged. "Bill has a cell phone, and calls his girlfriend in Chicago even though he's not supposed to have a cell phone. I used it eleven times. I owe you for the minutes."

Bill Field said nothing.

"I thought we had the jammers on," Ben said.

"You do, yes," Aleza said, "but for some reason, if you go back behind the pool house, you can get a signal. I only know that because I saw Bill there."

Bill shrugged. "Sorry."

"Jila talks in her sleep," Aleza continued. "But her comments are of a personal nature so I won't divulge them. Brenda Cox had an affair last year. She felt really bad about it. She finally told Mark, and now she respects him less because he didn't wig out. Ben wears a wig."

Ben chuckled, almost spilling his drink.

"I got nothing on you," she admitted. "Gordon here has about half a pound of marijuana in his toilet kit and a throwing knife tucked into a little pouch in each of his boots."

"Well done!" Maybach clapped. "You are a spy! You know I used to be in the Intelligence game myself. British Secret Service. I learned how to kill with a pencil. Do they still teach that?"

"No," she said. "Nowadays we use computers. They're heavier."

"So how come you didn't figure out Peterman?" Maybach asked.

Aleza shook her head. "I don't know. I thought it strange that he just popped in, but you all welcomed him so I figured he was part of your game. Still, it was obvious he wasn't a priest."

"How was it obvious?" Sandy asked.

"He said grace like a little girl. Also, about a month ago the Vatican ambassador got shipped off to Baltimore for chemo, so he couldn't have met with Peterman."

"Why didn't you say anything?"

"Give me a break. No one here says anything. Now show me these papers."

Sandy passed around the pages, and everyone read, in silence, an account of sorrow. Aminah Ibanez wrote of the two long years since her husband left for Peru, of how she missed him. She wrote of her fears for his safety, and how she spent part of each day staring out at the sea, waiting for his ships to return. She wrote of her hopes that her gift, hidden in a box inside a cask of flour, would give him comfort.

"So there is a box," Maybach said triumphantly.

Sandy shrugged.

"I knew it!"

"This doesn't really say much," Aleza said.

Maybach shook his head. "It says quite a lot. If it is true, and those bodies we found are in fact members of this expedition, then we can rewrite history. We can now establish an evangelical Islamic presence in Peru even as the Inquisition was consolidating."

Bill Field leaned forward. "It's a minaret," he said.

Everyone stared at him.

"The adobe tower. It's not defensive. It's not a tower, it's a fucking minaret. They built a mosque on the plaza." He stared at the copy of the diary. "Then the Christians came. They killed Diego Ibanez and they tore down the mosque and built a church right on top of it."

Jila drank from her liter of beer and Sandy lit a cigarette.

Bill shook his head. "You fuckers. You knew that already, didn't you?"

Nobody said anything.

"Fuckers."

"I told you it was a mosque," Maybach said. "I even described what the minaret would have looked like."

"Yeah, but I thought it was just another one of your goofy stories."

"I don't tell goofy stories," Maybach spat back.

"No? Not two days ago you prattled on for forty minutes about the time you played polo with Charles de Gaulle and you lost because de Gaulle's horse kept farting."

"It was like riding through a cloud." Maybach said.

Aleza glanced through the photocopies. "Two questions: how did you come by this document, and what on earth connects it to this site? This expedition could have landed anywhere on the coast, if they even got here at all."

"The document turned up in an antique market in Alexandria," Sandy explained. "An acquaintance of my landlady acquired it and sent it to her. She in turn gave it to me to investigate."

"Is there more of it?" Maybach asked. "This is a diary entry. Where is the rest of the diary?"

"To date, we have been unable to locate any other entries, though we have investigators in Cairo and Alexandria working on it."

"Why here?" Aleza asked.

"Because this is where the Ibanez expedition landed," Sandy answered. "All those looter holes weren't for nothing. Treasure hunters have been digging here for centuries. In 1954, an antiquities buff bought a ceramic goblet from a looter who dug it up right in front of our pyramid. On it was written the Shahadah in Spanish."

"The what?" Aleza asked.

"Shahadah." Maybach repeated the word. "There is no god except God and I declare that Muhammad is the Messenger of God."

Aleza bit her fingernail. "It could be a fake."

"It isn't." Sandy shook his head. "I've seen it."

Maybach lit one of his thin cigars. "So the Theatine connection was entirely fabricated?"

"Not entirely," Ben countered. "The Theatines were here first, and Carafa did become Pope."

"But he didn't come to Peru," Maybach said.

"No. Very likely not."

Bill Field jumped in. "So if the good friars aren't paying for this project, who is?"

Sandy hadn't prepared for that question. "The man who bought the document in Egypt is a scholar of Islamic history, and is quite rich. He is the same man who led me to the Cordoba documents, the documents that outlined the outfitting of the Ibanez ships. I'm fairly certain that both documents refer to the same expedition."

"And one thing more," Jila added. "The owner of the distillery is Walter Ibanez. He has some vague notion that his family has been here for centuries."

"So we can sum this up," Bill said, "by saying that some unnamed party wants this box found, while another unnamed party is decidedly against it. It seems fair to say that someone knows more about this project than we do."

Maybach laughed. "The man has a point. I've had kidney stones pass through my urethra with more ease than truth passes through Sandy Beckham's lips."

"The funding was conditional on secrecy," Sandy said.

"Why?" Bill asked.

"I don't know why."

"In any case," Maybach continued, "we know only a part of a larger dangerous truth. Whatever that box contains is of considerable value, beyond that of any archaeological significance. What could that be, a memento of religious significance? Muslims don't much go for that sort of thing."

"It's a genie," Jila said.

"A jinn," Ben corrected her, "and it's not a jinn."

"What's a jinn?" Aleza asked.

"A manifestation of thermal energy that can be compelled if contained."

"You've got to be kidding."

"It's not a jinn," Ben repeated.

"Then what do you think is in the box?" Maybach asked.

Jila dropped her empty bottle on the floor. "It would have to be a document of some kind, a promissory note or a financial instrument."

"What makes you say that?"

"It's the only thing that makes sense," she said. "Diego Ibanez was a Moor. He wouldn't have called himself that, but that's the word history uses to identify Islamic Spaniards. His family would have kept their faith hidden for generations. They got tired. That's why they left. Can I have one of those?"

Maybach pulled a fresh cigar from his pocket. "It's a blunt," he said.

"I know." Jila lit it from a candle. "Moors were used to hiding stuff. If they didn't, they got burnt. So what did they hide?"

"She has a point," Maybach said. "Excavations in Seville and Cordoba have uncovered numerous hiding places, large rooms and smaller spaces as well. Niches, false walls, metal boxes in flower pots."

"What did they keep there?" Aleza asked.

"Korans." Jila inhaled deeply and held her breath.

"And paperwork," Maybach added. "Korans don't have any physical value to the faithful. A preserved sixteenth century Koran might fetch a hundred grand at auction. Add the significance of finding it here, and it could be worth twice that."

"It would also be of enormous historical importance to a collector," Bill added.

"It would," Maybach agreed, "but it would not spur a murderous counter-recovery operation."

For a moment nothing could be heard in the room other than the collective inhalation of smoke.

"I say we finish this," Jila said. "We have six days left. Cox just about finished the map anyway. I think we're pretty close and I think I'm too pissed off to leave."

Bill shook his head. "I want to leave."

"I want to leave too," Ben said.

Jila looked up at him.

"I'm not willing to risk you getting hurt."

"It's going to rain soon," Maybach added. "I can feel it in my bones."

Jila turned to Aleza. "How are you feeling about our security situation here? You seem to have a handle on the guard units."

Aleza flipped her off. "You have enough guys with guns," she said, "but you can't control the surprises. I think you should pack up and leave."

"What if we were to seal off the area? No one gets in or out except the workers for the next six days. No cars, no tourists, no priests. Not even a rabbi. You think we can do that?"

"No," she said. "Not with a body lying around stinking up the place. We're going to have police to deal with."

"The body is already gone," Sandy said. "We have some friends who took care of that."

"Then we might be okay as long as nothing heavy comes our way," Aleza said. "I'll stay but I want a gun."

"You're not getting a gun," Sandy said.

"I want a gun too," Maybach said.

"You neither."

"I want to leave," Bill repeated.

Jila walked over and took Bill's hand. "I need you for a few more days," she said. "I need you to find something for me."

"What?"

"The box. I think I know where it is"

"Where?"

"I'll tell you tomorrow. There's one more reason you should stay."

"What's that?" he asked.

"Your plane ticket is for a week from now. If you want to change it, it costs about $75."

Bill nodded as Toro refreshed his drink.

CHAPTER 26

Santiago de Paz, Peru

"Incidents of bad luck come in threes, just like marriages," Sandy observed from the top of the pyramid. He was struggling to maintain authority over his pirate ship kite which now floated about fifty meters above the pyramid.

"You have to give it more line," Ben advised. The kite was magnificent, a miniature pirate ship with skulls and crossbones on its sails like no pirate ship ever had. The wind scooped it up as it whipped across the pyramid. "You think *El Niño* is here already, maybe a little early?"

Sandy shrugged, handing him the line so he could light a cigarette, which was difficult in the high wind. "I think I'm going to stop smoking," he said.

Ben spun out more line.

The first incursion came just before noon. Juan Carlos, in his role as the local authority figure, was given the task of repelling visitors. Two minibuses pulled up, and a pretty young nun made her pitch for a tour. She made a quick retreat into the bus when Juan Carlos told her about the Ebola outbreak.

The second incursion was more difficult. A hired car brought two professors from Stanford University who wanted a tour. Archaeologists share a code of sorts, a code that grants a non-negotiable welcome to any active excavation. They demanded to see Sandy before they would leave. Sandy stared through the binoculars. He recognized one of the men from grad school. "Loser," he said, exhaling. "That guy had this woman rubbing up in his face at Mardi Gras and he didn't even hand over the beads. That's what the beads are for. Tell them I'll meet with them in Trujillo the day after tomorrow," he told Juan Carlos. "Tell them one of the workers fell to his death and that I'm busy dealing with it. No wait, make it two workers."

Juan Carlos did, and they left unhappy.

The third incursion came just as the workday was over and the two minibuses pulled out, carrying the excavators back to Santiago.

Giuseppe Dante Porfirio diCasma was excited about this trip. He had returned to Peru only a week ago and was looking forward to sitting in his little garden in Lima. A palm tree shaded the stone bench where he liked to sit in the morning to contemplate God and politics.

As Papal Nuncio, Vatican ambassador, diCasma had spent nearly two years in Peru. This was to be his last post. At 84 years of age, he had served the Pontiff in a variety of positions. The highlight of his career had been his posting to Madrid, once the heart of Roman Catholicism. diCasma enjoyed his years in Madrid. The flowers, the wine, the women, even a priest could enjoy the women as superb examples of God's great grace and design. This posting to Peru required very little, a blessing here and there, a baptism, and the occasional mass.

Now, probably dying from the cancer though the doctors had been enthusiastic, he looked forward only to respite in his garden and his eventual repatriation to Rome where he intended to die.

Then one afternoon last week in Baltimore, as a tube dripped cancer-fighting poison into his arm, diCasma was visited by the personal secretary of an obscure Cardinal who had been charged with investigating allegations of desecration.

"It's probably nothing," the Cardinal told him, "but word has come to His Holiness that excavations of an early mission in Peru, in your part of the world, are problematic."

diCasma took in the information and vomited. He would investigate when time permitted.

Still weak from his chemotherapy, diCasma emerged from the back of the car, helped by his driver and his aide. The coastal breeze caught him and he smiled, remembering the Amalfi coast of his younger days.

Juan Carlos Cortez came out to meet them, then climbed the pyramid, quickly like a man accustomed to climbing pyramids, which he was.

"An emissary from the Holy Father himself," he said excitedly. "Can you please not play with the kite?"

"I don't like it," Sandy said.

"What don't you like?" Juan Carlos asked, stunned by his response. "We will be known in Rome. I would like to visit one day. I can ask to meet with the Pope himself and tell him of the fine work we have accomplished on his early Peruvian church."

"I don't like it either," Ben said.

Juan Carlos shook his head.

"Tell them they can come back in a week," Sandy said, giving the pirate ship more line.

Juan Carlos was outraged. "An emissary from the Pope," he repeated.

"Second one in a week."

Juan Carlos spat. "No, Sandy. Do you really think we should tell this man that he can't visit one of his own churches?"

Sandy managed the kite with one hand and lit a new cigarette off the last one, which had broken. "If it was up to me, I'd show him around," he said. "But it was up to me to let Peterman in, and I was wrong."

"You are not the boss of this project," Juan Carlos insisted. "You work here as a partner with us, your Peruvian colleagues who have roots here and who will have to deal with the impact of this refusal long after you are back in Wyoming. I can welcome this man here without your permission."

"I've never been to Wyoming," Sandy said, reeling in the kite, "but you have a good point, my local friend. Even so, I'm going to have to refuse. Tell him no. If you can't do that, then I'm going to pack up. And I'll take my money."

Juan Carlos growled. He made his way down the pyramid.

diCasma sat on a rock and drank from a water bottle, listening as his secretary argued with the man. It appeared that they were not going to be given the tour they had hoped for. He said a prayer for the souls of Peru, and when his secretary angrily reported that the site would not be available for their inspection, diCasma really didn't give a shit. "We'll call another day," he said.

"That didn't go well," Ben observed, dipping the kite and then letting it soar.

Sandy shook his head.

"We have another issue," Jila said, climbing up to join them. She pointed toward the beach where a large sailboat made anchor. "I saw it on the monitor. I tried to contact them by radio but they didn't respond."

"You're going to crash it if you keep dipping it like that," Sandy told Ben.

"It's a pirate ship," Ben said. "It's whole raison d'etre is to be evasive, to move quickly and unexpectedly. If you don't like the way I'm steering it, then take the helm."

"I'll do just that, but hold on a moment," Sandy said, reaching for the binoculars.

Jila grabbed them from him. "Gabriel," she read, "registered in Callao. Does that mean anything to you?"

"It does," Sandy said. "That's Mrs. Heydr's boat. She said she'd be coming by sea." He found his cell phone and dialed a number from memory. He spoke only a few words and hung up. "She says she wants to meet with Jila alone."

"Why does your cell phone work, Sandy? I thought we had the jammers on."

"I turned them off; they were of limited utility."

"Good to know," she said. "In any case, tell your landlady to go to hell. Who does she think she is? We just told off the Pope. Tell her I won't meet her without you and Ben."

"If the three of us leave," Sandy argued, "Maybach will smell a rat, as will everyone else. You two go. I'll tell the gang that you're on a date."

Ben winked. "I never lie. If that's the story, it's going to be a true story."

"I didn't agree to a date," Jila said.

"I didn't ask you on a date."

"You just assume I'd say yes?"

"So we're settled on this?" Sandy took the kite back from Ben.

"Yeah. I'm going to ask her about your $11 million."

"I told you, it's about a million and a half."

"Aleza said the wire transfer was for $11 million."

Sandy shook his head. "I wouldn't get into that with her right now. Just stick with the questions pertinent to this project, okay? And be cordial."

"Agreed," Jila said. "I promise that Ben will remain cordial."

"Don't screw this up, Jila," Sandy said. Unaware of how much line Ben had let out, he let out a bit more and discovered the line wasn't tied down. The pirate ship took off on its own, flew on its own for a few moments and crashed near the road. "There's going to be some repair work involved. And truth be told, it should never have come to this."

CHAPTER 27

SANTIAGO DE PAZ, PERU

Just after dusk, on a low sand dune behind the pyramid where they sat sharing a granola bar, Ben held Jila's hand, their fingers intermeshing as fingers do on sand dunes after dusk.

"I read this paper about college culture," Ben began. "It said that in the culture of American colleges, holding hands is even more intimate than sexual relations."

"I've heard that," she said. "Kids will jump from bed to bed, but holding hands means that you're officially boyfriend and girlfriend."

The sailboat was dimly lit by a few tiny signal bulbs but they were able to make out the launching of a rowboat that was now heading for the beach.

"Are you my girlfriend?" Ben asked.

Jila ate the last of the granola bar. "I don't know what to say, Ben. I'm not good at words. Why do you think I've never published anything?"

"You've published four major articles."

"Yes, with Sandy but Sandy wrote them. I'm not good with words. And I'm trouble, you know. I'm old. I've got patterns now. I fall asleep on the couch with the TV on, and I don't shower on Saturdays. I might be too old or too set for this."

Ben rubbed her hand. "Every Sunday I read the New York Times in its entirety, without interruption. I can't stand dust. Can you live with that?"

"Why did you leave me?" she asked as the rowboat drew closer.

"I didn't leave you. You didn't respond to me for a very long time.

"I was scared."

"So was I."

Jila nodded. "I remember sitting here with you years ago, in this very same place. I think you peed right over there."

Ben followed her glance. "I had to go."

"Maybe we had our chance, Ben."

He shook his head.

The rowboat scraped up on the sand and a tall Indian man stepped out.

"I need you to know that I'm thinking of you as my girlfriend," Ben told her.

"Fine."

"Fine? That's all you can say? Where's the romance in that?"

"I do what I can, Ben," she said, following him to the rowboat, taking his hand as he jumped in beside her.

The sailing yacht Gabriel had two masts, neither of which had carried a sail in decades. A large diesel motor had been bolted to the stern; it looked liked it had been salvaged from a tractor. The yacht was long past its retirement age, and much of the decking was covered in marine caulk. Barnacles had resurfaced the hull, and little worms made a comfortable home in the woodwork. Two fighting chairs on deck alluded to a more recent incarnation as a sport-fishing charter craft, but the decay and powerful odor of mold suggested that this had not been a profitable endeavor.

"I'm glad you could come," Edith Heydr said as Ben and Jila were led into the salon. "Please have a seat. We have much to discuss."

The narrow room was lit by a single oil lamp hanging over the galley table. Jila paused to read a plaque that told of the yacht's history as a hinterland for an American newspaper magnate many decades earlier.

"We're doing some renovations," Mrs. Heydr said. "Before long, we'll be the envy of the yacht club set."

"I'm sure." Jila sat on a needlepoint cushion so threadbare that it was impossible to determine what design might have originally been stitched.

Ben took a seat across from her and accepted a glass of wine from a the same man who had rowed them to the yacht, and who now wore a dinner jacket.

"I'm afraid I can't offer you dinner," Mrs. Heydr said. "Our cooking facilities are under renovation, but Tupac here has selected a fine Chilean white for our celebration."

"What are we celebrating?" Ben asked.

"Collaboration." Edith Heydr raised her glass for a toast.

Jila had never met her but had heard a great deal about her. She looked even older than she had expected "What's in the box, Mrs. Heydr?"

The old woman closed her eyes and exhaled. "I can't know what is in box because you have not found the box. I hoped that Dr. Beckham would be here tonight to hear what I have to tell because I think he would find it interesting. But I trust that you will brief him."

"We certainly will," Jila told her. "Who is Feyd Heydr?"

The man serving the wine had stepped back into the shadows but instinctively reached for his knife. Mrs. Heydr shook her head.

"That's interesting," Jila said. "Just the mention of the name evokes a response."

"Where did you learn that name?" Edith Heydr asked sternly.

"On the Internet. I couldn't find anything on you, but apparently this Feyd guy was some government minister in Egypt about a hundred and fifty years ago. There's also a Tiger Heydr who drives NASCAR, but I think he might be unrelated."

Edith Heydr frowned. "Can we not discuss my family? It's not easy for me to talk about the past."

Jila stared at what she thought was a stuffed bird sitting on the counter. "Hey, is that a real canary sitting over there? I think it is."

"It is."

"Does it sing?"

"It does not."

"Why not?

"I don't know."

"Interesting. Now forgive me, but I almost died here because you didn't feel comfortable talking about the past. So while I will be cordial, I am really quite disappointed in you."

Edith Heydr frowned, her eyes boring deeply into Jila's. "I have heard so much about you," she said. "Sandy loves you like a daughter, and Sandy is my friend. It occurs to me that there exists no other set of circumstances where I would not have you thrown overboard for your insolence."

Jila laughed. "Nicely said. Now why don't you start by telling us about Aminah Ibanez?"

Mrs. Heydr drank her wine. "Aminah Ibanez kept an extensive diary which she began sometime after her husband Diego left for the Americas."

"After he left for Peru," Jila added. "He was intending to land in Peru."

"He was," she said. "And he did. We know that only because of what you have found and because of the Ibanez line; Walter Ibanez traces his lineage to this event. And we have one Islamic cup that was found here. We believe Ibanez died within four years of reaching the shores."

Jila lowered her head. "That's not what I was hoping to hear."

"How do you know of this?" Ben asked.

"Because I have her diaries," Mrs. Heydr answered. "I've only shared a few pages with Sandy because I knew that he would sooner or later share them with whoever asked. And I cannot have that."

"But you have the rest of the diary?" Jila asked.

"I do. The father, Tomas, was arrested shortly after the mission was launched. Aminah had a suspicion that the older son, Miguel, informed the authorities about the Americas mission."

"Why would he do that?" Ben asked.

"I'm coming to that," she snapped. "The diaries reveal that Tomas Ibanez was again able to buy his freedom at considerable expense, and he did indeed emigrate to Alexandria with his son Miguel and his daughter-in-law Aminah. And in Alexandria they lived well, quite like monarchs."

"I hope he gave the son a shot in the ass or something," Jila offered, holding up her glass as the man approached with the bottle.

"If he did Aminah's diaries are mute on that aspect. She holds Miguel Ibanez in quiet contempt, but women of the time did not challenge men, and if they did, they were coy of it in their diaries. Aminah lost the baby she was carrying and never remarried. What is most significant for our purposes is that Tomas Ibanez renewed his faith and made his Haj with his son Miguel. Aminah's diary recounts in detail the expense of their voyage to Mecca."

"And she stayed behind," Jila noted.

"She did. She founded a cooperative school for girls that was still in operation when my great uncle Feyd took it over some centuries later, and made it a point of honor to continue Aminah Ibanez's work. The school is today quite vibrant, and instructs young women in literature and computer science."

"So what happened after the Haj?" Ben asked.

"After the Haj, Tomas Ibanez made his peace with God and with his son, and died the next year. His son Miguel spent the better part of his considerable fortune training and recruiting men to work for God. There were schools and military camps if I am to believe Aminah's diaries, which I do. Campaigns of a violent and spiritual sort ensued as the Ibanez sword cut through Suez and Palestine, drawing recruits from the dispossessed.

"And Miguel Ibanez led them, Diego's brother?" Jila asked.

"Yes. There was much fighting you see, and Miguel was good at it. In time they built a dynasty of militant Islam. That is all. That is all that the diaries of Aminah Ibanez reveal. She lived well into her seventies. She made an entry every year on the anniversary of her husband's departure but no ships were ever sent by Miguel Ibanez to search for his brother. To be fair, it would have been illegal and costly to send ships. But if it were your brother and you were wealthy as a pasha you might send ships. Aminah never forgave Miguel for that. That is almost all."

Jila shook her head. "Nothing of what you have shared informs our discourse here."

Edith Heydr stared at her. "Yes. This one last thing. What do you know of Islamic testamentary law?"

Jila shook her head.

Ben stared at the lamp's little flame. "I know that it's not a system of primogeniture like in Europe," he said.

"That's right. Islamic testamentary law requires that inheritance be split among children rather than given to the oldest son."

Jila caught the drift halfway through her second bite. "So when Tomas Ibanez died, his son Miguel took all the money for himself. Maybe he didn't send ships because he didn't want to find Diego. If he found him he'd have to share."

"But Miguel knew that his brother was still alive," Mrs. Heydr said. "There were Muslims all over the New World even in the 1500s. You know that, right?"

Jila nodded.

"One of them brought a letter back from Diego Ibanez. But Miguel did not respond, and did not share that letter with his father or his sister-in-law, though it has a place now in the historical archives in Cairo. The letter contains only four lines, and would make no sense to anyone unfamiliar with the expedition. As such, it cannot be used as proof of the expedition. But for us, it is an invaluable clue."

"So what did the letter say?"

"It was a request for assistance which Miguel Ibanez suppressed."

"Wait," Ben said. "So Miguel knew his brother was alive but he kept it a secret so that he could inherit his father's wealth."

"That's right," Mrs. Heydr said. "That's right. The Ibanez family was called Moors when they were in Spain. But when they relocated to Egypt, they retook their ancestral name."

"And what was that?" Jila asked.

"This is where this meeting becomes worth your while."

"I'm waiting."

"Saud."

"Excuse me?"

"Saud," Mrs. Heydr repeated. "Miguel moved through northern Africa, then into Sinai, leading a large following into Palestine and then back into the desert, building coalitions which grew in the centuries after his death. Growing ever more powerful."

Ben set down his glass. "You're saying that the Ibanez family was ancestral to the House of Saud, the rulers of Saudi Arabia?"

Jila's mouth hung open.

"Close it," Ben said, and she did.

"This is not public knowledge," Mrs. Heydr said. "The royal Saudi family does not make historical claims that far into the past, but we have it clearly documented."

Jila shook her head. "I think I get it now," she said. "If we find something in the box that proves Diego Ibanez made it here and had children, then in accordance with Islamic testamentary law, you can claim Peru as part of Saudi Arabia."

"Wrong," Mrs. Heydr spat. "Wrong!"

Jila sat back.

Ben's shook his head. "That's not it at all. You don't want to stake a claim on Peru for Saudi Arabia do you?"

Mrs. Heydr shook her head.

"You want to make a claim on the house of Saud for Peru."

"What?" Jila asked, not getting it yet.

Mrs. Heydr sat back in her chair.

"You're saying," Ben continued, "that if we can prove Diego Ibanez landed here, then under Islamic law you can make a claim to the throne of Saudi Arabia on behalf of his heirs."

"That's right."

"You have to be kidding," Jila said. "You think the king of Saudi Arabia is going to abdicate because we find a box? And then the heir, Walter Ibanez, rum and cocaine dealer, is going to be welcomed as the next king?"

"She has a point," Ben said. "Walter Ibanez is problematic."

"He is," Mrs. Heydr told him. "But his son Cesar is not. He's a devout Muslim, a scholar, and heir to the throne of Saudi Arabia. Testamentary law was set down by the Prophet. Ours is not a faith that is open to interpretation. If the claim is made and substantiated then the claim is valid."

"And you expect them to just give over the throne?" Jila asked.

"Of course not, I'm not stupid. But if the claim is made to the clerics, to the sharia courts throughout Saudi Arabia, the monarchy will fall."

"So how do you see this shaking down?" Jila asked. "Is it a new world order we have been working towards?"

"Perhaps. What do you say, Juarez?"

Ben stood and began nervously jingling the few things in his pocket fit for jingling.

"We've talked about the jingling," Jila reminded him.

Ben took his hands out of his pockets. "You don't intend for them to step down," he said. "But you figure they'll pay a lot to make this go away."

"That's right," Mrs. Heydr said. "I've been reading Aminah's diaries for years. I want to make her dream come true. I have her faith and her writings and her money in a foundation called Jibrail after the son she miscarried. I intend to make a claim on the House of Saud on behalf of Cesar Ibanez for ascendancy to the throne. If made publicly, the Islamic world will shudder and the House of Saud will fall. If made privately, the monarchy will pay, and they will pay dearly."

"And that's what you want?" Jila asked.

"Yes. I'll take a billion dollars a year to finish what Diego Ibanez began out there on your plaza before it was a church, when for four years it sang to Allah. I want to give Diego Ibanez his Caliphate."

"So it really doesn't matter what's in the box," Jila said, "as long as it proves that Diego Ibanez made it here alive to Peru."

"That's right."

"It could even be a grocery list."

"It could."

"You've told Walter about this?"

"Of course not."

"Wow, so that makes our excavation the key to the whole thing. I guess that's why you're paying us $11 million."

Mrs. Heydr stared icily. "I'm sure it was something on the order of a million and a half."

"But the wire transfer was for $11 million."

"Sandy told you that?"

"He did not. But he's not our only source of information. You take eleven million for the job then you subcontract it to use for a million and a half, I don't think so."

She laughed then, throaty and course. "No," she said. "You don't understand. I have a war to fight. I have terrorists to kill, corrupt policemen to castrate, and training camps to firebomb. This is expensive work I do. You're just one piece of a larger puzzle."

Jila stared at her. "I'm just a piece of a puzzle, am I? We'll I just became a more expensive piece. We're going to need a million dollars apiece for me and for Ben, on top of whatever else you're paying. This is a penalty for not sharing your information before now. This has been dangerous for us and it could have been safer."

Mrs. Heydr shook her head. "Would you have come if you knew the stakes?"

"Not a chance," Jila said. "Who shot us?"

"Assassins from Lima who were hired by Saudi intelligence operatives. They don't want this box found."

Jila nodded. "Is that right."

"Yes, that is right," Mrs. Heydr spat. "Four more operatives landed in Lima last Friday. I had them killed, but more will come. Can you find the box?"

"We can find the box. We're going to find the box in four days. Can you have our extra two million ready in four days?"

Edith Heydr nodded ever so gently and called for her attendant. "Tupac," she said. "My guests will be leaving now. Please take them back to shore."

"Thank you for your hospitality," Ben said.

Mrs. Heydr nodded.

Jila flicked a bug off of her pants. "I think your boat has worms."

CHAPTER 28

SANTIAGO DE PAZ, PERU

S andy smoked in the darkness of Sig's private suite as Jila told him of the meeting. He said nothing for a very long time.

"This makes me very nervous, Sandy."

"Me too," he said. "I understand the need for secrecy but this is bigger than I thought. I don't like the idea that there could be an entire government gunning for us."

"So is she some kind of terrorist?"

"No. She's not. I've known Edith Heydr for almost thirty years. I've even read intelligence paper on her that isn't widely circulated even in the CIA."

"Where did you get that?"

"From my wife, from my ex-wife. Also, many years ago, when I was just getting started in Peru, I was teaching in Kentucky back then, and two men came to the office without an appointment to talk to me. I was very busy. I was on my way to class but I had to take the meeting."

Jila smiled in the darkness; Sandy liked to spin things out slowly.

"Do you know who Simon Twinberries is?" he asked.

"No."

"Almost nobody does. He's one of the richest financiers in Bermuda. He's long retired now, but he was a senior member of the United Nations Security Council think-tank team on Islamic terrorism."

"What does Bermuda have to do with Islamic terrorism?"

"Nothing that I'm aware of," Sandy said. "So he comes to visit me in, tells me that a woman named Edith Heydr would be needing my help and that it was going to get deep. And that it might be messy but that I should consider working with her without worrying about her motives because

her motives were in concert with the program of the U.N. Security
Council. Also, he'd make it worth my while, help me out with grants and
appointments, money too."

"So you took him at his word?"

"I did," Sandy said. "I had him checked out."

"Who was the second man?"

"Jimmy Carter."

"Really?"

"Really."

"How is he involved?"

Sandy shrugged. "I don't know. He gets involved in stuff. He lends
legitimacy to things. You trust him right, like you trust Mr. Rogers."

"Mr. Rogers is dead."

"Yeah, but the authorities cleared Carter of any involvement in that."

"I'm glad to hear," Jila said. "Tomorrow can we have Aleza working
exclusively on the ceramics from the tumi excavations? And I want
Maybach and Juan Carlos to rip the hell out of the section of the plaza
where we found the minaret."

"Yes. Is that where the box is?"

"No."

He knew better than to ask. "Okay," he said.

•••

Bill Field followed Jila around the edge of the plaza. She led him to a
spot just north of the lab complex, behind the bathroom. Bill carried his
radar baton while three of the more seasoned workers brought the rest of
the equipment. "You're sure about this?" he asked.

"Quite sure," she said. "So sure that I made a big X in the sand to mark
the spot."

"Tell me why."

"Because the pirates used to do that."

"I doubt very much that they did," he said, "but that's not really my
question."

Jila stopped at the sign just behind the bathroom. "Peligro," she read.
"Danger. You see this area here, how it looks different?" She gestured to
the oval-shaped area behind the sign. The sand was a little darker, grittier
too, with bits of glass and plastic mixed in. Torn dog food bags that had

been empty for a decade poked out of the one ecological spot in the Americas that would forever refuse their inalienable right to decompose. Plastic water bottles poked from the sand like ancient relics next to the carcasses of three ruined pirate kites.

"Why here?" Bill asked. "This is a dump."

"Yes, it is." Jila sat cross-legged at the edge of the dump. "It's all about moons."

"Moons?"

"Yes, moons. Look at the area around the dump, what do you see?"

Bill squinted. "I see looters pits everywhere, craters, part of the giant kitty litter that comprises the whole north coast."

"Paul Theroux said that."

"Yes he did. Fifteen years ago teams of excavators worked this whole area, recovering bricks that had been moved or reused, bricks that had been torn of the face of the pyramid."

Bill sat next to her and drank from his water bottle. "And you're saying they found things right here."

"Yeah. Lots of adobe bricks with moons on them. Bricks that came from right over there." She pointed to the northern face of the pyramid. "So maybe around 750 AD, when the Moche made their final modifications, they built this side of it with bricks made by engineers and laborers from some local village that marked their adobes with moons. Okay?"

Bill nodded. "Okay."

"What do you think the excavators found right about here, right underneath where this dump in now?"

"Bricks with moons on them?"

"That's right," she said. "Arranged in a series of walls, the same irritating little fragments of walls that we find all over the place. Nothing made sense so they took the bricks and piled them up with the others, behind Temple 5, making sure to keep the moon bricks apart from the others so that they could someday be reincorporated into the pyramid."

"And then they gave up on this area?"

Jila shrugged. "Why not? It wasn't any different from any other area around here, and they excavated it pretty comprehensively because it had good bricks in it. But they gave up because the walls didn't seem to make any sense. Do you know why?"

"You're going to tell me that the walls were part of Diego Ibanez's house."

"Yes," she said. "I think they were."

"If they were part of Diego's house why wouldn't the Spaniards who built the church leave it intact?"

"Because the Spaniards were fanatics," she said. "Because whoever was in command here took offense. They didn't just tear down the mosque, they obliterated it. They could have just reworked it as a church but they didn't. They destroyed it because it was offensive and then they built a church from the same Moche bricks, using the same Moche architecture because somehow it wasn't as offensive as the Muslim architecture. Even as the Inquisition was all fired up back in Spain it burned hotter here - these guys felt themselves on the cusp of the Christian world. They weren't going to tolerate anything reminiscent of a Moor, not here."

"That's a nice story," Bill said. "But what's your evidence?"

Jila shook her head. "Limited. I'm still thinking it through. If you were Diego Ibanez, where would you build your house?"

"Someplace close to the pyramid," he said, looking around. "I'd want to be near the building material and near the mosque."

"Why not build your house on the plaza?"

He shook his head, sensing where she was going. "Because I wouldn't want to be between the mosque and Mecca."

"Right."

"I couldn't build my house west of the plaza because that's where the pyramid is. South is desert." He paused. "OK, it makes a certain amount of sense. But it could have been anywhere to the north, not just this dump. Why do you think it's in this dump?"

"Look around and what do you see?"

"Again, looters' holes."

"Fresh ones," she said. "This whole site has been worked steadily by looters for decades. All except here, the garbage dump. Looters take pottery and grave goods, they don't take walls. I doubt much remains of Diego's house but I think it was right here. Ben and I have been all over the documents. And every other square inch of this delta has been scoured. I think Diego Ibanez's house was under this pile of crap."

"And you want me to find the walls?" Bill asked.

"No I don't want you to find the walls," she said. "We just went over this. The walls were knocked down by the Spanish after they killed Diego

Ibanez. Then fifteen years ago, the excavators found the moon bricks and piled them up behind Temple 5. So you won't find any walls."

"So I'm looking for a house that used to be here but is no longer here?"

"That's right."

"Then what am I hoping to find?"

"A wooden box that Diego Ibanez buried under the floor of the eastern wall of his house."

Bill stood up. "You've been studying this for days and this is the best you can come up with?"

"It is."

"Even if the house was here he could have just as easily hidden the box in the pyramid somewhere. It would have been safer."

"He wouldn't have done that."

"Why not?"

"Because he was a Moor. Moors hid things in their houses, under their houses, or in hiding places in their houses. But always in their houses. Humans behave in predictable ways. If they did not, archaeologists would be without work. Did you have pornography magazines when you were in high school?"

"Excuse me?"

"Just answer the question."

"Did you?" he asked.

"No. Most teenage girls don't but you did, right?"

"Okay, sure."

"And you buried them in the garden? Or you kept them in the woodpile out back or under the cushions during winter in the neighbor's pool house?"

He stared at her.

Jila held up three fingers. "Here are your options. Under the mattress, in the closet under the sweaters, or, if you were a very brave boy, in the bookcase wrapped in a false cover."

Bill chuckled. "Okay. He buried the box under the east wall of his house. What exactly am I looking for?"

"You can set that thing for wood, right?"

He nodded. "Not exactly. I can't get that precise in terms of material. You see, the frequencies. . . ."

"But you can set it to find some light material mixed in with heavier stuff, something like that."

"Something like that. But there's probably wood all mixed in here."

"I doubt it."

"Why?"

"Because the guards sit out here at night guarding. They have been sitting out here for years. They light fires at night. Look at all the burn marks. There aren't any trees out here, so the guards would have used anything wooden for firewood. But the box we're looking for, here's my thinking, would be buried just a bit deeper than the original excavation trenches went. Fifteen years ago excavators dug down and found the base of a wall made of moon bricks and they stopped because it appeared to be sterile underneath. But it wasn't. Diego Ibanez built his floor to look that way. It was habit; he wanted a little hiding place under his floor. It was his nature. So the archaeologists didn't go down deep enough. We'll go deeper."

"How deep is the dump?"

"Hell if I know. Wait, I do know. I just read about it in the excavation logs. I think only about a meter and a half."

"Then we need to get some guys to clear it out."

"Yes," she said, "we do but that's a whole other ball of wax. First let's run it through with your equipment just for shits and giggles. There's something bothering me about this little trash dump. I'm just not sure what it is yet."

• • •

"It's hard to believe I was here in 1983," Sandy said, thumbing through his old field notebooks. "I had a brand new Ph.D. and had just finished my first year of teaching at Kentucky. Listen to this - 'August 27, 1983 - This has been a long week, tired of the hour-long commute each way from Trujillo to Santiago de Paz. Also, Trujillo is a miserable fetid dump of a city. Even cigarettes at twelve cents a pack aren't making me happy. Missing Marlena terribly, but the Moche roundtable conference has been informative. I think I might want to shift gears and work up here on the north coast some day. Yesterday Dr. Gordon Maybach gave the keynote speech. He's the guy who writes the textbooks. He was cool. I got to shake his hand!'"

"God, you really were a pussy," Ben said.

"Yeah, it would seem so."

"So what were you doing here that summer? I don't remember seeing that on your resume."

Sandy flipped forward another couple of pages. "I was working at a site just outside Lima that summer, which was nice—you could live right in the city, nightclubs and all. It was a blast, best time of my life. Marlena and I had this fantastic apartment in Barranco - the whole top floor of Mrs. Heydr's house." Sandy shook his head. "That was the best time for Marlena and me. Lima was something else then. You could walk three blocks and have any kind of food you wanted for a dollar. When I look back, I think she liked me best that summer, and we only had two summers, she and I. Anyway, I was just up here for a week, for the conference."

"Was Juan Carlos there?"

"No," Sandy said. "This was before Juan Carlos got involved. Before Sigmund Klein too, so there was no place to stay, that's why we had to bus in every day from Trujillo. I remember we got here on a Friday night, and we went out to the pyramid, and they had this shaman get us all loaded with San Pedro mescaline. It was the first time I'd ever flown above the earth on my own power. But after landing, it was bad. I've never vomited so much in my life. But here's the thing. I got food poisoning the next day from bad ceviche, and I spent the twenty-four crapping."

"I've enjoyed your story," Ben told him. "What might be the point of it?"

Sandy lit a cigarette. "Just that back in 1983, I did a lot of crapping here one fine day, and I don't remember the dump being here. We were taking shits on a camp toilet."

"So it was pre-dump," Ben suggested.

"It was pre-dump, yes. Then the next time I was here was in 1996 for the second Moche roundtable conference. Juan Carlos had been working here for a year or so already. No more camp toilet. The dump was definitely there by then, and they had this fucking wicker thing for an outhouse. Then I left for Bolivia when the guerrilla fighting got intense. I didn't come back until 2005. And everything was different by then. Sigmund Klein had built his mansion and already died, and they had built the lab and the bathroom. But this dump was still here. You came on board a year later, and Jila the following summer."

"You never met Sigmund Klein?"

Sandy shook his head. "Must have just missed him. He wasn't here for very long. He died pretty soon after he arrived. In any case, you're thinking the dump is important?"

"Yeah."

Sandy shook his head. "I'll tell you this much, I'm not going to excavate it. I'd be digging up my own turds."

CHAPTER 29

SANTIAGO DE PAZ, PERU

Aleza gave Toro a big hug when he brought her breakfast, and in doing so she snagged the keys to the Land Rover from his vest pocket. She had claimed stomach pains and begged off work, not easy, given that only three days remained of the project. She found the car key and then held up some of the other keys, thinking about them.

Watching as Toro made his brisk path back to the kitchen, she moved quickly to her room, thankful that Jila wasn't there. Inside the hard lining of the suitcase bottom, she found the Lucite press and the plastic key blanks.

She made the impressions quickly just like they did at the auto club when they made your spare plastic car keys. Seven keys and six blanks. She did the Land Rover key first, then the gate and the service door behind the garden. With four keys left and three blanks, she had to take her chances. One key looked brand new, no scrapes on the edges so she did that one. One was well worn so she did that one too. Thinking about the next one, she heard Toro moving around quickly and stuffed the kit back in her suitcase. She stood by the door of her room until she heard him pass and then walked quickly into the salon, poured a soda at the bar and left the keys on the floor next to the couch.

Back in her room, she cut the plastic, filing down the indentations with a nail file. She had several immediate goals. Learn more about the big field guns under the tarp in Margarita's laundry area between the kitchen and the bedrooms, then get into Sandy's inner sanctum and toss it. Find a gun, a little gun, the kind she could carry discretely. Finally, steal a car when the time came.

She had tossed her own room several times already to see what Jila had.

Aleza smiled thinking about that; she actually kind of liked Jila. Aleza had hoped to find a spare gun somewhere that she could use but far as she could tell Jila only had the two and she kept them with her all the time.

But much remained hidden until Aleza went searching. In the sock drawer, behind the socks, in a box marked 'para su salud rectal' and bearing a line drawing of an enema bag, Aleza found Jila's spare bullets—two trays of fifty 9 mm copper jackets.

Jila had a little lock on her shower bag, the kind of lock that little girls keep on their diaries. Inside were tubes of shampoo and toothpaste and a tube of fungal creme that smelled like plastique.

On the bedside table was a cheap ceramic cat with a bluebird in its paw. It was hollow, stuffed with odd coils of red resin-like substance which could have been explosives but which upon closer inspection turned out to be Twizzlers.

A roll of 35 mm film labeled 'Light Meter Calibrations - 2003' turned out to have no film in it at all. It had been emptied to make room for two cylinder keys to the ammunition boxes for the field guns in the laundry. Aleza had checked that really fast and dangerously one afternoon as Margarita hung her T-shirt on the line. No way to copy those, but good to know where they were.

A male action figure with an inscription reading 'Spiro Agnew, VP' rested on its side in the night stand drawer. A little compartment on its back was stuffed with birth control pills. *You are a shy girl*, Aleza thought.

And that was all she found.

She was filing the last plastic key when Margarita knocked on the door.

"Are you feeling any better?" Margarita asked.

"Still a little lightheaded." Aleza smiled gratefully, taking the cup of hot coca tea.

Margarita sat on the edge of the bed. "Why don't you come sit in the salon; I'll have Toro light a fire."

"Thank you. I was just having a little nap."

"With your shoes on? That must be uncomfortable."

"I'm fine, really," she said, taking a sip. "I'll come inside in a little bit. A fire sounds like a nice idea."

Margarita smiled. "I'm going to the market. Is there anything I can get for you?"

Aleza shook her head, then a thought came. "Actually yes, would it be possible to get some hair dye?"

Margarita frowned.

"I saw a woman in town yesterday who had reddish hair. I'm sure it's dyed. I've been so down lately I thought maybe dying my hair would make me happier. Does that sound crazy?"

Margarita kept frowning. "Your hair is beautiful."

"Could you find me some, please?"

Margarita kissed her on the forehead and left.

Aleza waited ten minutes. She was tempted to move on nine, but the errors she had made in life seemed to coalesce around impatience. So she waited, then crossed to the main house and into the salon. She tried the first key in the door to Sandy's lair. It didn't work but that might be because of the rushed tooling. The second key worked. There was a gate but Sandy hadn't been using it. She closed the door behind her and walked past the bathroom into Sigmund Klein's retirement bedroom.

Big bed. It was dark in the room with the shades pulled but she found the big desk. Two computers, a fax machine, a DVD player, a scanner, a TV, Play Station 2. Aleza flipped on the light and jumped back when she saw Toro sitting in the chair by the window. "You scared the hell out of me," she said.

"You stole my keys, Doctora."

CHAPTER 30

SANTIAGO DE PAZ, PERU

Jila took her shoes off and waded in the surf, the cold water washing over her feet. Bits of plastic washed onto the shore with each wave. Standing on her toes, she could make out the tip of the pyramid behind her, but nothing else of civilization. She had been walking along the beach for about an hour, thinking about Diego Ibanez, wondering where he anchored his ships. Probably not far from here. They would have used the longboats to come ashore, surprising a few fishermen who would have alerted the local lords.

The region would have been under-populated even then, as European diseases had already taken hundreds of thousands of lives. What would the locals have thought of Diego Ibanez with his ships?

They would have known hard times for some decades now; the Inca demanding tribute, forbidding them to travel on imperial roads. Now, strange new assholes pulling into port. Surely the locals who farmed around the pyramid, and it was a ruin even then, surely they understood that these newcomers were Spanish. But a different sort of Spanish, weren't they?

Atahualpa, the last legitimate Inca emperor, was executed in 1533, nine years before Ibanez arrived. Were there Spaniards already here on the north coast when those three shiploads of Moors arrived? Very likely not, Jila thought. Colonial documents mentioned only a few churches, only a few towns. But the priests would have milling about.

In some ways, the people living here when Diego Ibanez arrived were among the most cosmopolitan in the world, at least in terms of spirituality. They had exposure to all kinds of faith in the way that few Europeans did.

What would it have been like to have another group of overlords come into town with yet one more premise on how to be human and how to know God? Would the local lords have welcomed Islam? Unlikely. Would they have accepted Islam as their faith? That would depend on what Diego Ibanez could do for them politically. If we ally with you, can you keep us safe and tax us less?

Ibanez would have said yes. That much is without question otherwise his mosque would never have been built. But he failed. That too is without question, and when the Christian Spaniards came with their swords and their guns and their smallpox, those local lords and their constituents very likely learned about Christianity and said fine, what's the tax going to be like? Then leave us be.

Thoroughly depressed now, Jila made her way back towards the pyramid.

● ● ●

"Well, I have to say I'm upset," Sandy told her.

Aleza sat quietly in the big recliner, eating the empanadas that Margarita brought her.

Toro evaporated into the landscape as he had a habit of doing, leaving Aleza and Sandy alone.

"What do you want me to tell you?" she asked.

Sandy stared at her. "We agreed to share all information. So why did you break into my room? Are things not difficult enough already?"

"Are you not very competent?" she asked.

"It would seem that way," he said, "but I get a lot done." He paused to light a cigarette. "I have thirty-four publications, including five books."

"Impressive."

"You have no idea. Now what were you looking for?"

"Answers and weapons," she said, eating the last empanada. "Something is still not right and I can't put my finger on it."

"Try."

She shifted in the leather chair. "Why would Peterman try to kill me, and not you? Why not go after you or Jila or Ben?"

"That's a good question. What's your hypothesis?"

"I think he wanted to speed things up."

"How would that speed things up?"

"Because you would be scared, and you would start to work faster. I think he was here to assist and abet."

"Assist and abet who?"

She stared at him. "That's my point."

Sandy stared back. "You think we have another player here."

"I do."

"Who?"

"I don't know. It could be you."

"No, I'd know about it."

"It's not Jila because she couldn't keep a secret unless she believed in it. Can't be Ben, he might not be bright enough."

Sandy shook his head. "I trust Ben more than anyone else in the world."

"Fine. Maybach is too old and that leaves Juan Carlos, Bill Field, or the Good Housekeeping duo. I think it's Juan Carlos."

"No. I trust all of these people."

"Then you're shortsighted."

"Maybe, but I don't trust you," Sandy told her. "You'll be leaving us, heading back to Lima in the morning."

"I doubt that. I know too much. I know there was a homicide, for instance."

"Which you yourself committed."

"Details," she said. "I can shut you down."

"No you can't. I have very powerful friends," he said, pulling the cell phone from his pocket. "Actually, I really only have one very powerful friend, but as it turns out, she's quite chummy with your boss. We came to an agreement." He hit the redial button and handed her the phone. "It's for you."

She listened quietly as Jimmy Segura told her to stand down. Her assignment had just ended.

• • •

Jila crossed back over the dunes and back to the trash dump to check on Bill Field's progress. She spotted him from far away. He was seated by the edge of a looter hole as four excavation teams stared nervously at the dump. There was tension there, Jila could see it even from far away. The remote sensing radar equipment had already been put away. She ran the remainder of the distance. "What are you doing?" she asked.

"We're going to excavate," Bill said. "We're archaeologists; that's what we do."

Jila looked at the four two-meter square units that had been set up in the dump area. "No, no. What happened to the remote sensing? You were going to listen, to try to find some wood."

"I tried, but it wasn't working. The surface is too unstable; walking across it you can sink up to your ankles. There's too much interference. On the headset it comes out like static so I figured we'd dig."

She looked around. "Where's J. C.? Did he detail these guys here?"

"Juan Carlos called in sick. I detailed the guys. What's the problem? Are you afraid of what we're going to find down there?"

She nodded. "You could say that." She told the men to go back to the plaza to do cleanup work.

"You just made me look like an idiot," Bill said.

Jila stared at the pit. The surface was definitely unstable. "You're right; there is too much crap in here. This is where people used to shit, Bill. This is where people with typhus used to shit, and typhus might still be viable. All we need is a little wind kicking up and we could have an epidemic."

"You might have mentioned that," he said "So we're not going to dig?"

"We are," she said. "But we need to use the masks. Let's find the compass points for Mecca and match them to the eastern edge of the substructure. That's where Diego would have hidden his box, except now it has fifteen years of archaeologists' crap on top of it."

He nodded.

"We're going to have to do this very carefully, Bill."

● ● ●

At sunrise, Ben drove quickly to Betty Snow's pub to discuss the finer points of shutting down an unsuccessful season of excavation that had not lived up to their employer's expectation. They might still find the box; Jila was confident, but Ben didn't see it happening. How disappointing, he reflected as he drove through the cane.

"So, no box," Betty surmised.

"No box," Ben agreed, sitting at the bar, drinking the first beer of the morning.

"Are you any closer to finding it?"

"Yes. And we still have a couple of days left."

"If the weather holds, you might have another week. You need to find the box, Juarez. I'm serious."

"Don't tell me what I already know," he said.

"Do it this year, please. I can't see myself sitting here for another year watching Walter Ibanez bungle his cocaine smuggling. It's too depressing."

"Bungle it? I thought he was making a fortune."

"Not as much as he should be making. I think his heart isn't in it. Want some pretzels?"

"I do." Ben reached into the dish that appeared before him. "How long have you been here?"

Betty Snow poured herself another beer. "Coming up on eight years. I was in Puno before that but I couldn't take the altitude."

"Did you know Sigmund Klein?"

"No, he was already dead by the time I got here. He was only up here about two years, but he'd been visiting for a couple of years before that, long enough to get in a major pissing match with Walter Ibanez."

Ben ate a pretzel. "Say again?"

Betty Snow dried shot glasses with a hand towel. "What?"

"Do all bartenders at some point during the day have to dry glasses? Is it some kind of code?"

"Yes," she said. "It's part of the licensing."

"Pissing match?"

"Yeah. Klein and Walter hated each another."

"Why?"

"Soccer. Walter sponsored the local Chimu team, and Sigmund Klein was a minority owner of Pisco Chocolate and Wood until Nestle bought it, so they had this professional animosity. They'd have private games too. Klein would fly the team up, pay them outside of contract to play the Chimus."

"He'd come up here just for that?"

"No," she said, pouring Ben a shot of rum. "He came here because he loved that pyramid. But he loved soccer too, and the only team around here worth playing against was Walter's. So it turned into this major pissing match. Then Klein starts making noise about moving here, starts building his house, and Walter is ready to kill him."

"Walter is a big fish in these parts."

"Yeah, but Klein is one of the biggest fish in the country, could have been Vice President, except he didn't want the stress. He could take shits that were bigger than Walter Ibanez."

"So what happened?" Ben sipped the rum. It was the good stuff, aged like caramel brandy.

"Cheers," Betty said. "Juan Carlos had to run some major interference to keep the peace. Walter would get pissed off and tell his employees not to work on the excavations, and then Klein would call the head of customs in Puerto Chicama and tell them not to load Walter's crates. Klein knew Walter was smuggling because his bank did payroll loans for the dock workers union and for Customs."

"Sigmund Klein knew Walter was smuggling cocaine?"

"No." Betty gave him a funny look. "No. Walter was smuggling rum, not cocaine. He was exporting it without paying the duty. It's more profitable even after you pay off the dock workers and Customs. When they started looking at cocaine, they realized how much more money they could make."

Ben thought it through. "OK, but Juan Carlos was around back then. So he just turned a blind eye? Didn't want to get in Walter's way?"

Betty shook her head. "What are you talking about? Juan Carlos made a killing. He set Walter up with the only local airstrip that could handle a jet and be completely off law enforcement radar, because the airstrip was controlled by ex-Minister of Finance Sigmund Klein."

Ben stared at the rum bottle. "You're saying that Juan Carlos Cortez was using Sig's Place to run Walter's cocaine."

"That's right."

"Then how come nobody did anything about it?"

"You tell me," she said. "We could have taken down the coke smuggling years ago but we thought it might interfere with our objective. We care more about the Caliphate than we do about the cocaine."

"Jesus, on top of everything else, now we have cocaine smugglers working at the site. What's next, zombies? Why are you telling me this now?"

"Well, now is when you asked," Betty said, "Your spy girl knows too."

"Jila knows?"

Betty grinned. "What an interesting response, Juarez. Given the nature of our discussion, I would have thought that the mention of 'spy girl' would have conjured up an image of Aleza Sabatini, but yet you say Jila. You're not very discreet."

Ben shook his head. "That's not what I meant. You're saying that Aleza knows about this, knows that Juan Carlos is dirty."

"Yes."

Ben shook his head. "How does she know and I don't?"

"Don't know. Ask her," Betty said. "But you better hurry, there's a car coming to take her away."

CHAPTER 31

SANTIAGO DE PAZ, PERU

"**I** want you to know that I've really enjoyed your hospitality," Aleza said, her finger on the trigger of the artillery gun.

Margarita glared at her.

"The food was first rate." Aleza rolled her eyes and saluted Toro who stood just inside the laundry area behind the locked gate. He looked over her shoulder out onto the pool which didn't have so much as a single leaf marring its surface tension. He might have to kill this girl.

"And the service was like something from another world," Aleza continued, "from a kinder more punctual world, one which affords spotty glassware no quarter."

"I'm a soldier," Toro said calmly. "I don't think you can keep me here for long." He walked towards Margarita, and when he paused in front of her, she ran toward the door and quickly went inside. The door slammed shut behind her.

Toro grinned angrily, the artillery gun now pointed straight at him.

"That was good," Aleza said. "You covered her." This had not gone nearly as well as she had hoped; now the second she left, Margarita could let Toro out.

Toro grinned. He paced like a big cat in a cage, back and forth between the laundry lines.

"I wasn't really going to shoot her," Aleza added. "But I need to leave here, and I need your car. I have no intention of letting you hand me over to someone I don't know. I'm not getting into any car with this Betty person. For all I know, she's coming here to kill me, and I can't let that happen. And I still have to figure out why I got attacked. I'm not leaving until I figure that out."

"Margarita is inside," Toro said. "She will shoot you before she lets you leave."

"She might," Aleza said. "I'm going to have to take my chances with that."

Toro came right toward her then, toward the muzzle of the artillery piece that Aleza had positioned just outside the gate. He pulled a ring of keys from his pocket. "No, Doctora," he said. "I can't let you do this. I have the key to this gate right here."

"It's nothing personal," Aleza said. "I really did like you guys."

Toro moved his keys to the lock.

"I'm sorry about the lock," she said. "I filled it up with paste I found in Jila's bag. It's either fungicide or plastic explosive; it hardened pretty quick whatever it is. I have to go now."

No time now. Moving low and quickly through the house, she ran past Sandy's room, no time even to grab his laptop. She ran straight out to the Land Rover and found Margarita waiting for her in the driver's seat pointing a revolver at her abdomen.

"I need to leave," Aleza said.

Margarita smiled coldly. "A car will be here for you shortly."

"No really, I have to go," Aleza said. "I know you don't understand but it's important. There's one last piece of this puzzle that I need to figure out."

Margarita shook her head. "I spent three years in the cold mountains. I met my husband there. Before I met him, I killed one soldier." She stepped out of the car and pointed the gun at Aleza's head. "He deserved it, but it was terrible for me, a terrible thing. The next two were easy. I'm not going to tell you about them."

"Tell me about them," Aleza said, as Manuel moved quickly around the vehicle and grabbed the gun from Margarita's hands, shoving her against the car.

Aleza shook her head as Manuel tied her hands with plastic cuffs. She threw the gun onto the passenger seat and used her plastic key to start the engine. She motioned to Manuel to open the gates.

"I'm nothing without you," he said as she maneuvered the car past the big cactus.

She stared at him, unsure what to say.

"I could help much in your work," he said.

She smiled at him. He was young and beautiful, armed, uniformed, willing, and everything else that God blew out of his horn of plenty to please women.

"I have to go, sweetheart," she said. "Please be kind to Margarita."

"Tell me your address," Manuel said. "I can come to you."

Aleza gave him a big smile. "Thanks for saving my life. Open the gates for me please, Manuel."

He hung his head and keyed in the security code.

She blew him a kiss. "I like you," she told him.

"Wear your seat belt," Manuel cautioned as she shifted into second.

● ● ●

Ben drove quickly along the cane field roads toward the highway, toward one of Trujillo's affluent beach front neighborhoods. He was in a hurry now, he had to find the girl. If she was capable of getting past Toro and Margarita, who knows what else she might do. She might be gone, but maybe not. Ben had a hunch.

The *garua*, the gray mist that blankets the coast for nine months a year was lifting. Peruvians would return to the beaches soon after the Christmas holidays, but not before. "*Mal aire*," they would say, revealing the Peruvian's distrust of cool air.

Ben had been here only once before, many years back, when Juan Carlos was too drunk to speak let alone drive, and Ben had to drive him twenty minutes out of his way to one of the most beautiful neighborhoods he had seen.

A young lady had answered the door while Ben held Juan Carlos upright. The young lady was too old to be a daughter, and looked a little young to be a wife. And the terry cloth robe she wore was fetching and far too short, Ben remembered that much.

And quite a house it was. Small but right on the beach; Juan Carlos was rich by local standards. Balcony upstairs, attractive young woman in tiny robe downstairs; one could do worse. But that was some years back.

Ben was driving the little Suzuki jeep which didn't corner well but made quick work of the many speed bumps that lined the streets of the upscale neighborhood. This was clearly not a place for joyriding, not a place for rich kids to try out their fast rides, nor was it a place for poor folks to try out any rides. The private security men who lounged attentively in their little pavilions kept an eye out for that. But they didn't bat an eye at Ben. He looked too old or common to cause trouble, and this served him well since he intended to cause trouble.

He drove down a couple of the roads that led to the beach, trying to remember which one led to Juan Carlos's house, finding it on the fourth try. He parked the car and bought an ice cream from the one lonely woman who had her stall open on the beach. "Business is okay?" he asked.

"Sucks," she said, closing the freezer. "I moved here from Atlanta after the divorce. I've been writing poems about the seashore. You don't want to read them."

Ben gave her a hug, then walked along the beach to Juan Carlos's house. He climbed onto the porch and looked in the window. Nobody there. The door was locked, and the windows too. Looking back at the door, he noticed the splinters where the lock had been forced. With a little bit of shoulder he was able to push through quietly.

It was dark inside; the blinds were shut. Once his eyes adjusted to the darkness, he moved quietly through the kitchen into the living room where he found Aleza Sabatini gagged and taped to a heavy chair. The roll of duct tape was still attached, resting near her foot.

She shook her head and groaned.

Ben peeked into the bathroom and the bedroom, nervous now. Aleza had a nasty black eye which was swelling shut. When she started making noises he put his finger to his lips. "Where is he?"

She shook her head to the extent that the tape allowed and nodded her head up and down, staring at the duct tape gag.

"We'll get to that," Ben said. "Do they give you any sort of spy training at all? Because I've seen no competence whatsoever. You need a nice office job, something in the mail room. Where is Juan Carlos?"

She shook her head, lifting up her chin so that he could remove the tape.

Ben shook his head too. "Where's Juan Carlos? I'm not going to let you start shouting until I find him."

She rolled her eyes. Ben knew that look well from his prior relationships. He moved quietly toward the staircase and started up. He stopped suddenly when he heard the toilet flush.

He used the cover of the noise to vault the stairs and burst through the bathroom door.

Sandy Beckham spun and pinned him up against the door frame.

"Hey, boss," Ben said.

"You scared the hell out of me," Sandy said, letting him go. "What are you doing here?"

Ben took a deep breath. Juan Carlos was leaning over the toilet vomiting. "What's shaking, J.C.?"

Juan Carlos extended his middle finger briefly before grasping the toilet rim again.

"Sandy?" Ben forced a smile.

Sandy filled a glass of water and set it on the floor. "He was getting ready to leave, but in the process of getting ready, he got drunk and wasn't able to leave. Then Aleza kicked the shit out of him."

"Is that right?"

"She got here maybe half an hour before I did. She worked him over. She was still at it when I got here, then she pointed a gun at me so I had to clock her. I've never hit a woman before."

"You taped her up?"

"Yeah. I don't know how she got here. Toro was supposed to hold her until Betty sent the car."

"She locked Toro in the laundry room and stole his keys. What are you doing here, Sandy?"

"I came to have a chat with our project director here, find out why he got so nervous when we talked about excavating the dump. That was yesterday, and today he didn't bother showing up."

Ben told him what he had learned from Betty Snow, about the cocaine.

Sandy stared at Juan Carlos.

Juan Carlos shuddered and threw up whatever remained in his digestive system.

"Son of a bitch," Sandy said.

Juan Carlos groaned.

"I'm disappointed in you," Sandy told him.

"Aleza knows too," Ben said. "I had a hunch she might check this angle, finish her assignment before she left. Find out some answers from Señor J. C. here."

Sandy searched his pockets for cigarettes.

"What are we going to do with him?" Ben asked.

"Don't know."

"Nothing spells relief quite like an enema," Ben suggested.

Juan Carlos groaned again.

"Do you have any cigarettes around here?" Sandy asked.

Juan Carlos was breathing heavily, his head nestled between the toilet and the tub. "In the kitchen, in the drawer next to the stove."

Sandy turned to Ben. "Can you get them for me?"

Ben shook his head. "Get them yourself."

"Okay. Make sure he doesn't fall in."

"The cocaine has nothing to do with you," Juan Carlos said when Sandy left. "It has nothing to do with what happened in Chicama, so don't even ask me."

Ben punched him, a hard jab to the nose, and rolled him flat on the floor. "Bullshit. Because of you, Jila was almost killed, so now I'm going to beat you to death."

Juan Carlos's eyes bulged.

Ben shut the bathroom door, pressing the little button to lock it. "Sandy's not here now, just you and me."

Juan Carlos's eyes blinked from fear to anger.

"I'm going to ask only one time," Ben said, calmly. "And if you don't answer correctly, I'm going to kill you. Do you understand that?"

He nodded.

"Where's the box?" Ben slapped him hard across the mouth. "Not fast enough." Juan Carlos gasped, too afraid now to vomit, the adrenaline waging a war in his bloodstream against the alcohol, the adrenaline winning. He reached for the water glass which was outside his reach. Ben filled it from the tap and handed it to him.

"You don't understand," Juan Carlos said. He drained the glass and sat up, leaning against the shower curtain. "You don't know what it's like here day to day. If I have to let an airplane pass at night to get some money so that my excavators will come to work the next morning, I'll do that, okay, so fuck you." He vomited again.

Ben grabbed a towel and threw it at him. "Your face is bleeding. This is a beach towel, you know, not a bath towel."

Juan Carlos wiped the blood from his nose. "I live on the beach."

"I had one question, which you didn't answer. Where's the box?"

Sandy knocked at the door.

"In a minute," Ben said. He watched as Juan Carlos's eyes darted toward the left. "Don't get creative." He slapped him on the mouth. "Next one's going to drop some teeth."

Juan Carlos seethed with anger and discomfort, reaching that moment where fear takes over, not just fear of being punched but fear of everything.

"Who shot Jila and me in Chicama?

Sandy banged on the door. "Ben," he said. "I just spoke with Betty. She's sending her driver out here to come get Aleza. He's an hour away."

"Okay," Ben said as Sandy fiddled with the doorknob.

Ben stared at Juan Carlos. "Answer."

Juan Carlos heaved a little. "I don't know who shot you," he said, sitting up on the rim of the bathtub. "Honestly, I don't. It wasn't Walter. And I don't think it was about the cocaine. But from time to time. . . ."

Sandy knocked on the door. "Ben?"

"We're fine here," Ben said. "Go away."

"From time to time," Juan Carlos continued, "heavy guys would poke around. We'd tell them there's nothing here, but they would poke around anyway. Some say they're reporters, some say they're journalists. That's the same thing right?"

Ben nodded.

"Heavy though. Tough guys with guns. Dark guys, some Arabs but most were Colombians. You can tell by the accent. They would come around looking for the same thing you're looking for. We always told them to leave and they always did, eventually."

Sandy knocked on the door again. "I'm going to kick it down, Ben."

"Back off, Sandy. We're having a conversation."

"I don't know who shot you," Juan Carlos said. "But when I saw Jila looking toward the garbage area, I knew it was going to turn out badly."

"Why?"

"Because that's where we put the cocaine."

"What?" Ben took a deep breath. "Are you saying that you have cocaine hidden in the dump right now?"

Juan Carlos nodded. "Normally it never stays there overnight, but two big lockers came in just as you got here. The regular plane got a wheel broken in Ayacucho so we had to hide the lockers. We put them in the garbage because that was the one place no one would look."

"You couldn't take it out in a car?"

Juan Carlos looked down at the floor. "We're not allowed to use the Land Rover. Toro won't let us."

"Does Toro know about this?"

Juan Carlos looked up as if Ben were insane. "Are you joking? He'd kill us. We asked Walter for the keys to the lockers so we could take the packages out and carry them individually, but he said no."

"So you hid your cocaine shipment in the garbage dump?"

"Yes."

"How many people know about this?"

Juan Carlos reached for a box of dental floss that had fallen behind the toilet and set it on the edge of the sink. "Everybody knows about it."

"Everybody?"

"Half the men on the project knows about it. How much money do you think they make? About nine dollars a day for your excavators, that's what you pay. And they're glad for those nine dollars; that's more than they could earn in the cane fields. But they know to expect a bonus for looking away when the shipments come and go. If you try to excavate the garbage dump, you'll have trouble."

"Where is the box? Is the box in the garbage dump?" Ben asked.

"I don't know where the box is," Juan Carlos said, lowering his head.

Sandy was outside the door again. "Open the door, Ben."

"In a minute."

Sandy kicked the door off its hinges. He walked in, pulled Juan Carlos to his feet, and hauled him downstairs.

Ben washed his hands and looked out the window, thought it looked darker than it should be. Heavy clouds floated low over the ocean. "Sandy," he called out. "Sandy, look out the window."

"All I see is the street," Sandy said a moment later.

"The other window. Look out at the beach."

"Not good," he said, a moment later.

Ben went downstairs, walked past Juan Carlos who was sitting on the couch across from Aleza. He found Sandy outside on the porch. "Storm."

"It looks like it."

The wind was already blowing hard.

"Hurricane."

"Not a hurricane," Juan Carlos called out. *"El Niño."*

Sandy shook his head.

"You ever see an *El Niño* before?"

"Yes," Sandy said. "In Piura, four years ago. I was there with you."

"Did it look like this?"

Sandy stared out at the ocean, watched as the clouds hovered over the water, a thin layer of fog between water and cloud - a seamless blue rainbow. "Yeah," he said, "it looked like this."

"I'm going to call Jila," Ben said.

"I'm sure she knows about it. It's the same ocean, and Santiago is only about forty miles north of here."

"She needs to know about the dump. If she starts excavating it, some people are going to get angry. Walter Ibanez is going to get angry and that could be trouble." Ben told him about the cocaine in the dump, then called the kitchen phone at Sig's Place. The line was dead.

"It stopped working about a month ago," Juan Carlos said.

"Would you please untie her," Ben said, pointing at Aleza. "Do you have your cell phone, Sandy?"

Sandy tried the number for Toro's cell phone. A recording informed him that the mobile network was temporarily unavailable. "No good," he said.

"I'm going back," Ben said.

"You won't get past the airport," Juan Carlos told him. "They close the highway when the storms come because of all the crashes."

"Hey, you know what," Ben told Juan Carlos, "you could start by un-taping her mouth first and do the feet last, OK?"

Juan Carlos began gently peeling the tape from Aleza's mouth.

Sandy shut the door just as the power went out. He walked across the room and looked out the window to the street. No power in any of the other houses either. That was good. Otherwise it would be easy to get paranoid.

He locked the door, checked the windows to make sure they were locked and pushed the kitchen table up against the back door.

"Are you okay?" Ben asked.

"I'm not liking this. She won't excavate, right? Not in this kind of wind.

Not if it was going to rain, right?" Sandy paced. "Out at the site there'll be little bits of bone flying around. She wouldn't work in that."

Ben nodded. "Maybe she would; we only have two days left."

"She's going to dig it," Sandy said. "I'm going back."

"What if they close the highway?"

"I'll drive on the beach. The jeep has four-wheel drive."

"Let's go."

"We can't both go," Sandy told him. He pointed at Aleza. "Someone has to make sure she gets in the car. That car is on its way, storm or no storm."

Aleza rubbed her jaw and spit bits of tape onto Juan Carlos's carpet. "I'll get in the car on my own," she said. "I'm done with you assholes." Juan Carlos untaped her face and arms, but as soon as he untaped her leg, she kicked him in the shoulder."

Juan Carlos screamed when his head hit the couch.

"Good Christ," she said. "That's a couch; it's soft."

He lunged at her, got his fingers around her neck.

She boxed his ear repeatedly with her one free hand until Ben pulled him off her.

"Misplaced aggression," Aleza said.

Ben yanked the remaining tape from her arm and pulled her up by her shirt. "I am getting tired of you," he said, handing her the duct tape. "Here's what we're going to do. You're going to tie him up."

Juan Carlos groaned.

"My pleasure," she said.

"Then you're going to sit quietly in the chair until your babysitter comes. Can you do that or do I tape you up too?"

"I can do that."

He let go of her and turned to Sandy. "Go. I'll take care of this end."

"You're sure?"

"Go."

Aleza wound a piece of tape around Juan Carlos's head then ripped it off quickly, pulling away tufts of hair. "We'll start with the head," she said as he cried out.

"Be careful here," Sandy said.

"There's one thing you need to know," Aleza told him. "This asshole has been using the site to run cocaine."

"Old news," Ben said. "How did you know?"

"One of the guards told me. Also you need to know this, the priest wasn't working alone. There's someone else on the team. You have to tell Jila because he'll kill her first if she does find the box."

"Who?" Sandy paused at the door.

"Maybach," she said.

"No way."

"It has to be Maybach," she said. "I've come at it from every angle and it's the only scenario that makes sense."

Ben shook his head.

"This is my job," she said.

"Yes," Ben said, "but you're not very good at it."

CHAPTER 32

SANTIAGO DE PAZ, PERU

"**D**id it just suddenly get dark out here?" Bill Field asked.

Jila looked up at the sky, then out toward the ocean. "Holy shit. Rock me like a hurricane."

"It's not a hurricane," he said. "What time is it?"

"You have a watch."

"It's in my bag. If it's not too much trouble you could just tell me."

"About noon," she said. "I was wondering where everyone went."

"They're having a break." Bill stared out at the surf. "This could be bad. Let's go have an early lunch."

"Can we do one thing?" she asked.

"Just one thing?"

"Can we just keep it between me and you - the fact that we're really about to tear though this area with very little stratigraphic control?"

"Why?"

"Because I don't trust everybody; I'm having feelings of paranoia."

"You trust me?"

"I do," she said. "Whatever games are afoot here, you're not part of them."

"I can be crafty," he said, half-pleased and half-offended.

"No doubt. But you couldn't be dishonest if you tried."

He stared at her, weighing her. "Everybody thinks that about me. I wish it were true," he said as they started back toward the house. "A few years back we had a job search for an assistant curator in Medieval Costumes. Three applicants made the cut. One of them was a new grad out of Michigan who just finished a dissertation called 'Cossacks and Cassocks' which was marginal at best. She slept with me after the interview, after the museum had closed, in the rare fabrics room. We hired her. She only stayed about a year."

Jila smiled. "Janine Pace," she said. "I knew her in college. I always wondered how she got that job."

The color drained from Bill's face. "I. . . I'm telling you this in confidence."

Jila laughed. "And in confidence it shall remain. Was there a point to this admission?"

"No, I guess. Just that I can be unpredictable."

Back at Sig's Place, lunch had been set for three. Aleza's things were gone, as apparently was Aleza.

Margarita was two steps behind her, excited, looking ten years younger. "This is the door, okay," Margarita began. "You're Toro. Look at this, I just walk past him and into the kitchen. He covered my exit."

Jila grinned. "So she's gone? Where the hell is everybody?"

"They're looking for her." Margarita jumped from point to point, elaborating on her escape from Aleza. "I did it just as you said—wait until the person is between you and the gun and you can move."

"Where's Ben?"

Margarita grabbed her to keep her still. "So listen, I would have been locked in with Toro but when he walked in front of me, I ran out the door. That was how I was able to get outside to stop her."

"But you didn't stop her. She left."

"Well, one the guards helped her."

"And where is she now?"

"I don't know. She took the Land Rover."

"Where's the guard?"

"Out back by the garden. Toro is beating him with the big spoon."

Jila closed her eyes. "You did great, Margarita."

"I did, yes."

"I'm getting nervous. Let's call Sandy."

"Service is down" Margarita said. "Ben drove off to try to find Aleza."

"Where is Juan Carlos?"

"He didn't come in today."

"Where's Maybach?"

"In his room. He was out at the pyramid with the GPS, checking whatever Mark Cox did, then he came in for a nap."

"Are you sure you're OK?"

"Better than OK," she said. "But Toro is mad. He's going to stay mad until we find the girl. I'm going to go make some sandwiches. *El Niño* is coming."

Jila washed her face and hands, then made her way into the salon.

"Two days left," Maybach said, sitting at the head of the table. "Not counting this afternoon, of course. You'll still have a few good hours today. Are we going to make it?"

Bill Field shook his head as he loaded his plate with salad.

Jila sat and drank some lemonade. "So how goes the mapping?"

"Fine, fine," Maybach answered, staring at her. "How go the excavations?"

"Not well. I think we're at a standstill. The garbage dump is not looking as attractive as I had hoped."

"So we give up?" Maybach asked as Margarita placed the bowl of soup in front of him. "Where is your husband, dear lady?"

Margarita sat heavily in one of the big oak chairs. "He's very upset about what happened today." She recounted the adventures of Margarita and Toro and their imprisonment. "He's still out back with the big spoon."

"So that would explain why our leaders are absent," Maybach concluded. "But that aside, it appears that we are now facing a severe geoclimatic perturbation that will result in downpours, high winds, and flooding, a phenomenon otherwise known as *El Niño*."

"Well put," Jila said as Margarita returned to the kitchen. "It's already raining offshore."

"Will we be wrapping things up?" Maybach lapped at his soup, creating a mess on the Hindenburg place mats.

"It would seem so," she said. "We can come back next year."

Maybach snorted. "I don't think so. I'll be 89 years old. I have no intention of coming back."

"We'll have one last try at the garbage dump," Bill said. "Gordon, would you be willing to take some workers out and backfill the burial trenches on the plaza?"

"And what will you be doing?" Maybach asked.

Jila jumped in. "We'll poke at the dump a few more times, but I think we might be timed out here."

Maybach paused as Margarita set a platter on which several tiny carcasses had been arranged.

"Is this what I think it is?" Maybach asked excitedly.

"*Cuy*," Margarita said.

"Guinea pig." Maybach clapped his hands.

"It's a delicacy," Jila reminded him.

"I know that," he said, poking around the platter with a fork. "Shall I start with a breast or a wing?"

"Just eat it." Jila speared a piece that looked to be well done.

Maybach did the same. "So you two are going to work the most promising area of the whole site while I backfill away."

"I don't know what's promising about it," Jila said, "but I think we can say that this season was not what we hoped it would be."

"I should say not," Maybach agreed, "but you know as well as I do that excavations become most productive the moment they are about to end."

• • •

"It's dark out here," Jila said, speaking through her face mask.

"Trust in the force," Bill Field said through his mask.

Only six workers remained. The rest had melted off into the town when the wind kicked up. "Let's go," she said to the remaining four, pointing at the pile of face masks next to the garbage dump.

One man bumped another, and that man bumped another. They were all young men, Jila noted, men who had not been working on the excavations for very long.

"Doctora." One of the workers stepped forward, mask in his hand. "I don't think we should work here. It's not healthy."

Jila lifted her mask. "I agree, Gustavo, but the masks will keep you clear of any contaminants."

Gustavo scanned his associates for help and found none. "I think we shouldn't dig here."

"I know," she said. "The wind is kicking up, but it's not deep. A meter and a half. We'll do it fast and you can take tomorrow off."

Gustavo looked down at the tenuous surface of the garbage pit. "The other guys say to stay away from this area."

Bill stood up. "Why?" He looked at the men, all clearly nervous. "What are we going to find here?"

Gustavo, the leader now, maybe for the first time in his life, knowing that he would be cutting cane with everyone else here once the gringos had left, shook his head. "I don't know," he said. "But I think we have to go now."

Jila watched as the rest of the men nodded in unison. "Okay. Then go work with Professor Maybach on the plaza, but I need two guys to stay and just move dirt for me. Bill and I will dig if that's what you're worried about, but we still need some help." She pointed to Chino who was the youngest worker and Daniel who was probably the oldest. Chino looked up at Daniel and said nothing until Daniel nodded.

The rest of the men left.

"So I guess it's just you and me," Bill said, kicking at the surface of the dump. "Chino and Daniel carrying dirt but you and me in the trench doing the heavy work."

"You'd think that," Jila said, as Toro strode forcefully toward them. "I think we might have some help after all."

Toro rubbed his eyes and reached down for one of the masks.

"Why do you want to do this?" Jila asked.

Toro stared at the mask as he tore off his jacket. "Dr. Klein loved this place," he said. "Do you know what work I did back in Lima before I met him? In Lima I shined shoes. Dr. Klein brought Margarita and me from Lima. I want to honor him and I want this to end."

Jila's eyes opened wide. "Want what to end?"

"I'll show you." Toro slapped the mask on, grabbed a shovel and began ripping through the garbage dump as the wind picked up and drops of rain the size of grapes were quickly absorbed by the sand.

Jila and Bill jumped in, shoveling layers of sand debris and dried excrement out onto the surface, moving quickly down, thirty centimeters, then fifty as the rain picked up and the ground turned muddy. Daniel and Chino moved quickly to shovel the debris into large pails at the edge of the trench.

Bill yelped as his pick bounced off a surprisingly resilient surface.

Toro put his shovel down next to the pick axe he had planned to use and wiped off the surface of Bill's find. Inch by inch, the box became clear, a plastic locker of some sort, like a high-end cooler or a thermal container.

"Open it," Jila said, when the cover was exposed.

"Oh-oh," Daniel said, crouching on the edge of the trench. "Doctora, a lot of trouble this is. People will not be happy."

"Open it," she repeated.

Bill used his shirt sleeve to wipe the mud from the locks. "It's locked," he said. He smiled then, summoning up the best of Bill Field. He grabbed the pick axe, and with two deft chops, sheared the intricate metal locks from the plastic box. "That's what I'm talking about."

"Open it," Jila told him.

Toro leaned in and opened the box, lifting the big plastic lid.

It was empty, though it quickly began filling with rain.

Daniel's eyes bulged. "*Madre de Dios,*" he said.

"What were we expecting?" Jila asked.

Daniel shook his head. "It's not a thing for me to know."

Toro kicked the box. "Cocaine."

"Cocaine?" Jila stuck her hand in, feeling around the contours to find anything in the way of a clue. "Cocaine?"

"Walter's cocaine. Juan Carlos hides it here for him." Toro stared down at the mud.

"Juan Carlos hides it here for him," Jila repeated. "How about that." She felt betrayed, not only by Juan Carlos but by her own sense of judgment.

Bill tossed the locker out of the trench. "Get rid of this piece of shit, will you."

Daniel said something quietly, and Chino carried the locker away.

Toro grabbed the pick axe and began chopping away, clearing debris and old bricks and incongruous diapers and old water bottles and bits of newspaper and the accumulated broken beer bottles of a decade of cautious and semi-cautious stewardship of cultural patrimony.

The next locker was not far from the first. "Smugglers is what they are," Toro said angrily. He punched through the locker with a pick axe before Bill had a chance at the locks. This one was also empty.

"Fucking Juan Carlos," Jila shouted. "I'm going to smack the shit out of him before I shoot him."

Toro stepped out of the pit and wiped his hands against his slacks, leaving trails of mud. He stared out toward the ocean where the sky was darkening. "It's going to start raining a lot harder, maybe in five minutes, maybe ten.

"Let's do this," Jila said, her clothes already drenched. She looked out at the coast where the rain was socking down onto the beach. It was a little better up here at least, not yet quite as muddy as the low delta. Maybe that's why the Moche chose this high note on the delta, maybe because their kings and gods benefitted from a little bit of relief. A divine king needs only a few hours of respite to affirm his power.

"Screw this," Bill said, his shirt now soaked. "I think we've already found whatever we're going to find."

"No," Jila said. "We're already down a meter. Let's finish this. We'll get wet, but we've been wet before."

Bill looked out at the beach, at the fervor of the storm, a storm that would move mountains, but not today, he concluded. Not when only fifty or sixty centimeters of mud lay between him and what he might find. He picked up his shovel and began digging.

Toro smiled, though no one saw it through the mask.

Jila stood at the edge of the trench and saw menace in the storm. The rain was picking up now; larger drops like water balloons smacked loudly onto the sand and onto the top of her mask. She had seen this before, a lighter storm four years ago. *El Niño* was here. She picked up the shovel and began sloughing through the layers of garbage.

With only Daniel remaining to haul away the debris, the dirt and garbage began to accumulate on the surface. As the wind picked up, tiny fissures began to form on the edge of the trench and the floor became softer and less stable. Jila flailed angrily with the shovel. They were too close to have it end now. She found herself thinking about Puerto Chicama, remembered looking down at the bullet holes, remembered calmly running her fingers along her back to find out if the bullets had exited.

"Doctora," Toro grabbed her arm, startling her. "Doctora, we are at the bottom. The garbage is gone from this area."

She looked down and noticed that she had been chopping through adobes for the last minute at least, not even noticing them in the mud. She dropped down on her knees. "Help me with this, Bill. I need to see some moons. *Lunas*," she told Toro, as the three of them knelt in the small space, using picks and fingers, using their already soaked sleeves to wipe away the mud and find the edges of mud bricks before they melted in the rain.

"Tear it all up," she said. "Toss the bricks on the surface. Get as many of them up as we can.

"This is a floor?" Toro asked.

Jila could barely hear him. "Yes, this is a floor. And Moche did not use bricks to build floors. They would have puddled the adobe, like it's puddling here right now. This is not a Moche floor."

"And we are trying to see under the floor?"

"Yes we are," she said. "There's going to be something hidden there." She scooped out the water with the blade of her shovel. Little reeds floated in the pooling water. She poked her trowel down as hard as she could, found nothing but the hard semi-yielding resistance of the adobes. She did it five or six more times until the trowel bit into something different.

Six hands worked furiously, their motions choreographed by haste and adrenaline. Bill came down on a woven mat, accidentally ripping through it before he switched to the brush.

"It's a mat," Toro said, "a piece of a mat."

Jila grabbed a segment of Moche burial shroud and used it as a towel, sopping up the water and clearing off the ruined surface.

"It has an image on it," Bill said excitedly. "This could be it, the cover of the Ibanez box." He brushed excitedly while Jila mopped and wiped.

"It looks like a ship," Bill said excitedly. "A gray ship." Much of the fabric had been damaged or burnt but it appeared remarkably well-preserved for its age, even for Peru. "And look, the moon."

Jila frowned.

"The background is blue, the sky or ocean. This could be his ship."

Jila sat back and threw off her mask. She opened her mouth to the rain.

Bill continued brushing. "There's lettering here. Help me clear it."

"Don't need to," Jila said. "I already know what it's going to say."

"What are you talking about?"

"It's the Hindenburg," she said.

"What?" Bill tore off his mask, put down the brush and used his trowel to roughly scrape the sandy goop from the surface of the mat. There it was, majestic in its implications, the dirigible Hindenburg floating on one of Sigmund Klein's place mats.

"At first we had twenty-four of them," Toro said. "Now we have only eleven."

Jila felt the water seeping through her pants. "The fucking Hindenburg." She hoisted herself onto the edge of the trench, nearly slipping in the process. "I think that's a wrap, boys. But hey, at least we found some empty cocaine lockers."

Toro stood up and stared out at the ocean.

"Are you saying you're done?" Bill asked.

"I'm done," Jila said.

"Don't you want to keep going?"

No, I don't," she said. "It's just garbage, Bill. It's a place mat."

"If it was in a museum it would be," he said. "But archaeologists get their most important information from context. There is often more information in the position of the artifact, in its angle of repose, than in the artifact itself."

Jila folded her arms. "It's a place mat, Bill."

He smiled. "A place mat that turned up under an adobe floor, which is not where it should be."

"That's actually a good point, Bill."

"We need to see what's under the place mat," he said.

When Toro knelt down, everybody resumed their earlier positions. Jila ripped up the remnants of the place mat and they began carefully troweling through the softer mud beneath it.

"There's nothing in here but mud," she said looking up. The sky was almost black.

"It's been backfilled," Bill agreed. "Somebody dug through this and took something out and then backfilled it and put a place mat on top. Somebody already got the box, Jila."

"Let's find the contours," she said. Daniel had wandered off unnoticed sometime during the past half hour, so it fell to Toro to bail the water from the pit. He used the more intact adobes to create a tiny levee around the area where Jila and Bill worked, then dug a quick pit behind him, channeling the rainwater as lightening snapped over the pyramid.

"I have one wall here," Jila said. The sand that had been used to fill the pit was considerably softer than the walls of the tiny hole Diego Ibanez dug almost five hundred years ago.

Bill found the opposite wall and within a minutes they had defined the roughly half-meter square pit where the box would have sat. "Look," he said, reaching down, grabbing roughly with the glove, holding up two thumb-sized fragments of dark wood. "This could be from the box."

Jila took off her gloves, grabbed the wood fragments, and closed her hand around them. "We found you," she whispered. "You're not what I expected, but we found you."

"This is the floor," Bill said. "The pit is only about 20 cm deep. It would have been a shallow box."

Jila quickly wiped off the muddy floor of the pit and poked her trowel through in a dozen places. No surprises. A larger chunk of wood still rested along one of the edges. About as long as a pencil and twice as thick, it had been stained a dark black. "You're not from here," she told it happily. "You're from Seville or Verona or some fucking European place. A good lab will put us within eighty miles from where you began as a seed."

"This is a good thing?" Toro asked, staring at her. "This little splinter makes you happy?"

"There's nothing else down here," Bill said. To be sure, and because the rain was going to erase any clues anyway, he sliced through the little pit, destroying half of if with his shovel, poking around roughly. "There's nothing else down here." He took the coordinates and the measurements, writing them down on his sleeve with a Sharpie. He drew a sketch of the little pit, then got the digital from his backpack and took twenty quick pictures, walking around the edge as he snapped them, pausing every minute to wipe the rain from his lens.

Jila laughed. "A finer job of precision site recording I have never seen."

"Why are we happy?" Toro asked, collecting her gear. "Did you find what you were looking for?"

"No," she said. "But I never really do. Let's go."

"I'm right behind you," Bill said, tossing the drenched camera into his pack.

CHAPTER 33

SANTIAGO DE PAZ, PERU

In the dream she was sitting at a sushi bar in Dublin with a ski instructor named Dolph. "Come diving with me," he pleaded. "I know a lovely beach just outside of Berlin, practically deserted this time of year."

"I can't," Jila said, pouring blueberry syrup on her waffles. She smiled a little sadly and the dream changed. The image was hazier, and it crackled like an old transmission. She saw an old woman sitting on a balcony brushing her hair, staring out at the sea through a wooden lattice. Men called out prayers from Alexandria's minarets as Aminah Ibanez stroked her long gray hair and cried for her husband.

Jila opened her eyes and reached back for the dream but it dissolved quickly. She could make out the glow of a little fire that had died down. She stretched, twisting around in Sigmund Klein's big recliner. She had a blanket over her; Toro must have put it there when she fell asleep. The house was mostly dark though a triangle of light spilled out under the door to the library. "Hello," she called out.

She heard a chair scrape back on the tile floor, and Sandy Beckham came in. "Hey there, sweetheart," he said, sitting on the leather couch. "I thought you were going to sleep all night."

"What time is it?"

"About three in the morning."

"When did you get here?"

"A little after midnight. A power line went down over the Pan-American and they closed it for about two hours. I sat in the gas station by the road drinking coffee. I figured I'd cut through the cane fields and move along the beach but by then it had stopped raining."

Jila turned to look out into the yard. No rain. "When did it stop?"

"A few hours ago."

"So it's over?"

"No. It will start up again in the morning. Today was just a preview."

"Where's Ben?"

"He's at the hotel in Trujillo. He's coming back in the morning. The phone lines are temporarily back up, and I spoke with him a couple of hours ago. He stayed at Juan Carlos's house until they came for Aleza." Sandy gave her a quick review of the commotion earlier, and about the cocaine.

"What a mess," she noted. "So where's Juan Carlos?"

"Ben left him in the house taped to his couch."

"That sounds about right. Those cases that were supposed to have cocaine in them were empty, you know."

Sandy lit a cigarette. "Bill told me. You figure Juan Carlos was ripping Walter off?"

"I do," she said. "Did you see what we found today?"

"Yeah. I cough up bigger chunks than that every morning."

"I'm sure you do. But even so, that's our box."

"I think you're right. Overall, I'd say this was a successful field season. We consolidated a number of Moche friezes. We moved a huge amount of dirt, found an Islamic burial, found the earliest mosque in the New World, and the house foundations of the first known Muslim conquistador, plus a couple of splinters that connect it all to historical documentation. As for whether or not we get to blackmail the Saudi Arabian government, I couldn't give a shit."

"Well when you put it like that it doesn't sound half bad." Jila yawned. "What about Mrs. Heydr and her Caliphate? Is she going to be disappointed?"

"I imagine," he said. "We might have the remnants of the Ibanez box, but. . . ."

"It is the box, Sandy," she interrupted. "It is the box. It was exactly where the box should be. So we fulfilled our contract and thus deserve our paycheck."

He nodded. "Well, I think we had all hoped that the box would contain something significant, like a King Arthur's sword or one of Moses' tablets or something, but it didn't."

"But it did. Somebody stole it recently, at least within the last ten years, probably Juan Carlos."

"You think?"

"Yes. Thing about it, the dump is his sandbox, where he hides things. He found something there and sold it without knowing what it was. We need to ask him."

"Yeah, you know what though? If he did steal that cocaine, he's probably halfway to Bolivia by now and looking over his shoulder every thirty seconds half expecting to see Walter."

"That's probably true," she said. "I think I want to have a talk with Walter."

Sandy shook his head. "I think it's best to leave this one alone. Let's clean house tomorrow and then bug out of here. We'll go back to Lima, have a nice dinner and leave the Moche alone for awhile."

"Where will you go?"

He stubbed out his cigarette in the ashtray. "I'll stay in Lima for a few months, see how this settles. Then I'm not sure. I've been here so long it feels like home. If I get bored I can teach classes at the University or shine shoes in the park. Maybe I'll go to Ecuador later in the year. What about you?"

Jila pulled the blanket up over her shoulder. "Maybe go back to California. I think that's home now."

"And Ben?"

"And Ben," she repeated. "Yeah, I guess we should talk."

"You'll get your chance in the morning. For now, you should get some sleep. Breakfast is in about four hours."

"I'll be late," she said standing up and stretching. "Good night, Sandy."

• • •

In the dream, she was sitting in the fighting chair of a skiff off the Florida Keys working a porpoise she had hooked fast with a number three catfish lure. The gruff captain shook his head. "Ye can't be catching no porpoise," he said. "A porpoise be a mammal."

"Be a mammal," the captain's parrot repeated.

She took a deep breath of warm salty air and felt the wind in her hair. She opened her eyes to find Ben, his fingers in her hair. "Hi," she said.

"Were you dreaming about me?"

"Aye," she said. "I was. What time is it?"

"Seven-thirty. You missed breakfast."

"Did you see our treasure?"

"Not yet," he said, "but I used some of those new toothpicks that were sitting in the lab. They really do a good job."

"Very funny. It's the box, Ben, all that's left of it. What's going on today?"

"Not much. It's gray and windy but not raining. Sandy and Bill took the final photos earlier and now they're backfilling the plaza. Maybach is down sick in bed. He thinks he caught a flu yesterday. We're wrapping it up."

"Thank the sweet lord for that," she said. "It's time to go home."

"Yes it is. Want to take some time off with me, maybe head up to Machu Picchu for a week?"

She held his hand. "We could do that. That sounds nice. What will we do after that?"

"I don't know," he said. "What do you want to do?"

"I asked you first."

"I got a nibble from a job in London. University College. I don't know if it's going to happen but if it does, you could come with me. We'll get a little flat in Chelsea and eat chips from paper cones. On Sunday afternoons we'll drink pints of frothy beer."

Jila grinned. "I'd be a British house-frau?"

"You could frau," he said. "You could make a passing British frau."

"And if you don't get the job?"

"I don't know. I'm thinking maybe I could go to law school."

"What?" She looked up at him.

Ben laughed. "Just kidding."

"That's the scariest thing I've ever heard you say."

"Sorry. It won't happen again."

"There's one more thing I want to do here, Ben. I want to talk to Walter. I want us to have a little chat with him, just you and me. You should have seen the tension on the workers' faces yesterday. It wasn't good. And they're going to have to continue working here after we're gone."

"Sandy won't go for it. And Toro won't let Walter near the house, no matter who tells him otherwise. Walter isn't a good guy."

"No he's not," she agreed. "But he's part of this, and there are some things he needs to know. I want to tell him the whole story."

"Sandy definitely won't go for that," Ben assured her.

Jila shrugged. "He doesn't have to. It's time this all became public record. Tonight. Meet me in the tomb after dinner, like around eight. Don't tell anyone."

Ben closed his eyes. "This sounds bad, Jila. Let's just go home and be done with it all."

"Can't," she said. "It's not quite over yet."

CHAPTER 34

SANTIAGO DE PAZ, PERU

"Poor little wood chippies," Jila said to the three fragments of the Ibanez box. "You'll be in a museum soon. No glass case for you, I won't lie, but at least a nice acid-free box, and you'll be right next to a zinc button and some sail canvas from a dead body. I hope that doesn't frighten you."

"Are you talking to the wood?" Ben asked. He was boxing up the laptops and the cameras.

"I'm talking to the wood."

"So we're just going to leave this all here?" He pointed to the monitors and the larger computers that hooked into the security system.

"Yeah, Sandy said to leave it. He thinks he might come back next year if everything quiets down."

"What about the tumi?"

"Tomorrow we'll take it to the museum in Trujillo."

Ben nodded. The security alarm beeped and he looked up at the monitors to see a figure descending the stairs, coming down toward the tomb. "No," he said. "Please tell me you did not tell Walter Ibanez to meet us here."

"I couldn't have him come to the house," she said, switching off the alarm and the monitors. She didn't want any of this recorded.

"This isn't good." Ben watched the figure in the monitor climb down into the well. "He could kill us both."

"I told him to be sure he wasn't armed."

"That comforts me."

"I'm glad you could join us," Jila said as the man entered the tomb.

Then she frowned. It was Maybach, and that was definitely not part of the plan.

"Is this part of the plan?" Ben asked.

Gordon Maybach grinned. "This is part of my plan." He held Sigmund Klein's old Army Colt in his hand.

"What's this, Gordon?" Ben asked. "What's with the gun?"

"There are about six or seven loops here that I'm not part of," he said. "And I'm not leaving without what I came for. Now where's the box?"

"We didn't find any box," Ben told him. He began walking slowly toward Jila, trying to get between her and Maybach. "They found three little clumps of wood which is all that's left of the box. . . ."

"No, no," Maybach said, pulling the hammer back on the pistol. "I learned that move before you picked up your first trowel. You stay put. I know the little girl is armed but I doubt you are. I need you to sit down in that chair."

Ben sat.

"Show me what was in the box."

Jila looked into his eyes, into the little pilot lights deep inside. This would be the end of Gordon Maybach, a celebrated career spanning six decades. Unless nobody ever knew about what was happening right now, unless nobody but Gordon Maybach survived what would be called a horrific robbery. She saw that in his eyes as he nodded gently.

She'd never get a shot off. And a forty-five round at close range was not something you normally recovered from. The gun was an old model, and Maybach would have to cock it before his next shot, maybe giving her a second or two before he had a chance to shoot Ben, but she might die from that gunshot, a bullet that big. "I can show you the fragments," she said. "Do you want me to show you?"

Maybach shook his head. "I want the box you excavated yesterday in the rain after you sent me off to work on the plaza. You found it, you dug it up and you took it here. Where is the box?"

Jila pointed to table where a little cardboard tray held the wood fragments. Maybach didn't even look at it, his eyes firmly on Jila. He found the contours with his free hand and reached inside. "This is just little bits of crap."

"Yes," Ben said. "It's all that's left of the box. It was removed sometime during the last ten years. We think Juan Carlos took it."

Maybach glanced at him for a second. "No," he said. "No."

"We're looking at the maker's marks again, to see if we read something wrong. We might have made a mistake."

"So maybe there's another box buried out there?" Maybach shook his head. He was agitated now. Whatever happened, it was over as soon as he walked out of this room. There are some things that you can't apologize for. "Let me tell you how this works," he said to Jila. "I count to eight and then I shoot Juarez. Then you get eight more before I shoot you. You can stop me at any time during either of these counts by showing me what was in the box."

"Are you doing this on your own time, Gordon?" Jila asked. "Or are you working for someone?"

He smiled icily. "It started out as a favor to British Intelligence who has no interest in seeing a friendly Saudi monarchy overturned. But mostly I'd have to say I'm doing this for myself. I'll get two million pounds for whatever I give them."

"There's nothing here," she reminded him. "It's not worth anything."

"I'm too old," he said. "I've spent my money already. Two million pounds will allow me to retire in some measure of comfort. Now where were we? Oh yes, I was about to count. One."

Jila saw the figure in the hall behind Maybach, moving slowly.

"Two." Gordon Maybach had played this game once before, many decades ago in the guest room of a little chateau by the Dardanelles. It required great concentration. Nobody ever waits until eight. They always do something. "Three."

Jila kept her eyes locked on his as Walter Ibanez peered into the room, trying to get a sense of the situation. "What if I showed you on the map?" Jila asked. "Then we can go there right now. Ben and I will dig."

"Four."

Ibanez stepped quietly into the room, hugging the wall. He reached over and gently wrapped his hand around the hilt of the tumi.

"Five."

Jila could still bluff, but not yet, not when there was still plenty of time. Not when Walter Ibanez drew back the tumi and stepped forward.

"Six," was the last word Maybach spoke. The tumi connected at the side of his neck, finding the mark it was manufactured to find, but dull and fragile now after thirteen centuries of neglect, it snapped in half.

Maybach bled but not badly; he turned and dropped Ibanez with a single shot. He spun around and saw Jila standing right where he left her, but she had guns in both hands now and they were flashing like strobe lights.

Jila breathed slowly. She remembered the little Palomino horse she used to ride as a girl. She remembered the taste of brie and dark coffee and a distant time when she had been an elite part of something that required serenity in dense situations. *I'm just not normal,* she told herself. She intended to keep shooting until the gun fell from Maybach's hand or until chunks of Maybach began to dislodge. Ultimately these events transpired simultaneously.

Ben moved quickly toward Maybach, kicking the gun away though there was little chance of him reaching out for it. His last breath had already been exhaled. "I think you hit him about twelve times," Ben said.

Jila didn't hear him. "Fourteen hits," she said as she set the guns down on the table.

In designing their tombs, the Moche paid scant attention to the acoustic repercussions of rapid gunfire. As a result, Jila heard nothing but a high whine with a little buzzing behind it, as if her brain were a modem dialing to connect with some font of information that could make sense of senselessness. She knelt down next to Walter and ripped open his shirt. He tried to sit up but she shook her head. She turned him over and probed the exit wound.

"Are you all right?" Ben asked her, holding her face in both hands.

"Get an ambulance," she said. "Get Toro and the jeep."

"I'm not going to leave you right now."

"You have to," she yelled above the buzz. "You need to tell Sandy. Get Toro and the jeep and some of the guys to come and carry him."

Ben nodded and ran.

"It's bad," Walter said.

"Yes it is." She grabbed a towel and a couple of the cloth artifact bags, and pressed them to the wound. She put some of the cloth under his chest and laid his head down. "Thank you, Walter," she said.

"I'm going to die."

"No, you got shot at close range, which isn't good, but it's a clean shot. You're very lucky, it went right through you. If we can keep the blood inside you, you'll be fine."

Walter held up his head, looked down at the blood. "I won't make it to Paradise," he said. "I'm not a very good man."

"Yeah, well I think you just redeemed yourself."

"It's too late."

"It's never too late for redemption," she said.

"You're not allowed to repent with your last breath," he said weakly. "It says as much in the Koran. As the Red Sea came rushing back, the Pharaoh of Egypt told God that now he believed, and God told him it was too late."

"Then let's not make this your last breath, Walter." Jila picked up another bag and set it on top of the others, keeping the compression firm. "You'll have some explaining to do, especially about the cocaine. I don't think that's really Allah's thing, but you did a good deed here."

"The angel is here, Jila, the angel of death. Can you feel his presence?"

"I can't," she said. "But if he's here, he's here for Maybach, not you."

He watched her for a moment before speaking. "I have the book in my floor safe. You can look at it if you want."

"What book?"

"The book that Tomas Ibanez gave his son."

"What? How do you know about that, Walter?"

She had to move closer now. He was too weak to yell and she was too deaf to hear.

"They found it about ten years ago. Juan Carlos sold it to me for $6,000. I looked at it again last night. I tried turning the pages but they come apart in your hands now. When we found it, you could still read the pages. Tomas Ibanez wrote an inscription inside the cover to his son, Diego, wishing God's fortune to bear on his American Caliphate."

"Why didn't you tell me this before?" she asked. "You could have saved us all quite a bit of trouble."

"I wasn't sure if that was all there was to this. Such a fuss for just a little book."

She felt like she was hallucinating. "What was in the book, Walter?"

He watched her as she held the cloth firmly against his chest. "Poetry. Islamic poetry translated into Spanish. Songs to God, nothing more," he said as he began to lose consciousness. "They were quite beautiful."

CHAPTER 35

Rio Amador, California

Ben was nervous because his life was going to change today, one way or another. It was early February; an army of red paper cupids held their positions in neighborhood windows. That had to be a good omen.

A burst of warm air hit him as he opened the door to the Rancho Maidu Museum. Stepping inside, he found Duncan propped up behind the counter. Pants up to his ribs, wearing the same bolo tie, he looked like he hadn't aged a day since the last time Ben was here. Still a spry ninety.

Duncan shook his head. "You've got some explaining to do."

Ben walked through the hall and out the back door. He heard her voice before he saw her. She was surrounded by little bodies moving about, kindergarten maybe, listening as she told them about Maidu burial mounds.

She saw him when she stood up, but didn't miss a beat. "Okay, does anyone have any questions? No, okay then. Now if you go back inside, Duncan will show you how the Maidu raised their dead."

The students stared at her silently.

"I mean made stone tools, how the Maidu made stone tools, or made fire or something. Duncan is talented. Just tell him what you want to see."

Ben put his hands in his pockets, suddenly shy too.

"I've been expecting you," she said as the students marched off. "It's been more than a month."

He was breathing deeply now, his eyes watering.

"You never really did say a lot, Ben. But when you do, it's always a thrill. Are you going to say something to me?"

"You ran away again. I turned around and you were gone. We had just put Walter in the ambulance and you were just gone. Why?"

"I don't know," she said quietly. "I felt like part of me got ripped open again. I had to be alone to fix it."

"Is it fixed?"

She shrugged. "Patched up. I think I'm beyond fixing."

He moved forward and hugged her. "Little Bird," he said.

"If you make me cry, you better make it worth my while," she said. "What does Little Bird mean, you used to call me that?"

"I'll tell you some day," he said, pushing back his tears. "Walter is recovering. The bullet went right through him but it clipped a lung. They had to take part of it out. He's weak and he walks with a cane now. He's building a mosque in Santiago and another in Chicama."

"Yeah. He sent me an e-mail."

"And Parana, you know about what went down in Parana?"

"Yes," she said. "I saw it on CNN. The Parana Massacre. Paramilitary forces, who no one is claiming, routed the terrorist networks. They took out the whole leadership at a secret meeting, leaving the bodies of Miguel Ali Hassan and the other terrorist leaders for a bewildered Paraguayan police force to deal with." She pulled away and turned to discretely wipe her tears as Ben did the same. "You think Mrs. Heydr organized that? Maybe that was what the rest of the money was for?"

"I wouldn't be surprised."

"What about Sandy? Have you heard from him?"

"He's staying. Walter agreed to pay for another season of excavations and also for some high quality roofs to protect the friezes. Sandy thinks they can finally prepare the site for visitors, bring tourist wealth to the local economy and show the pyramid to the world. It's a good plan."

"And Juan Carlos?"

"Nobody's heard from him. I asked Walter if he killed him but he said not yet."

"So what happened to the book?"

"Officially, it is now being worked on by archival specialists in Seville," Ben said. "But in fact, Bill Field took it back to Chicago. They have conservators who will work on it quietly. Sandy gave some photos of it to Mrs. Heydr who showed them to the Saudi ambassador to Peru. Apparently some arrangement was made; Jibrail Holding, via Twinberries Hamilton will be receiving $34 million annually to build mosques and promote peaceful Islamic initiatives throughout South America."

"Not bad," she said. "And the little box fragments?"

"Field Museum. Bill said it should take about a year but minimally, the book and the fragments of the box and the chemical analysis of the sail cloth from the burial will establish that the Mecca skeletons are Diego Ibanez and his lieutenants, and that they died at the hands of an Inquisitor intent on putting an end to the American Caliphate."

"And they almost succeeded," Jila said. "Maybe they would have if not for us."

"That's true," he said, thinking about it. Maybe it's up to Walter now."

"And Mrs. Heydr." Jila took a deep breath. "You came to stay with me, Ben?"

He kicked an acorn, sent it on a low arc right into a bedrock mortar. "I got the offer from University College, London. Associate Professor of Archaeology. It's a plum, Jila. I wrote in my application that I was an Indian. They might have misinterpreted, thinking I was from India. Serves their imperial asses right but they made me an offer. I want to know if you would come with me."

Jila kissed him, lacing her hands together on the back of his head. "I can't," she said. "I need to stay here. I have a job here, and I don't want to fly in an airplane; they're too dangerous."

"We could go by sea?"

She shook her head. "You can stay here with me. Duncan is retiring for the third time. His arthritis is getting worse and all his stone tools are turning out like shit. So there's an opening if you want it."

"How's the pay?"

"There's no pay, strictly volunteer, but if you worked out, I would be willing to double it after a three month probationary period."

Ben looked up at the sun, let it wash into his eyes for a moment before closing them. It was the same sun the Maidu had been looking at for millennia. "I'm quite wealthy," he said.

"Me too."

He nodded and took her hand.

CHAPTER 36

MONTEVIDEO, URUGUAY

Jimmy Segura sat on the balcony, taking in the view of the beach. It was late but the bathers were still there and the music would last for hours. He had suffered a little breakdown after delivering the third packet of Parana intelligence to Edith Heydr. Then after the Parana Massacre, he jumped on the next flight out of Peru, hoping it would be headed for Paris or the middle of the ocean, but Uruguay was as far as he got. That was seven months ago.

He sent a confession by e-mail to Salvador Montes, who threatened to hunt him until he died. But before long, Montes reconsidered. He had personally gotten a fair bit of juice from the events that transpired at Parana. As Chief of Section for Islamic terrorism in South America, he was credited with much of the victory. He asked if Jimmy would consider staying on in some capacity that would be defined and redefined on a long series of later dates and Jimmy had agreed, feeling uninspired to turn his back on $86,500 per year.

"Sit with me and listen to the music," he said as Flor came onto the balcony.

"Quiet," she hissed, stroking the baby. "You'll wake Baltazar."

THE END

ABOUT THE AUTHOR

William Doonan is an archaeologist and professor of anthropology in Sacramento, CA. He has spent many years conducting excavations in Central and South America. William is also the author of two mystery novels, Grave Passage, and Mediterranean Grave, which recount the adventures of Henry Grave, an octogenarian detective who solves crimes on cruise ships. William lives in Sacramento with his wife and two sons. For more information, visit www.williamdoonan.com

14276418R00150

Made in the USA
Charleston, SC
01 September 2012